Creative Texts Publishers products are available at special discounts for bulk purchase for sale promotions, premiums, fund-raising, and educational needs. For details, write Creative Texts Publishers, PO Box 50, Barto, PA 19504, or visit www.creativetexts.com

CATCH THE STINGER, BEFORE IT STINGS YOU!
by E.R. Pomeransky

Cover design by Laura Roth

Published by Creative Texts Publishers
PO Box 50
Barto, PA 19504
www.creativetexts.com

ISBN: 978-0-692-54892-9

CATCH THE STINGER, BEFORE IT STINGS YOU!

by

E.R. Pomeransky

I dedicate this book to
the people of Cornwall

CHAPTER ONE

The pilot of the Hercules C-130 had no interest in human misery, as he flew towards the Horn of Africa on that April morning in 1998. The half a dozen or so men sitting back in the fuselage were playing cards, surrounded by empty cans of lager. Rough looking men, unshaven, scarred faces; as if they had seen the battleground of life upside down and inside out. A couple of teenage boys sat in the cockpit alongside the pilot and co-pilot, in awe of their first flight.

'Sebastian flew this same route, didn't he, sir?'

'Yes, son,' the pilot replied to the youth. 'And I flew alongside him.'

'Did they ever catch who murdered him, sir?'

'That's still a work in progress.'

One of the men in the fuselage suddenly shouted, 'over eight hours we've been stuck in this fucking sauna, how much are you paying us again?' He was a

Brummie, heavily built, wearing only jeans and a vest that exposed *LUCIFER* scrawled across one bicep, a skull drawn on the other.

'More than you're worth,' the pilot replied.

'What did you fucking say?'

'Better than the trawler or tug though,' the co-pilot tried to defuse the situation. 'At least we can't get seasick.'

'Why this plane and not one of yours?'

'Because they won't associate the drop with us, and because the boss said so,' the pilot mocked.

'I suppose the great Sebastian also flew with the boss, sir?' the other teenager asked.

'Yes, many times,' he softened his tone.

'Wish I could meet the boss one day.'

'The boss is a very private person.' Turning around in his seat, he shouted, 'not much further, lads, we've done about 4,250 miles, only about another 50 to go.'

'Hope it's going to be worth it,' the youth whispered to his pal, offering a stick of Wrigleys.

Playfully the pilot made a grab for the gum. 'Ha-ha. Anyway, don't you two kids worry about it being worth it, there's good money to be made. Do you know it only costs $2.50 a tonne to dump here? Elsewhere it's over $250 to $1,000, not that I'm paying anything, of course.'

'What are we dumping today, sir?'

'Nothing much today, son, it's a test run. Just a bit of uranium. But, there again, it is radioactive,' he chuckled. 'We've also got cadmium and mercury on board. But, soon it will be the big drops, you know what I'm talking about.'

'So did Britain develop the chemical weapons, sir?'

'Us, don't be daft. It was the fucking Germans.'

'Don't let him fool you, boy,' another member of the crew called out from the fuselage. 'We produced the most deadly chemical weapon of them all, VX.'

The pilot reached for a can of lager nesting in a cold bag. After pulling the ring he drank the ice cold liquid.

'I hope you don't mind my asking, sir, but is this legal?'

'Everything's legal, so long as there is money in it.' The pilot pointed to the barrels lined up against the side of the fuselage. 'They contain nerve agents, it affects the nervous system. Just takes a single drop on your skin, or even if you breathe in a miniscule atom, it can cause your lungs, heart and everything to be paralyzed.'

'So, if a bit touches us, then we drop dead just like that?'

'It's contained, so it can't hurt you,' the co-pilot assured him.

'But, having said that,' the pilot tormented the youth. 'Once it drops we don't know what will happen to the Somalis, if it accidentally splits or spills. If it touches them in any way, their symptoms will be sweating, vomiting, even convulsions.' He paused to change the settings on the controls.

'What, a bit like an epileptic fit, sir?'

'Worse, much worse. They'll lose their sight, shit themselves, won't be able to breathe and then they'll die.'

'That's pretty awful, sir.'

'No, not really,' the pilot shrugged. 'The country is already on its way out. They've been fighting a civil war for years, and then they had the floods last year, killed over 1000. And then there was the famine in 1992 that killed over 200,000. Probably millions, if the media could get their sums right,' he scoffed. 'No, we're doing them a favour, son, putting them out of their misery.'

'So if the boxes break on hitting the water or shore, the contents will kill the local population, sir, even the children?'

'Who gives a fuck?'

Down below, the turquoise waters of the Indian Ocean flowed gently towards the Seychelles, and onward to the Arabian Sea. Bordered by soft white beaches and tall palm trees, that cloaked the devastation behind the facade.

'Right, lads, get ready to drop!'

'You'd better get a hernia job then, ha-ha,' a voice roared.

The pilot was not used to men like these, lazy, rude and unprofessional. Back on base his own men were trained, would serve to the death without a complaint.

Leaving the controls in the hands of his co-pilot, he hurried to the back of the aircraft and opened the ramp.

'Ready to go!'

He could hear them rise from the floor, still moaning.

'Enough, let's get this done and the sooner we'll be home.'

'So long as we gets us money, that's all we care about,' the tattooed Brummie grunted, as he grabbed hold of a barrel and manoeuvred it towards the opening. The others followed his lead, relieved to feel the fresh air on their faces.

'It might look like Shangri-fucking-la, but it's not, I assure you,' the pilot lectured. 'These waters are full of fucking pirates.'

'What, Long John Silver, oo-ah me hearties?' one of them jeered.

'Piracy here isn't about pieces of silver, it's about taking hostages, and threats to international shipping with hijacks, and in some cases murder.'

'So is that the plan for us, sir, are we to become pirates?' one of the teenager's asked, causing a roar of laughter in the fuselage.

By now the plane had slowed down, almost hovering above the sea where children were playing and diving for fish.

'Sir, there are children in the water.'

'Close your eyes then. Listen, the MOD used to pay me to do this, and they will probably start again, once the media back off.'

'You didn't mention kids,' the Brummie complained.

'Look, lads, Europe has been doing the same here for years, so don't take the guilt on your shoulders.

Anyhow, the kids won't be hurt, these barrels are sealed tight.'

'Make sure they're lined up,' the co-pilot instructed.

Grunting their replies, they re-aligned the barrels.

'You know the real reason why they chose to drop their chemical waste here, don't you?'

The co-pilot shook his head.

'For the oil, of course, why else do you think they are using the country as a dustbin? To get rid of the population so we can take it back.'

Pushing each barrel out through the ramp, they watched in silence as the cargo descended like bombs, and then landed on the white beach. The few that missed the shore hit the ocean, exploding its contents across the waves only a short distance from the children. The pilot knew that when the monsoons came, any spilt gases and liquid would be shared equally among the nations.

The men grabbed their cigarettes and lit up, relieved as much for the nicotine as for the fresh air.

'Well done, boys.' The pilot began handing out wads of notes to each of the crew. After counting their money they shook hands, more than happy with their pay.

'When we arrive back at base there'll be a hosepipe by the airfield,' the co-pilot said. 'You'll need to hose yourselves down thoroughly, and then remove your overalls and place the washed overalls in a pile.'

'Burning them?'

'Of course, they're contaminated.'

'So what is the next drop?' the Brummie asked, swigging back the last dregs of beer from his can.

'Flowers I think, violets,' the pilot smiled, now feeling more upbeat.

'Why don't your own RAF men help you, sir?'

'His own men fucked off to RAF St. Mawgan, son. Had enough of him,' a crew member laughed. 'They're probably poncing about practicing for the public air show.' 'Will you be using my father's violets, sir?'

'Why don't you also use the Kaleels' lavender?' the other youth joined in.

'Lavenders blue dilly, dilly,' a crew member began to sing. 'Lavenders green, when I am king dilly, dilly, you'll be my queen.'

'Is that what you sing to your missus?'

'You be a saucy git for your age, boy,' the man laughed. 'Of course I does sing it to she, but I always change the dilly for willy, ha-ha'.

The pilot grinned. 'Isn't the song Sweet Violets more appropriate, the old one by Dinah Shore?'

'You sing it to us,' one of the men suggested. The rest of the crew joined in clapping.

The pilot cleared his throat.

'Sweeter than the roses covered all over from head to toe, covered all over with sweet violets,' he began. By the end of the song most of the crew had joined in. 'Which just goes to show, all a girl wants from a man is his sweet violets.'

Suddenly, the radio bleeped. The pilot answered the call.

'I'm on my way back, job done.'

'Guthrie's in Redruth,' the voice at the other end complained.

'Yes, I know, he's been there a while.'

'Why the fuck didn't you tell me?'

'Nothing to tell, so long as he is kept under surveillance. You said not to finish him off.'

'You should have kept me informed.'

'Okay, but I didn't think it that important. Just give the nod and he's history.'

CHAPTER TWO

Redruth was in mourning since the closure of South Crofty tin mine that previous month, March 1998. It was 3,000 feet deep and had been the livelihood of the Cornish town for over 400 years since the 17th Century, although tin and copper mining in the area dated back to long before then. At its peak Redruth was known as one of the richest towns in the world. Now *FOR SALE* signs hung everywhere, shops were being sold or boarded up and a large percentage of its youth were moving away.

Henry Guthrie, known to one and all as plain Guthrie, was well aware of his infamy in the town even though he had only lived there for about two months. The reason behind his fame was not due to the fact that he was one of the only black men there, but because he had recently appeared on the front page of the tabloids for having been released from prison due to an appeal. Not the best form of introduction, but thankful that the murder conviction had been reduced to manslaughter six months earlier. His buffoon of a lawyer had then called for a mistrial and the conviction was quashed. But the memories still haunted him, the arrest, the beatings by the police and prison officers. Almost the 21st Century and nothing had changed.

His first floor flat, a one bedroom hovel that should have had an *UNFIT FOR HUMAN HABITATION* sticker across the door, was next to a fish and chip shop in Green Lane, living off their chips most nights.

Grabbing a packet of Marlboro from the bedside cabinet he lit up and inhaled a few drags; and then, lay back down on the pillow, oblivious to the stained mattress and damp bedding. The radio played in the background, Percy Sledge, one of his mother's favourites.

'When a man loves a woman, can't keep his mind on nothing else...' He sang along to the words, thinking back to Stella's funeral, surprised that the authorities had let him attend. His mother said it was lucky they had no kids, but he did not feel so lucky.

'Look at you, six foot three, good looking, like a young Cassius,' she had said, as they had walked away from the graveside. *'Not many girls could deny a sexy Essex boy. You're only 39 years old, you'll meet someone else.'* But he had no desire to meet anyone else, still sleeping with her photo under his pillow, his beautiful, beloved Stella.

Despite his efforts he had no idea where her post-mortem had taken place, probably done in Antwerp, he surmised. What did not make sense was, why the man who had killed her had not also killed him. If only the coin they had tossed had landed in her favour, she would still be alive. But, the year inside had given him time to grieve, his mind not as numb, his heart not as fractured. Now he could concentrate on finding her killer, and he would find him, of that he was certain.

Peering out of the bedroom window, he glimpsed the distant outline of Carn Brea Hill rising up through the thick morning mist, overshadowing the small Cornish town. Rolls of steam were sweeping down the rugged side of the brae, blanketing the gypsy encampment below. Once a Neolithic settlement, it was now crowned with a medieval castle and 19th Century monument to Lord Francis Basset. Perhaps he would climb to the top some day and enjoy the views.

Flicking his cigarette ash onto the neighbours blue striped canopy, he liked to observe the customers below who queued for their lunch and supper. Today in the queue – a couple of young mums wanting to silence their kids with a bag of chips, teenagers in school uniform, and half a dozen workmen in overalls. He could also see his Harley parked over the road.

The smells from the fried, vinegary food rose up into the flat. Yet, he did not care where he lived so long as it was in Cornwall, he had his reasons.

Deciding that it was time to get ready, he headed off to the shower. It felt good to be able to wash whenever he chose, even if it was in a rusty closet that sprayed tepid water.

Ten minutes later, dripping his way across the worn, brown, bedroom carpet, he caught sight of his reflection in the mirror. Shaking his belly to see how much it wobbled, over 17 stone at the last weigh in, that came from sitting in a cell all day eating fodder. His long black ringlets danced about his head as he shook, causing the water to run down his broad shoulders. Along with his dimpled cheeks he looked like a rock star, or so numerous folk had told him. The anomaly was his glassy green eyes, where they came from nobody knew, but they were a magnet for the girls. Although, he had never married and had no children, none that he knew of.

Reaching down to the bed he grabbed his silver crucifix, kissed it, and then put the chain round his neck. Looking at his belly from a different angle in the mirror, he caught the reflection of a painted wooden clown sitting on the chest of drawers, between the rosary and his Walther PPK pistol. His weight gain no longer seemed to matter, now moving away from the mirror towards the window, overcome by memories.

Throwing the cigarette stub into the kitchen sink, he filled up the kettle and placed it on the hotplate of the small Belling cooker, better suited to a camper van. It did not matter, he had no intention of staying for long. Depositing a Typhoo teabag into a chipped mug he realised that he had run out of sugar. He used Typhoo only because his mother always bought it. She was a good woman, the best; raised him to be honourable, decent, and he had let her down badly. Not just with the constant lies, but she had envisaged him being someone great, a lawyer maybe or a doctor. Perhaps he should have gone down that route, saving lives, she would have been so proud. Ironically, his only motivation during his year in prison was the knowledge that he would kill the man responsible for Stella's death. After all, his only raison d'etre for the past 17 years was murder; he was an expert at it.

Sitting down in the torn, stained armchair, with a mug of tea and a Marlboro, he leaned back and closed his eyes. Immediately, images flashed before him, demons waiting in the wings, one after the other like a reel of film. Where were these memories stored, in his brain? What if his brain crashed like a computer, would he lose all the programmes and files, would she be erased from his thoughts forever? Yet, he knew that it was too late for regrets, they should have quit while ahead, got married, settled down like normal people and had a family. Too late, he always left it too late.

Perhaps he would move abroad when all this was over. He fancied the Greek islands where he could sit theorising over Plato's *Republic*. Maybe stand in a market place debating the theory of forms, or the illusive shadows in a cave. Kos would be ideal, he had always wanted to live near a harbour.

Opening his eyes, he caught sight of the packages lying on the floor, delivered to his post office box number. This was the fifth package he had received, all still unopened and all postmarked: *Albert Embankment - Vauxhall Cross*. He wondered how much they knew. The problem was, there was a mole in the works, some evil bastard who had set him up. One thing was for certain, it would not be long before they found him.

CHAPTER THREE

The entrance into the long, tree-lined driveway of the Penventon Park Hotel was covered in pink blossom. The large Georgian mansion was grand by Redruth standards, hosting 64 bedrooms. The grounds outside the hotel accommodated a nightclub and a small pub for teens and twenties.

Guthrie headed towards the hotel dressed in a pair of black trousers, white shirt and new grey tie to match his grey tweed jacket. As with all his coats and jackets, this one was lined with bullet proof fabric, slimmer than the conventional vest but more effective.

A Mercedes was blocking the door into the hotel reception. Dropping his cigarette butt he squeezed through the gap behind the car boot, and entered the hotel vestibule. Of course, he had not come here for pleasure; it was merely the start of a long process of elimination. Who killed Stella? Who had set him up? Who was the mole? As far as he was concerned, everyone was a suspect.

Piran Trelawney was already seated at one of the tables in the restaurant when he entered. His friend had not changed much since they had first met as freshers; retaining his blonde Adonis looks and big blue eyes.

'Ah, Guthrie, I'd like to introduce you to my father-in-law, Jonathan.' He focussed on the tall, grey haired man sitting opposite. 'Jonathan, meet my good friend from university, Henry Guthrie.'

The men shook hands.

'Jonathan works in bio physics,' Piran explained. 'He's based at a private hospital.'

'Actually, we've met before, sir,' Guthrie smiled at the older man. 'At your daughter Olivia's wedding.'

'Oh, yes, I forgot you'd met at my wedding,' Piran laughed.

'I was still married to Olivia's mother then,' Jonathan explained. 'As you probably know I've since remarried and have two more daughters."

'So how's life treating you, Piran?' Guthrie asked. 'And how's Olivia?'

'She's still trying out new diets, nothing seems to work.'

'Oh, dear. I have heard of a new drug that can burn fat, perhaps she could try that,' Guthrie suggested. He felt sorry for Olivia with her frizzy ginger hair, round spectacles and weight problem.

'Have you heard of this drug, Jonathan?' Piran asked.

'Yes, I have actually.'

'Can't you prescribe it for her?'

'No, unfortunately not, Piran, it hasn't been licensed here yet.'

'Well, surely you could slip her a bottle of them, not tell anyone, or say it's a clinical trial.'

'Certainly not. I have never done anything underhand in all the years I've been a doctor, and I don't intend to start now,' he retorted. 'You'll just have to continue with your philandering like you've always done.'

Guthrie loved Piran like a brother, but he knew his best friend had never been faithful to his wife, and sadly for Olivia, she also knew.

'So how's your family, Guthrie?' Piran digressed.

'My mother still lives in Ilford, but finding the shops too far to walk these days. My youngest sister has just divorced and moved in with my mother, along with her two children.'

'Well, at least she'll be able to help your mother, I suppose.'

'Doubt it, she'll be out clubbing every night knowing her,' Guthrie laughed. 'At least they live near the park, which will be nice for the kids.'

'Oh, I know the one you mean,' Jonathan joined in. 'Valentines Park, it has its own boating lake. It used to have a swimming pool. Lovely place, I had a colleague who lived in Gants Hill.'

'Oh, yes, I know it, just on the other side of the park.'

'There was a fairly large Jewish community living there in the 60s. But now, they've all moved out due to the immigrants,' Jonathan complained. 'All one sees there now are saris and burqas; one can't see a white face for love nor money.'

Guthrie did not say a word, but he caught sight of Piran, face to the floor, fists clenched tight.

After a few moments of awkward silence, Piran said, 'Guthrie wants to ask you about the job on offer at Treliske Hospital.'

Recalling the recent phone conversation with Piran, regarding a vacancy for hospital courier, Guthrie had been more than surprised to learn that Jonathan had agreed to get personally involved.

'Piran, you should know by now that's it's no longer called Treliske, but The Royal Cornwall Hospital,' Jonathan corrected his son-in-law.

'Just because they've upgraded the buildings, Jonathan, doesn't change the fact it started out life as Treliske. Everyone in Cornwall still calls it that and will continue to do so.'

Guthrie observed them both, the young man calm and happy-go-lucky, as always.

The older man, pale and agitated, as if he did not want to be there.

'I hope you don't mind, Guthrie,' Jonathan said, 'but I've already discussed it with the relevant people and they have agreed to take you on a trial period, if that's okay with you?'

Pouring a glass of iced water from the jug, Guthrie smiled. 'Thank you, Jonathan, much appreciated.'

'Only a three month trial on basic pay, after which, if they're happy, you'll be offered a contract and pay rise. You can start this afternoon if you like.'

Piran looked to Guthrie eagerly.

Guthrie replied with a nod.

'There you are then, all done and dusted,' Piran laughed, trying to keep the mood upbeat.

During their meal they made small talk, until Piran brought up the inevitable, Stella's death.

'Jonathan, what has always puzzled me is, how was it that Guthrie was charged with that woman's murder, what's your take on it?'

'Well, from what I read in the report, the bloods were found to be contaminated with Apitoxin, honey bee venom.'

Guthrie bit his lip, too painful for so many reasons. Of course he had never told Piran that Stella was his lover, it was safer that way, only his family knew.

Jonathan wiped the edge of his mouth with a serviette. 'I believe the lady who died was your colleague at a courier firm you worked for, is that correct, Guthrie?'

'Yes, we'd gone for a long weekend break to Belgium. With my other workmates I mean, about a dozen of us,' he lied, wanting to dissolve into the white tablecloth. He needed a cigarette.

'Arsenic was also found on the inside of the corpse's mouth. Well, according to the media,' Jonathan added, crossing and re-crossing his legs. 'Apparently, a syringe was found in Guthrie's hotel room in Antwerp containing the said chemical.'

'My defence also mentioned a dead bee that was found near her body,' Guthrie added. 'They wanted to run more tests on the bee, but the prosecution wouldn't agree to it, and then, suddenly it disappeared.'

'How on earth could a jury or even the police think you did it?' Piran asked. 'I mean, if you were guilty then why would you have kept the incriminating evidence in your hotel room?'

Before he had a chance to respond they were interrupted by the waitress with their desserts.

A pianist began to play the baby grand in the corner, beside a window that looked out onto a flower bed. The flowers reminded him of Stella's painted, wooden clowns that she made as a hobby. Covered in blues, reds, greens and yellows; just like their couch, table and remote control. Everywhere he looked there was a memory of her, in a floating cloud, a feather pillow, even in the biscuit tin. He missed her as if she was just a heartbeat away.

'So what brings you down to the west country?'

'Don't know really, Jonathan, just fancied a change, and Piran suggested I moved nearer to him.'

'I see, how thoughtful of you, Piran.' Jonathan focussed on the strawberry Pavlova, eagerly dipping his spoon into the meringue. 'So you both met at Exeter University, lovely campus. Did you also read law, Guthrie, is that how you and Piran both became friends?'

'No, I read philosophy.'

'We first met on the university cricket team,' Piran laughed. 'And then we found ourselves in the same class for jurisprudence. We got on so well we decided to share a room.'

'So, you didn't go on to make your fortune after graduating, I presume?' Jonathan almost sniggered. 'Well, I'm afraid to say you need ambition. Without it, then what's the point to life?'

But, there was something crucial that Guthrie had not told him, such as the 15 years immediately after graduation. Headhunted by British Intelligence during the university 'milk round', he had signed up then and there. Although, he had told his mother that he was in Italy teaching English as a foreign language. Even Piran did not know about those missing years. He could have been a millionaire several times over by now, but had given a large chunk of the money to his family. The rest was in investments and policies, which he was unable to access until December, when he turned 40, and that was 8 long months away.

'I wouldn't be where I am without ambition,' Jonathan continued the lecture. 'It's lucky you haven't got a wife or how would you support her? You need to learn a trade, get some training.'

Guthrie wanted to smack him on the chin. Before he got the chance to respond, Piran and Jonathan nipped off to the toilet.

Taking the opportunity to have a quick drag on a cigarette, he thought back to his own training, it was the best. In those first years he trained with the commandos, marines, SAS and Interpol to name but a few.

Stella knew about training, she was also an agent; he had lived with her for 3 years. They usually worked separately, but, on that last contract in December 1996, they had decided to join forces to get the job done by Christmas. It was code-named *Marzipan.* Their mission had been to assassinate an arms dealer by the name of Sebastian Dubois.

It had been easy to track him down to Ostend. They had chosen to stay at a hotel in Antwerp, a safe distance from their target. The flipping of a franc decided who would do the deed. Stella lost, and stayed back at the hotel to do some Christmas shopping, while he went off to sniper his prey. As there were as many diamond clusters crowding shop windows, as there were Hasidic Jewish clusters crowding the Antwerp streets, he had wondered if that trip would be the right time to suggest the inevitable. Antwerp was the perfect place to buy an engagement ring. But, he never did buy one, as the moment he returned to the hotel room he found Stella lying in a pool of blood. Before he had a chance to check her pulse the door burst open, and a herd of armed gendarmes rushed in. He could still hear their voices, shouting, yelling; could still feel the kicks and punches.

Judge, jury and lawyers were all in a hurry to close the case to get home for the holiday, justice came last. The problem that he was unable to disclose where he had been at the time of the murder, due to the nature of his work, did not help. It took a year before he was finally released, which confirmed there was a mole in the works, as his contact in MI6 had failed to respond to his numerous requests for assistance. Whoever had orchestrated this, had wanted Dubois killed, but why kill Stella? That was the riddle yet to be solved. Taking another drag on his cigarette, he thought how ironic that Belgium now had the Euro and not the franc; maybe if a Euro had been tossed it would have landed in Stella's favour.

Suddenly, he noticed an envelope lying on the floor near Jonathan's attaché case. Slyly retrieving it, he took a quick glance at the address on the back of the unopened letter. It was from the director of the Eden Project in St. Austell, it was addressed to a Matthew Trembath at a Cornish bee farm.

When the men returned to the table they were deep in conversation.

'What utter rubbish, Piran,' Jonathan laughed. 'I've never heard of bees used for chemical warfare.'

'It has been known that during the cold war the MOD used fleas injected with arsenic.'

'Well, I have never heard of that, think you've been watching too much TV,' Jonathan mocked. 'I mean, do you seriously think a country at war would have the time to get enough bees to take down an enemy country?'

'I bet they've experimented.'

'There wouldn't be enough bees on the planet to sting millions of people with some sort of chemical weapon. And why would they sting, unless every person was drenched in sugar or something of that sort?' Jonathan continued to scoff. 'I've never heard anything quite so ridiculous. You'll be telling me next that there's going to be a flea circus.'

Guthrie decided to take the bull by the horns.

'Have either of you heard of the Eden Project?'

'No, I've no idea what that is, sorry,' Jonathan replied. 'Talking of arsenic, I recall when I was married to Phyllis, Olivia's mother, and we went to see Arsenic and Old Lace performed by the local am-drams. Well, that night they'd actually used elderberry mead wine, without the knowledge of the actors. And so, they were all blotto by the curtain call, ha-ha.'

But Guthrie was not listening, he was wondering if there was more to Jonathan than met the eye?

CHAPTER FOUR

Truro is a small Cathedral city. In fact, it is Cornwall's only city, where the rivers of Kenwyn and Allen converge becoming the Truro River. Residing between St. Austell and Redruth on the main train route from Penzance to Paddington, the area had been a settlement since prehistoric times once boasting a Norman castle. But now, it was the magnificent cathedral, and the new NHS hospital situated on the outskirts of Truro, that was the apple of the city's eye.

It was just gone 2.30 when Jonathan and Guthrie pulled up in front of the main doors of The Royal Cornwall Hospital in a mini cab.

'The personnel officer is expecting you, her office is just inside the doors to the right.'

'Thanks very much.'

'Well I must dash, good luck with the job.'

'Thanks, appreciate it.'

Before clocking in with the personnel officer, Guthrie decided to make a quick tour of the hospital.

The buildings were numerous, and of various shapes and sizes. The complex was impressive. They had used Cornish driven names such as *The Trelawney Wing, Lamorna House, Pendragon House* and *The Mermaid Centre.* One of the wards was named after the Redruth tin mine, South Crofty. Soon he would have to waste valuable time riding up and down the dual carriageway in his new job as courier. His only consolation was, that it would only last a fortnight at most. Treliske Hospital was the reason for his move to Cornwall, due the cryptic letter he had received in prison. Now that he was here, everyone was a suspect. Stella's murderer could be here, a nurse, a cleaner, he had no idea.

Sitting down on a nearby bench, he took out the letter and re-read it for the umpteenth time.

Hi Mr Guthrie, sorry to learn of your current plight and hope it's not too bad in there. They don't allow gifts or else I'd have sent you a book or something. Anyhow, I thought I'd write you a poem to cheer you up, seeing how you are a philosopher I thought you might like it: -

'This reasoned evidence law is key. And is a high flyer with its new wing of the eagle numbered SW673455. A crown as sweet as honey on French Pancake Day, sweet as marzipan, sweet bee, the same day the star returned to heaven. Mine is the last of tin puzzles.'

Good luck, Tom Smith

Of course, he was not getting any younger, and even though it was not written in formal code, it still took longer than usual to decipher. But, time was something he had not been short of in prison. Taking the initial letters of each word on the first line it spelt *TREL*, and then, by adding, *'is key'*, he eventually worked out Treliske. Of course, he would have worked it out much sooner if he had known that such a place existed. By the time he looked it up on the web, Treliske Hospital in Truro had changed its name to *The Royal Cornwall Hospital.*

He still did not know what high flyer meant, it could refer to an entrepreneur or politician perhaps. *The star returned to heaven* was easy, an obvious reference to Stella. As for *the wing*, well, the hospital certainly had a new wing, must have cost a bob or two. Brand spanking new, it had only just opened at a cost of £27 million.

The reference to honey most probably a reference to the bee found near Stella's body. Yet what did pancakes have to do with anything? *Marzipan* was easy enough, but, who else would have known the code-name of that Belgium contract? Was the letter from someone with good intent, or was it from the mole himself, hoping to lure him out into the open?

'Eagle,' he said aloud. But, there were no eagles that he had noticed. Although, there was some sort of bird sanctuary near Hayle. Even so, he could not see what that would have to do with anything. On the other hand, the bald eagle was the symbol of the United States, perhaps Stella's killers were Yanks.

Taking out his notepad he wrote down:

1. Treliske 2. Bees

'You a doctor?' a Cornish voice interrupted his jottings. It belonged to an elderly man wearing a blue striped dressing gown. He sat down beside Guthrie.

'No, mate, about to start work here as a courier, so what are you in for?'

'Gall bladder.' His old, arthritic fingers fumbled about with sparse strands of tobacco in a tin.

'Here, have one of mine.' Guthrie offered the man the open packet.

'Thanks, don't mind if I do.'

'So, what's it like, you know, staying in the hospital?'

'Well, 'ee have to laugh, don't 'ee? I mean to say, they've spent Lord knows how much on these 'ere buildings, probably come to a billion. Yet, the wards are still as dirty as ever.'

'Oh, I'm sorry to hear that.'

'My wife died in this place. She'd had a stroke, but her nurse just shouted at her all the time. Told her that she could do more than she said she could,' the old man confided. 'Do more? She couldn't damnee speak, couldn't even walk. Yet this nurse shouted at her and made her cry.'

'Perhaps you should have told someone?'

'I demanded that she be given a different nurse, they promised they'd sort it, but never did. By the end of the week she was dead.'

Guthrie threw his cigarette stub to the ground not knowing what to say, nor having the time to say it.

'Hello, Ray,' another old man sat down on the bench. 'What did 'ee think of the dinner? I quite enjoyed the fish.'

'Would rather have had a pasty.'

He knew this was his get out and go clause.

After several wrong turnings Guthrie found himself near the mortuary. Debating whether or not to take a look, he found himself walking through the doors.

It was as he anticipated, a flag of hygiene waving across the highly polished floor and spotless walls. He wondered if they put as much effort into cleaning the wards, recalling what the old man had said.

The lights hung down from the ceiling and walls making the area intensely bright. The length of one wall was lined with refrigerated storage units. The other wall supported stainless steel sinks. In the centre of the room were rows of sterile examination tables, thankfully empty of corpses. The last mortuary he had visited had walk-in refrigerators, storing up to 15 bodies on their individual rolling tables. The mortician there had explained, that the tables were tilted towards the corpse's feet where there was a drain. To perform a post-mortem, they were moved to the sink, so that any blood and body fluids drained away.

A side door was open leading into an office. Guthrie took a peek inside the room. There was a desk supporting a phone, a vase of carnations and a large Compaq computer.

Glancing around to check he was alone, he snuck inside.

The Eden Project he typed into the oblong space. An illustration came onto the screen showing a large grassy complex within St. Austell's china clay hills. It appeared to be overrun by large objects that resembled giant golf balls. Below the illustration was a page of text:

"*The Eden Project will combine ecology, horticulture, science, art and architecture. It will provide an informative and enjoyable experience while promoting ways to maintain a sustainable future in terms of human global dependence on plants and trees. The exhibits we hope to include will be at least 100,000 plants to represent the five thousand species from many of the climate zones of the world. This Project is to be constructed in an unused china clay pit. The world's largest greenhouses will be the artificial biomes. There will also be an apiary.*"

The golf balls were apparently the biomes, igloo shaped domes with hexagonal cell-like patterns covering them. They were there to house and protect the plants that came from all over the world. It was not due to open to visitors until 17th March 2001.

Yet, what surprised him most was, the illustration on the next page. There, right in front of him, was an outline drawing of a sculpture of a giant bee.

'Good afternoon, can I help you?' a grey haired, bespectacled woman interrupted. A tweed skirt poked out from beneath her white coat.

Guthrie handed her his MOD security card, although, he was well aware that the card was out of date. He was supposed to have handed it back over a year ago, and, of course, this was not an MOD job.

She inspected the card before returning it.

'Is there a problem?'

'Firstly, I need you to ensure my visit here and my identity is not revealed to anyone, not even to the hospital executive.'

The mortician nodded. 'Jane Tresidder', she shook his hand.

'Good to meet you, Jane. I apologise for using your computer, but desperately needed to research something on the web, I hope you don't mind.'

As she did not reply it was apparent to him that she did mind.

'As I noticed your door open, I thought I'd pop in and ask a question.'

'Yes?'

'Well, a friend of mine died in Belgium, do you know where she might have had her post-mortem performed?'

'Can't really say, was she buried in the UK?'

He nodded. 'Yes, near to where she lived.'

'Well, it will be on record.'

Then suddenly a thought came to him. 'I'm just wondering; would it be possible that she had the post-mortem done here?'

'What was her name?'

'Stella Johnson.'

'Oh. Yes, I do remember.' She looked surprised, now sweeping back the fringe of her hair which had tumbled down onto her spectacles. 'The late Colin Brodie started the post-mortem.'

Guthrie nearly jumped in the air. The tip-off he had received while in prison was not just about the identity of the killer, but far more.

'Why do you need the information, is there a problem?'

'No, not really, just a few technicalities to clear up.'

'I didn't fill in the death certificate,' she admitted. 'And Colin was told not to fill it in.'

'Didn't Dr Brodie think it unusual not to fill in the death certificate himself?'

'Well, perhaps this is a breach of protocol but it needs to be said,' she confessed. 'Colin was furious at the time, as he had initiated the post-mortem. He was only about a third of the way through it when they insisted that he let someone else finish it for some reason. He died soon after.'

'Do you mind if I ask who they is?'

'Well, the hospital executive we presumed. By the way, Miss Johnson died abroad,' the woman volunteered. 'But, for some obscure reason, her body was brought here for the post-mortem. I mean, she didn't even live in Cornwall.'

'Anything else you can remember?'

The woman looked puzzled, as if there was something she could not quite recall.

'Did he find anything unusual on the body or in her belongings?' he prompted.

Her face suddenly lit up. 'Yes, that's it. Colin found two small cellophane packets in Miss Johnson's pocket. One packet contained violet seeds and the other packet contained saffron.'

'Oh, well, that is interesting.'

Stella had told him that she would go Christmas shopping on the day he had gone to Ostend, but, now he realised that she had done nothing of the sort. It made him smile to think that she had been a true professional until the very end.

'The packets disappeared on the night Colin died.'

'Can you confirm what Miss Johnson died of?'

'Well, at first it was thought she died of arsenic poisoning, but then, we also found traces of a bee sting.'

Leaning back against one of the tables she explained, 'we found sucrose in the sting, sugar. Sucrose decomposes at 186

Centigrade and turns into caramel. Colin thought it probable that some other heating device had been added.'

He was out of his depth and had no idea where this was leading. 'Sorry, I don't understand.'

'At some point in the bee's lifecycle this sugar would heat up inside the bee turning liquid into solid,' she continued. 'It would cause the bee major discomfort, and, no doubt, trigger them to sting their nearest victim.'

Guthrie suddenly felt nauseas. Was this how Stella died, in agony?

The woman held open the office door hinting for him to leave.

Smiling, he stood up and walked back into the mortuary.

'Did Dr Brodie find anything else?'

'Yes, he discovered that the sting contained traces of cocaine, and...'

'Go on,' he prompted.

'It also contained a chemical weapon of mass destruction.'

CHAPTER FIVE

Less than 250 yards from the Treliske mortuary was a large portacabin, separated from the main hospital buildings. The laboratory was filled with stainless steel cabinets and shelves that hung precariously above the sinks and worktops, most filled with surgical equipment. A small refrigerator stood in a corner, an empty cage balanced on top. In the centre of the sterile room stood an examination table and a three column theatre trolley, watched over by sophisticated lighting equipment that dropped down from the ceiling.

The Professor was exhausted, he wondered if he was anemic. His wife said it was due to pressure of work. He had to concede that she was probably right, he had hardly been home to dinner all month due to work.

A large cellophane packet filled with a white substance lay open on the table before him. Carefully scooping up the powder, he tipped it into the pan. These were not modern laboratory scales, but cast iron kitchen scales which he had owned since graduation, a gift from his late father. Positioning the small black weights onto the scales until he was satisfied with the balance, he carefully tipped the contents of the pan into a funnel attached to a large glass vial. As he pushed the stopper into the top of the vial he remembered the day his father had handed them to him. 'So proud, son,' he had beamed. Would he still be proud? He very much doubted it.

It was just as he was in the process of opening the liquid nitrogen tank to inspect the cell cultures, when he was suddenly interrupted.

'Good afternoon. I haven't seen you for ages.'

'Oh... hello, Simon, what a surprise,' he did not like people creeping up on him in the lab.

'So, tell me, why are you out here in a tin hut when Treliske has new state of the art labs? By the way, you've lost weight, is your hernia still playing up?'

The Professor ignored the interrogation.

'What brings you into this neck of the woods, working back here again?'

'No, I'm still at Derriford in Plymouth.'

'Really, I thought you'd gone to Barts.'

'Yes, that's right, but it was only a temporary post,' Simon explained, gazing around the sterile room. 'I've only popped back to see my daughter. She's still boarding at Truro School.' Simon suddenly noticed the stack of large cardboard boxes near the door. 'Busy man, you should have an assistant.'

'Yes, no rest for the wicked, as they say.'

Simon moved closer. 'So, what are you up to, cloning Dolly mark 2?' Picking up a box of growth hormone injections from the worktop, he studied the small print on the side. 'Made in Belgium, eh, so what's going on in Belgium?'

'I'm modifying some growth hormone for an endocrine patient,' he replied, hurriedly locking down the lid on the tank. 'They manufacture it in Belgium.'

'Can't they do that in pharmacy?' Simon removed his jacket as if he intended to stay. 'Anyway, I thought growth hormone could be ordered directly from Pfizer marketing in Kent.'

He had forgotten that Simon had done the occasional stint in the endocrine ward.

'Pfizer HQ is based in Belgium. I'm researching a new form of this hormone.'

'What, in liquid nitrogen?' Simon frowned. 'Oh, by the way, congratulations on the new wing at Treliske.'

'Thanks, still smells of paint. Now called The Royal Cornwall. You should go and take a look at it.'

'Perhaps I will on my next visit. By the way, nice BMW outside, good reg.'

'Yes, bought it as a Christmas gift to myself, ha-ha.'

'Great views from here, you can see right across the golf course and even Treliske's helipad,' Simon digressed, as he peered through the barred window. 'Anyway, why I've popped in is because I'm having a few drinks this evening with some of the old cads in The Trelawney. I thought you might like to join us, say around six.'

'Fine, see you then.'

After Simon had left the lab, the Professor walked towards a small cupboard. Taking a key from his trouser pocket he opened the locked door, and carefully removed a capsule. He took the capsule over to the tank of liquid nitrogen. Retrieving a phial from inside the tank, he unplugged the stopper and poured the liquid contents into the vial of white powder along with the contents of the capsule. Although he knew there was a risk of explosion, as vapour phase cryogenic storage and not liquid was now the accepted practise, but he had little choice in the matter. As he mixed up the substance he failed to notice the shadowy figure behind the small barred window.

*****

Wing Commander Paul Trembath sat opposite his wife in the restaurant of the Trelawney pub, usually full of hospital staff. Suzette was a stunningly beautiful woman with her high cheekbones, large green eyes and long, black hair. Her tall slim figure was complemented by a red silk dress and matching high heeled shoes. Trembath was also dressed for the occasion in a smart, grey suit.

It was a quaint restaurant, with fishing nets hanging from the black beamed ceiling, and a couple of old kegs standing between the pew-like benches. Photos of fishing boats and fishermen lined the walls, in between a rusty anchor and a steering wheel from a ship.

They had chatted throughout their fish supper, although, both were tired from the day's activities.

'I'll tell my father about the chimney when he's gets back, Suzette. Probably needs a sweep, I mean a professional sweep.'

'I expect you're right, not nice a dead blackbird falling into the hearth.'

'Incidentally, I spoke to the boys and they'd be happy to landscape the garden for you.'

'It's not my garden, Paul, it's your parents' home,' she gave a soft sigh. 'Anyhow, why would I want your boys doing it? I would hire a professional landscaper. I'd want a tree-house for the girls. Maybe a couple of water features, and a sundeck. Even a swimming pool, that's how it's done nowadays. Not just a piece of rockery and a few plants.'

'Yes, I suppose you're right as usual,' he replied. 'By the way, we have to go through the accounts soon, there have been a number of overheads recently.'

'Let's not talk shop, darling. Let's talk about the girls.' Suzette placed her fish knife and fork down on her empty plate, wiping her mouth with a serviette.

Trembath had also finished his meal, and was now smoking a Gaulois, savouring every inhalation.

'I know you aren't happy with them boarding, Suzette, and I miss them as much as you do. But, they get a better education than at some plebby local school. And they make contacts for life.'

'But, they are so young.'

Suzette always got her own way, but not in this case. He had insisted that they went away for several legitimate reasons, although, she had chosen the school, paid for by a trust fund left by her late father. This had been their first term away and she was missing them like crazy.

'Marietta said she needed new hockey shoes when she phoned last night. So we must add that to the list.' Suzette opened her bag and took out her lipstick and compact, and proceeded to replenish her pouting lips with a glossy pink haze. 'And Elise needs a new racket. I told her she could buy one from her teacher and we'll send the money. Or perhaps we'll go and see them?' Suzette loved her daughters more than anything in the world. 'Did I mention that Elise has passed her grade 1 on the flute and Marietta won second prize in the school gymkhana?'

'About a hundred times. Elise obviously takes after you with her music. I suppose I'd better start saving for when she wants to enroll at the Royal College of Music,' he joked.

'So, Paul, what do you think about going to see them?'

'I've told you before, I can't get away until the autumn, we'll go then. You could always pop up next week to see them if you want to, stay at a local hotel. Be a nice break.'

'No, I'll wait for the autumn, you're right there's too much to do here. Anyway, you must be exhausted after the flight.'

'Pretty much, but I couldn't miss taking you out for your birthday.' He blew his wife a kiss. 'How are the pottery classes going?'

'I've not bothered this term.'

'You should, you'd become another Bernard Leach.'

'I don't think so, but thanks for the vote of confidence. Think I'll go back to painting, it's easier.'

Re-filling their glasses with Chardonnay, he asked, 'Is Marietta still doing pottery or is it drama? Or has she given that up like everything else?'

'Don't be so cynical, she's only 9. Anyway, she's very good at arty things.'

'I thought we'd take the girls to Spain to see my parents when work eases up, they miss them,' he suggested.

'I've got a better idea; we'll invite your parents to Florida. We promised the girls we'd take them to Disneyland.'

'Okay, when this job's finished we'll go to Florida. I'll take early retirement and move anywhere you want to go.'

'I was thinking; we could move nearer to where the girls are boarding.'

'Gloucestershire? Not to my taste, Suzette. Anyway, you'd miss the sea.'

'Oh, you'd love it, darling. It's got a wonderful race track, Gold Cup and all.'

'You'd be bored.' He flicked his ash into the ashtray. 'I just can't imagine you socialising with a bunch of hobbits that strayed over from Wales on a wet afternoon.'

'Ha-ha, that's not very nice. No, I was thinking more of the Cheltenham Arts Festival,' she grinned, revealing her sensuous dimples. They have a jazz fest, science fest, and even music and lit fests. It would be a great place to live for a while.'

'I think you should have an exhibition in St. Ives,' he digressed.

'Maybe. I'd like to do some family portraits, you know, with the girls.'

'You've got such beautiful eyes,' he winked. I think it's about time we had a son.'

Suzette responded with a sneer.

'Cheltenham does sound quite nice, it sort of grows on you,' he laughed. 'By the way, I've bought you a small birthday gift.'

'You've already bought me a new flute.' She glanced down at the instrument protruding from a straw bag by her feet.

Kissing his wife on her cheek, he handed her a small box. Inside was a gold ingot and chain. The ingot was embossed with the shape of a honey bee resting on a honey pot.

'Oh, it's absolutely beautiful, thank you.'

'Happy birthday, glad you like it.' He loved his wife more than anything, loved her as passionately now as on the day they married.

The waiter approached with the bill.

'Thank you,' he nodded, placing his card and a £10 tip into the dish.

Just as Suzette was wrapping a black shawl around her shoulders ready to go, a uniformed RAF corporal walked in through the door, and headed towards them.

'I knew we should have gone to Perranporth,' he whispered to her.

'Sir, operation is ready for dispatch.'

'Well done, Corporal Mylor. Take a seat.'

'I didn't mean to disturb you, sir. I didn't realise you had company.'

'This is my wife, Suzette. Have you met before?'

'No, sir. Nice to meet you, Mrs Trembath,' Rob Mylor gave a nod, his eyes catching sight of the flute.

'Suzette's a musician.'

'I can play the penny whistle, sir,' Rob laughed. 'What do you play, Mrs Trembath, if you don't mind my asking?'

'Piano, saxophone, flute, violin, and cello.'

'Wow. If you don't mind my saying, Mrs Trembath, you look like a film star.'

'Ha-ha,' Trembath laughed, leaning back in his chair.

'My husband's laughing because I did a little stage acting when I was younger,' Suzette smiled, her dimpled cheeks adding to her sensuality.

'Her father made her give it up. He claimed she was too intelligent and packed her off to the Sorbonne, and quite rightly.'

'Oh, what a shame, you'd have made a great film star.'

'It doesn't matter, it's what you make of your life that counts,' Suzette smiled graciously.

'Suzette, why don't you order a liqueur or another coffee while I have a chat outside, shouldn't be more than 15 minutes.'

Once they were outside the pub Trembath lit up another Gaulois.

'Are the flowers ready?'

'Yes, sir, the crates are ready to go.'

'And how are you finding it, not too much?'

'Not really, sir. More like a challenge. And I really liked seeing the Indian Ocean, never seen it before, it was fantastic.'

He gave a nod of approval. 'You'll be travelling to Belgium soon, are you up for it?'

'Oh, yes, definitely, sir.'

'Glad to hear it, Corporal. I have a position for someone of your calibre. Play your cards right you could go far in the for...' Something suddenly caught his eye.

It was raining by the time the Professor left the pub. He had departed early, bored with all the nonsense they spouted. Simon, the golden boy, had constantly self-praised, as the foolish junior doctors danced around him like some demi god.

The pavement was daubed with puddles bombed by the rain, but he did not notice, walking straight through them, his shoes and trouser legs soaked.

As he neared the hospital he heard footsteps behind him. Turning round he was disconcerted to find nobody there, apart from an elderly couple sheltering at the bus stop. He should have been at home now, with his family. Playing with the children, putting them to bed; making love to his wife. They were supposed to have been planning their summer holiday this evening, but now a holiday seemed out of the question. He had missed every parents evening, every nativity play and for what?

A red helicopter flew overhead, away from the hospital. His eyes followed its trail along the night sky, embossed with grey rain clouds.

The hospital car park was packed when he entered the grounds, it was visiting time.

Footsteps - they were right behind him. He walked faster, but so did the footsteps, crunching over the uneven wet tarmac. Hurrying through the main doors of the hospital, he made a dash for the shop.

Hiding behind a pyjama stand, he wiped the perspiration from his forehead with a handkerchief. Maybe he had imagined that he was being followed, it would not be the first time.

Deciding that he needed to go home, he made his way to the car park.

Just as he was about to climb into the driver's seat he felt a hand come down hard on his shoulder.

'Hello.'

The Professor jumped with fright, his face paled on seeing the familiar figure standing before him.

'What the hell are you doing stalking me?'

'You didn't return my call.'

'I've been busy.'

'You're late with the order.'

'What do you mean I'm late?' he yelled. 'I handed over the order late because of your arseholes.'

'They most definitely aren't mine,' the man sneered. 'Just make sure you deliver on time. We'll need a batch by next week. I've found another buyer who's interested.'

'Listen, and listen well. I've told you before, I will not be bullied by you or anyone, is that clear?' he demanded, his face contorting. 'If you continue in this vein I shall just throw down my cards and go to the police and tell them everything.'

'Ha-ha, I don't think that will be beneficial to either of us. Goodbye.'

Once he was inside the safety of his car, the Professor dropped his head down into his hands and wept.

Unlocking the glove compartment, he carefully removed a bottle of Scotch he put it to his lips. When he had drunk at least quarter of the bottle he returned it back to its hideaway. Instead of locking the compartment, he removed the object lying behind the bottle, a black revolver. With trembling hands, he put the gun against his temple. Making the sign of the cross he slowly pulled the trigger. Click. But, to his deep dismay, he discovered that the gun was out of bullets.

CHAPTER SIX

It was gone 8 p.m. by the time Guthrie returned home after his first shift at work, and he was exhausted. The past 4 hours had been spent riding up and down from Truro to Derriford Hospital in Plymouth.

Lying on his bed, he thought about the letter that he had just picked up from the post office box. More like a package than a letter, in an A4 envelope. It was different to the previous correspondence, in that there was no sender's name or postmark. Yet, the envelope was written in the same handwriting as the letter he had received in prison - from the person calling himself Tom Smith.

Well, too bad, he did not have time for riddles, he just needed to rest. But, as his mother used to say, there is no rest for the wicked.

As the tea was brewing he went into the bedroom to change.

'Ride a white swan like the people of the Beltane, wear your hair long, babe you can't go wrong,' he sang, while climbing into a pair of dated black trousers. After all, he was not going out for pleasure. Really he should shower, but tonight an extra spray of deodorant and after shave would have to suffice.

In the street outside the local youths were making a din. They had probably downed a few bottles of cider from the local off licence on Fore Street. Well, he had done worse himself as a teenager in Ilford, sneaking into the clubs and pubs underage. Smiling, as he recalled the pubs that both he and his friends had entered, barely 15, *The Cauliflower, The Cranbrook,* and even one named, *General Havelock.*

After eating half a cold pasty, he decided that it was time to take a look at the contents of the envelope. Ripping it open, he discovered a thin document inside. The cover read: *MINISTRY OF DEFENCE, TOP SECRET*, along with a motto and emblem. But, he had seen enough papers like this to know they were rarely Top Secret.

Turning the first page, it showed a map and a large photograph of a desolate air base.

He was even more puzzled when he turned the next page and discovered that it was not written in code. What was the point in writing the first letter in code? Guthrie seethed. It had merely caused him the unnecessary problem of deciphering it. There again, the original note had been sent to him while in prison, and that meant anyone could have read it.

The first line of text read:

"Nancekuke Common became a Chemical Defence outstation of Porton Down Wiltshire."

Of course, he already knew that Porton Down was an MOD agency. It was a government military science park, a defence research institute. It had often been criticized for developing and testing out weapons of mass destruction on animals and humans.

He continued reading down the page.

"Nancekuke Common manufactured the nerve agents, sarin, CS and VX, Illegal

under the Geneva Convention of 1925. Churchill had wanted to increase production there, but his plans were halted when he suffered a stroke. In 1969 there was a protest by locals and others against the manufacture of chemical weapons at the base, as seals, fish and birds were dying in the area. Although the MOD assured the public that production had ended in the late 1950's, it was known that it was still being manufactured until at least 1980. They claimed to have destroyed all the buildings when it was given back to RAF Portreath, which is now 'officially' just a reporting post for RAF St Mawgan. But they lied! Not all the buildings were destroyed. Nancekuke Common produced 20 tons of the nerve gas sarin during 1951 to 1976 and 35 tons more after, 41 men died from working there, 9 of them during their time of employment. That was 41 out of the 150 workers employed on the base – and production is continuing. There are five dumping areas for chemical waste on the hill top. Some of the chemical waste was disposed of down mineshafts."

What was the person thinking, sending this letter to him? After all, he was not an agent anymore so why would he be interested?

Irritated, he turned to the next page.

"The squadron from RAF Portreath were sent to the former Republic of Yugoslavia in Jan 1997. 34 Sqn RAF Regt were presented with the Wilkinson Sword for Peace 1997 jointly with 1 Sqn RAF Regt for providing humanitarian support throughout Operation LODESTAR. During their absence the Wing Commander was made second-in-command over RAF Portreath.'

'So what have you been up to when the boys were away, I wonder?'

Taking another look at the note that he received in prison, he scrutinised the words until he came to the line,

"And is a high flyer with its new wing of the eagle numbered SW673455."

Perhaps, if he had done better with formal logic at university, this deciphering might have come easier. He guessed that SW must mean the south-west of Cornwall.

Opening his wallet, he removed a small travelling map of Cornwall, it had Ordinance Survey numbers on the back pages. Deciding that it would be best to start with the west coast towns and villages first, he traced his finger down the page:

OS - Grid Ref: SW475306 - Penzance; OS - Grid Ref: SW756540 - Perranporth.

He continued down the page until he came to OS - Grid Ref: SW673455 – It was the RAF base.

Nancekuke Common and RAF Portreath were one and the same.

*****

Riding the Harley along Penberthy Road into Portreath, less than 3 miles from Redruth, Guthrie noticed Nance Wood, a dense fortress of trees. A great hiding place for a camera or spying eyes, to view any visitors heading up to the airbase, he thought. Turning off into Tolticken Hill, he rode up the long winding lane bordered with trees and thick foliage on each side. At the top of the lane he was confronted by a noticeboard pinned to a large steel gate. It read:

MOD - RAF PORTREATH – NO ENTRY - TRESPASSERS WILL BE PROSECUTED

The gate was flanked by high fencing and barbed wire, it appeared to be connected to electricity cables.

Feeling slightly uneasy, he pulled out his Walther PPK pistol from his pocket and carefully attached the silencer.

A rodent of some sort was digging a hole near the fence, confirming that the electricity was not turned on.

Using his flick knife, he cut a large hole in the wire and then climbed through. The silence unnerved him.

Looking through his infra-red, optic and night vision goggles, which allowed him not only to see his own breath quicken, but also the body heat from unseen enemies, he noticed that the whole terrain was densely bordered by trees.

Ten minutes later he found himself inside the complex. Running breathlessly through the trees and across the uneven ground, he eventually came to a lane that led into a small empty car park. It was surrounded by sporadic single storey buildings and a couple of tall chimney stacks. Some buildings resembled derelict 1950's prefabs, others, warehouses, like the buildings at the factory shops just down the Portreath road. Even the row of barracks looked more like a museum piece than a functioning defence unit.

Many of the stone buildings were badly damaged, which made him question why they had not been pulled down.

Obviously it was vastly different to 1941, when the base was an RAF Fighter Command Sector Station and Overseas Air Dispatch Unit.

He needed a cigarette. The lighter failed to light on the first two attempts, but did on the third. It reminded him of when he was at school, and his classmates' warning never to take the third light. His mother had told him that the superstition came from the war years.

After a few deep drags he decided to crawl towards a long, single storey block, designed on a similar scale to the barracks, but this was much smarter. Beige walls, brown window frames and sloping slate roofs. There was a tree outside on the walkway, by the made up road. Paths led from the road to all the front doors, giving the impression that this was a normal block of bungalows or offices in a normal street in the centre of town. Except for the large blue notice stating: *ROYAL AIR FORCE PORTREATH.*

The lawn was neatly trimmed, with a few daisies sprouting up around the signpost. A garage stood at the end of the block with a metallic blue BMW convertible parked outside. A parked car meant that the driver was somewhere about. Maybe that was why the electric fence had been turned off.

Rubbing off the gravel and stones that had imbedded into his dusty palms, Guthrie decided to take a look at the car. Keeping down as low as possible, he ran across the open space towards the vehicle.

Sliding across to the driver's seat, he reached into the glove compartment. There were just some gloves, a map, and a half empty bottle of whiskey. On the back seat were several children's toys. Just ordinary stuff you would expect to see in a car, now feeling disheartened, it had been a waste of time.

Sliding back out of the vehicle, he dropped down to the cold ground. Crawling along on his belly he suddenly noticed the bridge over a narrow stream. Moving towards it he noticed a small dilapidated utility building resembling a garden shed. The windows were secured with iron grates, the door padlocked. It made little sense why this ramshackle concrete shed would be secured, unless it contained something of value. But a padlock did not stop him.

A nasty stench greeted him as he entered. It was empty, apart from an Air Force badge on the floor with the motto, '*Ever Alert*'. Dirt and cobwebs filled every corner of the ceiling. Paint was patched and peeling and the wooden floor had descended into the earth below. The only furniture were two cupboards. Opening one of the cupboards he found it thick with cobwebs, now wondering if there was any point in continuing with the search, he was running late as it was. An empty jar caught his eye, perched on the dusty shelf, labelled Trembath's Cornish Honey. Holding the jar to his nose he could smell traces of honey. There also lingered another smell, probably mould. On the top shelf of the next cupboard was a grubby book about wild flowers, there was a bookmark inside advertising *KING BEE HONEY*. But the *King* had been crossed out with a pencil and *Queen* had been scribbled in its place.

Bending down to inspect the space under the shelf, he found a large bundle wrapped in a polythene sheet. Pulling off the sheet thick with dust, he was disappointed to find only a long black gabardine coat, a large brimmed hat, a fake black beard, and two ringlet lengths of hair.

Gripping tight at the fake ringlets, he tried to remember where he had seen them before. And then it suddenly came to him. It was a Hasidic costume; like those he had seen worn in Antwerp. What if one of the men in Belgium had not been an authentic orthodox Jew? Maybe, someone used the disguise in order to watch them, follow them? Was the owner of this costume the man who had murdered Stella, if so, why keep the costume? Unless of course, the wearer had plans for future use, or maybe just keeping it as a trophy. But, more importantly, who was the author of these letters, this Tom Smith? Could he in fact be the murderer, just enjoying playing mind games? Then suddenly he saw them, a row of gas canisters that had been hidden behind the polythene.

*****

The music pounded loudly, as the dancers wiggled their hips and the drinks flowed. The Twilight Zone was packed to overflowing. Pseudo trendies of all shapes and sizes filled the dance floor. Overlooked by spectators seductively draped around the spiral staircase, that led up to the balcony where more drinks were to be had.

Guthrie leaned over the balcony to see what talent there was on offer, if any. Yet, if truth be told, he just wanted to go home to bed and sleep. Checking his watch, it was 11 o'clock. Perhaps the hospital noticeboard had given the wrong date for the hen night. Wishing it was not quite so noisy he took another gulp of the neat Scotch - And then he spotted them, a group of nurses dressed as French maids with their caps, aprons, stockings and suspenders and not much else.

They headed towards the bar tottering on their high heels, shrieking and giggling for attention, as the bleary-eyed males leered. They did not look much like nurses that was certain, with boobs and bums flashing around. He wondered which one he should approach.

Returning to his table in the corner, he swigged back the remainder of Scotch. About to make his move, he was suddenly interrupted.

'Excuse me, is this seat taken?'

She was around 30, blonde streaks, very pretty face and curvaceous, but not quite as slim and toned as he normally went for. Anyway, he was not looking for romance; just a quick shag with a brainless nymphette who might be willing to do his bidding.

About to refuse her request she sat herself down.

'You a body builder?'

'No.' He made a move to stand up and walk away, when she suddenly grabbed his arm.

'Do you want a drink?' She was obviously drunk.

He did not reply straight away, weighing up his options.

'I'm with the hen party,' she revealed, on noticing the direction of his gaze.

'Where are your stockings then?' he mumbled disinterestedly, peering beyond her to the young, suspender-glad nurses.

Suddenly, out of the corner of his eye he caught sight of her huge breasts overflowing their harness.

'Are you a Treliske nurse?'

'Used to be, hope to be going back there soon. I still do a bit of part-time when they're stretched. So, what are you drinking?'

'I'll buy you a drink instead. Let's go downstairs.'

Leading the way down the winding staircase he headed to the bar.

'What would you like?'

'Bacardi and coke, please.'

'Why don't I buy a bottle at the off licence and take it back to yours, where do you live?'

'Strawberry Lane, do you know it?'

He nodded. It was the local council estate.

She hooked his arm as they headed off, her tottering on high heels, him staring at her cleavage.

As they neared the council estate he stopped outside an off licence, and purchased a couple of bottles of Bacardi, and cans of Coke.

'Fancy the chippy? I'm starving.' He had not eaten since lunch, and it was almost midnight.

'I'm sort of on a diet,' she giggled.

'Oh, you don't need to worry, got it in all the right places.' He thrust his arm about her waist and squeezed her tight.

They ate the hot vinegary chips on the way home, passing small groups of youths eager for battle, and couples fornicating in the shadows.

The pubs had closed for the night, but that did not stop the drunks from hanging around outside.

Her house was tiny but clean. The beige wallpaper was torn in places and the room needed a lick of paint. A 1970s red and black settee filled most of the room. In one corner stood an armchair, in the other, a TV and a music centre. The speakers had sellotape holding them together. On the small coffee table was a party political leaflet, he peered down at the small print.

Redruth has a population of 6,800. It has the fourth worst antisocial behaviour rate in Cornwall. According to statistics from the Cornwall and Isles of Scilly Safety Partnership, which comprises local authorities and the police, it has the most poverty-stricken three per cent in the country. 45 per cent of the 1,800 people in this area of Redruth North are on some kind of benefits.

Jonathan had mentioned over lunch, that during the 18th and 19th centuries Redruth had been one of the wealthiest mining towns in the world.

'I won't ask if you're a Labour supporter.'

'I'm not particularly; none of them are any good,' she said, her voice nervous.

Perhaps she was regretting his presence, if so, there was still time to get back to the Twilight Zone. Although, most of the nurses would be taken by now.

'Oddly enough the Tories usually get in here, not certain why. Perhaps they don't want to build more council estates in Redruth.'

He was not listening, his attention now fixed on the photographs that lined the tiled mantelpiece. Most were of a boy of around 3 years of age; a couple of the prints were of a man and a woman.

'My son's sleeping up the road with my neighbour for the night,' she explained guiltily.

'Cute looking boy,' was all that he could think to say.

Through the gap in the curtain the full moon hovered in space, like a white witch casting spells on tides and minds. Rod Stewart sang in the background as they shared the bottle of Bacardi, chatting about menial topics. He quite liked the singer's raspy voice.

Moving across to the sofa to sit next to her, he focussed on her breasts as he placed his arm around her shoulders. Pulling her close, he kissed her. By the time it came to the track, Waltzing Mathilda, Guthrie had finished the bottle and was Waltzing Mathilda into her bed.

CHAPTER SEVEN

Two miles away, a black Mercedes was reversing onto the abandoned terrain of South Crofty tin mine, that rested in the shadows of Carn Brae hill. A row of terraced houses were sited directly opposite the headgear. Beside it, stood the engine house and tall stack, cast in silver by the moon.

Three men stood near the car smoking.

'You're certain this is the right entrance, Mo, as there are other mine shafts in Pool?' Aabid, the handsome 24 year old, asked the leader of the group.

'South Crofty is an amalgamation of twelve mines,' Mohammed replied.

'I've told you before that I didn't want this done in public for the whole world to witness.'

'It's not my fault, Aabid.'

'Well whose fucking fault is it?' Aabid raged. 'We were supposed to have done this before dawn this morning.'

'Yes, but the tug didn't pull into Falmouth until two hours ago. It couldn't be helped. Anyway, don't worry they don't have any CCTV here.'

'What about CCTV in the street itself, have you checked that? And anyone might see us from their window. We'll never get away with this,' Aabid warned. 'Sheik Amir doesn't have a clue that there are houses nearby.'

'Yes, but the cage is right over the back there, behind the buildings.' Mohammed pointed across the barren ground to the derelict constructions. 'Nobody can see it from the road.'

'It's a fucking full moon, the whole fucking world can see us! Why not go for broke and do it outside the police station?' Aabid threw his cigarette stub to the ground. 'Even I can see the cage from here, it's in full view.'

'Not that cage, ours is in a derelict shower block that hasn't been used for years!' Mohammed barked, leading the way to the car boot.

Rashid, the youngest member of the trio, kept his head down, as he slunk across the rough gravel, following in the footsteps of his two co-conspirators.

Mohammed unlocked the boot. Inside was a small steel trunk.

'How will the lift work if it hasn't been in use for years?' Rashid asked.

Mohammed was annoyed at their neurosis, his black moustache beginning to twitch. As the eldest of the trio they should respect him.

'Show me some respect. And it's not a lift, it's a cage!' he shouted, taking a large torch from the boot. 'I've been informed that it's been set up ready for us in good working order. I'm not totally stupid, you know.'

After several more mutterings the men grabbed the handles of the small trunk and tried to lift it.

'It's too heavy with all that gold,' Rashid complained.

'Look at the size of it,' Mohammed said, switching on the torch. 'It's a miniature chest and only a third full.'

'It doesn't feel like a third full.'

'Look, you're not holding it right, idiot.'

'Don't call him an idiot!' Aabid shouted. 'He's not an idiot. You're the idiot for getting us into this crap.'

'I only obey orders.'

'Why the fuck, as a grown man, don't you think for yourself? Aabid demanded. 'We've been set up here by Trembath, and you know it! They should have flown it directly back themselves rather than all this nonsense.'

Struggling beneath the weight of the trunk, gripping hard at the handles, they headed across the rugged terrain ignoring the warning sign:

DANGER — DO NOT TRESPASS

They could still see the stack and headgear in the distance, standing like redundant monarchs overseeing their realm that was disintegrating around them. Deserted by their subjects, only the abandoned buildings remained, along with a few broken locomotives trapped inside their cages.

More warning signs greeted them outside the fence guarding a concrete building. They placed the trunk down onto the dusty ground.

'For goodness sake, I suppose now we've got to cut through this.' Aabid brushed down his clothes.

'No, don't worry, we won't have to cut anything,' Rashid mocked. 'Because Mo doesn't have any wire cutters.'

Mohammed scanned the perimeter of the fence.

'Look, it's already been cut, see, you wasters!' he raged. 'What, you thought I was an imbecile?'

The main door of the shower block looked to be in a bad state of disrepair, under the glaring beam of the torch. The padlock was broken and rusty, the paint was peeling off the door. Inside, they were greeted by a row of broken showers filled with garbage. *CAPTAIN'S OFFICE* was painted on a side door in bold blue lettering. When they reached the cage at the far end of the shower block, they dropped the steel trunk to the floor, and climbed into the protective orange overalls they found hanging on pegs.

'We should have parked the car in a side road,' Aabid said breathlessly. 'If someone looks over here they'll know we're here because of the car.'

'Who's going to walk all the way here?' Mohammed asked, putting on a helmet with two lamps attached.

'Police, clubbers, you name it,' Aabid replied sarcastically. 'Look, the notice on the cage says no more than 8 persons to ride in the cage, what does the chest weigh?'

'What's that paint for?' Rashid interrupted, noticing the small pot of paint in Mohammed's overall pocket.

'Ready?' Mohammed asked, ignoring the questions.

They grabbed the handles of the trunk and squeezed into the rusty, steel cage.

Mohammed opened up a map.

'You'll never be able to read that once we're down there, it will be pitch black,' Aabid scoffed.

'That's what torches are made for.' Mohammed pulled the bell. 'There should be some lighting on down in the mine. They charged the cage up just for us.'

'I'm so pleased,' Aabid said. 'It's my life's quest to be trapped inside a mineshaft and no one to know I'm there.'

The cage began to move, squeaking and jolting as if about to break. Their hearts pounded. Their eyes desperately searching for a spark of light, but there none. There was only darkness, as the cage bumped its way down into the black abyss.

The cage shook and squeaked like a door off its hinges, as it descended into the depths of the earth, a world where most never ventured.

Then suddenly, it picked up speed, now racing down like a free fall drop ride at a funfair.

'Allah, save me!' Rashid screamed, as they plunged down into a bottomless pit.

It seemed as if they had descended miles before it eventually slowed down and then juddered to a halt. The men dropped to their knees, overwhelmed by their experience. Once they had caught their breath, they crawled out of the cage into the black void.

The damp stench overwhelmed them, as they found themselves in a narrow stope. The arced ceiling only inches above their heads, forced them to remain on their knees. With only the lights on their helmets to guide them, they crawled over the rocky ground, attempting to drag the steel trunk along with them.

'This is just a large pipe, we'll never get through it,' Aabid said, sliding across the lumpy ground on his belly. 'Why isn't this mine like others where you can stand?'

'Because, Aabid, this is a very old part of the mine, it has not been used for many, many years.'

After crawling a few metres they arrived at a ladder, it led down into another seam.

'We can't carry this chest down a ladder...oh!' Rashid yelled.

'What?'

'There is a big hole right beside me!'

The three men beamed their lights down at the large cavity penetrating through the rock, a stope that was filling with water.

'Okay, we'll have to turn around and go back to the cage, and go down that way,' Mohammed suggested, straining to read the map.

'You're lost, aren't you?' Rashid accused Mohammed. 'I bet you sent the cage to the wrong floor.'

'I bet you're right,' Aabid concurred. 'Doubt we'll ever escape from this fucking dungeon. Did you hear that, Mo? We've come the wrong fucking way!'

'We'll probably get silicosis,' Rashid mumbled, as they headed back to the cage.

As they descended to the lower seams the temperature rose. The deeper they went underground, the hotter and wetter it became. As with every 100m deeper, the rock temperature increased by 1°C. By the time the cage rattled to a halt all three men were stripped down to their underpants.

Once again, they began the trek along the rough, rocky ground, but this stope was swathed in water. For the next hour they hobbled and crawled along the dark labyrinth of tunnels and stopes, the cavities where ore had once been extracted. Broken cables and wires hung precariously from the walls and ceilings. The beams on their helmets were unable to stop them from bashing their bodies against hidden protrusions, or entering blind alleys. Often they found themselves wading knee high in water, pushing and pulling the small trunk over the rough ground.

Mohammed occasionally stopped to paint a red cross on the damp walls along the way, as a guide for future treks.

Eventually they arrived at a man-made tunnel, a steel and aluminium construction. A large Clayton battery locomotive stood before them, attached to a tipping wagon.

'The loco's been charged up for us,' Mohammed said, signalling to his companions to lift the trunk into the wagon.

‘Look, there’s another tunnel over there with its lights on. We came the wrong fucking way!’ Aabid ranted.

‘I don’t believe it,’ Rashid dropped to his knees with exhaustion. ‘We’ve just gone through all that for nothing; we got off at the wrong level again!’

After climbing onto the wagon, they travelled for about 3 miles in complete darkness. Then suddenly, in the distance, they saw a bright light at the end of what looked to be a cave, it was the moon.

‘The sea, it’s the sea!’ Mohammed shouted.

Exhausted, the men lifted the trunk out of the wagon.

‘Why couldn’t we have brought the chest in this way by boat, instead of half killing ourselves going the long way round?’ Aabid groaned, yet, pleasantly overcome by the salty fresh smells from the ocean, as he entered the cave flooded by moonlight.

‘Because we didn’t know which cave led from the sea to the tunnel until we walked the walk,’ Mohammed puffed.

'What a load of shit!' Aabid shouted. 'If someone could set up the cage and charge the loco for us to get here, then they could have given us a map to sail here instead of this crap.'

'We might have been seen if we came here by boat.'

'Seen by whom?' Aabid demanded.

'Seen by the security at RAF Portreath, the base is right above us. There must be security cameras everywhere!' Mohammed shouted, annoyed by Aabid's whining.

'They're having a laugh at us,' Aabid raged. 'They just wanted to make fools of us! If they can drop their chemical waste from a plane, then they could also collect the gold.'

Mohammed scoffed, 'we're not supposed to know about the drops, that's supposed to be top secret, Aabid.'

'I don't know how they get away with it.'

'Forget that now, we're in Portreath and that's all that matters at the moment.'

'So how do they get it out from here?' Rashid asked, inspecting the cave.

'Secret entrance,' Mohammed pointed to a padlocked door in the cave wall. 'It leads into one of those bunker type things on the base.'

'Still don't know why they couldn't have picked it up in Belgium, and flown it directly here.'

'How many times, Aabid? How do you propose they hide gold bullion in an RAF aircraft? It's not easily hidden if anyone should want to inspect it.'

'Well, they manage to smuggle RAF guns in the aircraft easily enough, when they fly them out to Sheik Amir.'

'Good point, Aabid, I hadn't thought of that,' Rashid nodded. 'If they are dropping off guns in Dubai, wouldn't it make sense to pick up the gold then?'

Mohammed was fed up, exhausted. He just wanted to go home to his wife and family back in Dubai.

'Here, help me lift the chest over there.' He pointed to a small cemented area, in front of a small door. 'That must be the other entrance out of the base. Behind the door are steps leading out onto the side of the cliff, above Lighthouse Hill.'

'Where's Lighthouse Hill?'

'It's a residential road, Rashid. It terminates just below the airbase.'

'Oh, this RAF base is very secure then, surrounded by lots of neighbours,' Aabid gloated. 'So, why couldn't we have driven the chests up the cliff and brought it in that way, as the CCTV cameras would presume we lived there?'

'The cliff's too steep to carry them from the road, like the side of a mountain.'

'Oh, and the mine was so fucking flat and easy to walk along,' Aabid replied. 'What's the point of the RAF having a security system on their base, if you can just enter it by the back door?'

Mohammed fumed. 'This cave is part of South Crofty tin mine, not a military base, remember? And the actual back door, as you say, is a bunker built into the side of the cliff, well-hidden and secured.' He dipped into his pocket. 'See I have the keys.'

'How many more chests do you expect?' Rashid tried to defuse the hostility.

'At least five more, and that's only this batch,' Mohammed replied, unlocking the door.

'Why can't they wait, why does it have to be done now?' Aabid snapped.

'Because this mine only closed down last month in March.' Mohammed wiped the sweat from his head. 'That means the water hasn't had time to flood all the lower seams.'

Aabid and Rashid sat down on the rocky ground and lit their Turkish cigarettes. Their tired eyes now focussed on the black ocean, that lapped up to the edge of the cave, illuminated by a sliver of moonlight.

'The other chests will follow once Sheik Amir receives his payment.' Mohammed joined them on the ground.

'What in guns?' Rashid sneered.

'If only it were just guns,' Aabid complained. 'What glory it will bring to Allah, blessed be He. I always had ambitions of being involved in smuggling chemical weapons of mass destruction.'

'You must never mention the contents of the case!' Mohammed ignored his taunts. 'You refer to it only as, Sweet Bee, is that clear?'

Aabid continued to snigger whilst blowing out rings of smoke. 'It's not going to be just one suitcase-load of bee serum, is it? And why were we chosen above all others, because of our great expertise, Mo?' he looked to the older man grinning. 'No, of course not, it was because we were the only idiots out of Sheik Amir's workforce who spoke English, and didn't have a criminal record.'

Mohammed did not reply. Instead, he removed the paint pot and brush from his overall pocket, and made his way towards the end of the cave where it met the sea. Dipping the brush into the pot, he proceeded to paint a red cross on both the inside and outside walls of the cave.

'Can't miss it,' Mohammed said proudly, admiring his handiwork.

'Picasso couldn't have done any better,' Aabid sniggered.

'We'll now return to the Penventon,' Mohammed said, leading them out through the side door. 'We'll get a few days rest, before the next chest arrives.'

'Great, so looking forward to it,' Rashid groaned, as he trudged up the steep flight of stone steps.

'Don't worry, boys, you're right. We'll do it at night next time, and come by boat. It will be much easier so long as we're not seen.'

'What about their security, is that no longer an issue?' Aabid asked sarcastically.

'I'll give Trembath an ultimatum. Either he turns off the CCTV or else we won't deliver.'

CHAPTER EIGHT

The following morning over a mug of strong tea, she hinted about seeing him again but Guthrie did not reply. She wore a candlewick dressing gown over her naked body. Her face looked pale without make-up, her eyes puffy and red, caused by her drinking spree the night before.

'You like living here?' he asked, stirring more sugar into his tea.

'Are you joking?'

'It's got a nice name, Strawberry Lane.'

'Well, I haven't seen any strawberries have you?' she laughed.

Guthrie wanted to light up, but thought she might object.

'The father of your son...'

'My husband, Tom, died a month before our son was born, lung cancer. I named the baby after him, Tommy,' she explained, her eyes watering. 'We owned a lovely house in St. Agnes, overlooking the sea. Had a lovely nursery ready for the baby. Tom had spent months redecorating the house and landscaping the garden. And then, when he got sick, all our savings were eaten up with lawyers, and other crooks when we tried to sue the company.'

He felt sorry for her, for what he had done. Pity was an emotion he rarely felt for his victims, and she was a victim. He wanted to say, 'yes, I understand your grief, my girlfriend died too.' He so wanted to say it, but failed.

'He worked in the mines, you see. Mostly Geevor, but that closed down in 1990. Tom wasn't a miner but a geologist, he had a PhD.'

'Wasn't he life insured or anything?'

'Yes, of course. But the insurance company wouldn't pay up because they said it was the mining company who were liable, because he died from working down the mines.'

'Radon gas?'

'I'm not certain,' she shrugged.

'Mind you, there are numerous lung diseases from working down mines. Well, so I've been told.'

'The mining company won't pay out as they tried to deny liability. They said that the life insurance company should pay and vice versa,' she explained, buttering a slice of toast. 'Waiting for it to go to court, but the solicitors here are rubbish. Have some toast.' She pushed the plate towards him.

'Thanks.' He took a slice and buttered it. 'Do you often bring men back?' Guthrie regretted it as soon as the words had been spoken.

'Last night was the first time. I was drunk. It's also the first time I've left Tommy with a babysitter overnight, apart from when I work. But, I'm not going to make excuses.' Her blue eyes watered. 'Last night was the anniversary of Tom's death. I just didn't want to be alone.'

'How do you manage, I mean financially?'

'I used to be a full-time nurse, a ward and theatre sister in Treliske,' she volunteered. 'But I had no one to look after my son every day. So, apart from the occasional stint there when they're short staffed, I have to make do working as a chamber maid at the Penventon until he goes to school next year, and then I can go back part-time.'

'I suppose child minders are expensive.'

'He comes to work with me at the moment, I only do mornings. Start at nine finish by two most days,' she sighed. 'They don't mind as he's very good. I wouldn't leave him with a stranger, especially not after he's lost his father.'

'What about the person who babysat last night?'

'Oh, yes, well the old lady takes care of him if I have to go to Treliske on emergency cover, but she's too old and frail to look after him daily.'

'What about your family?' He wondered why he was bothering to ask so many questions to a one night shag.

'My family live in Ilford, it's in Essex. But, I wouldn't be eligible for a council house there now, even if I wanted to go back. And I definitely can't afford to buy one.' She put down her mug of tea and laughed. 'Ha, you've asked all these questions about me, and I know nothing about you.'

He gave a wink, shocked that she came from the same place he did, Ilford.

'Actually, I noticed you yesterday lunchtime at the Penventon, whilst I was cleaning one of the bedrooms. I saw you walking out of the reception with two men,' she said, buttering a slice of toast. 'I laughed at the mix up with the attaché cases.'

'What mix up?' he asked, helping himself to more toast.

'It was the older man who was with you, he put down his attaché case near the porch,' she explained. 'It was right near to the case belonging to one of the Arabs who are staying at the hotel. I noticed that they each picked up the wrong case. I tried to wave to them but no one saw me, and by the time I got to reception everyone had driven off. I hope your friend got his case back.'

'So, what do you know about these Arabs?'

'Oh, not a lot, just that they're very good tippers. I think they're from Dubai, you know, the United Arab Emirates.'

'Are they here for work or pleasure?' He tried to sound nonchalant.

'I think they have something to do with South Crofty. I found some maps of the mine on a table when I cleaned their room. They're probably studying at the Camborne School of Mines. They take a lot of foreign students.'

'They'll obviously be very rich when they return home to wherever, you should get in with them,' he teased. 'Or do you prefer us poor Brits?'

'Sorry, I drank too much last night.'

'Don't worry about it. So, you sometimes work at Treliske, what's your name again?'

CHAPTER NINE

Tehidy Country Park was 3.4 miles from Strawberry Lane, Redruth. Two hundred and fifty acres of spectacular woodland thick with trees and shrubs, and nine miles of nature trails, giving the opportunity for mountain-biking and horse riding. There were even trails for the visually impaired. The large mansion house that stood in the grounds, was once home to the wealthy Bassett family, who had made their fortune from tin and copper. Now the mansion had been transformed into apartments.

Riding his Harley into North Cliff car park he wondered if he should forget today and go home to bed. He was tired, only been in the job a week, but, after spending a year just sitting in a cell he was feeling the strain.

A haze of bluebells greeted him on entering the woods, rocking to the tune of the westerly winds. Thick with foliage and flora, the country park offered protection to numerous creatures, including bats, badgers and foxes. Two grey squirrels ran over hoping for a treat, alerted by his feet crunching over the broken twigs. Of course, this was not the easiest route to take, in order to get where he was heading; but it was definitely more interesting.

Information posts were scattered across the park, giving the names of the vegetation, and other scientific data. Following a stream along its course, he eventually reached Otter Bridge, where he stopped to light up. The information post told him that the stream flowed from Tehidy Park right out to the sea at Godrevy Point. He wondered if this stream was connected in any way to the red river, that Redruth was named after.

Continuing along a daffodil bordered path, he arrived at a lake that gave refuge to swans and emerald headed ducks. The blossoming trees were in abundance here. Maple, conifers, horse chestnut trees, towering above the bushes and shrubs; casting shadows along the paths and lakes.

As he walked beneath the shadows of the trees, along the paths carpeted in pink and white blossom, he was unable to fully appreciate the beauty of his surroundings. His mind focussed only on Stella.

The signpost read:

TEHIDY BEE FARM

Bees had been the second word on his agenda.

Rows of white beehives were lined up in the distance, resembling miniature beach chalets. He would feign he was a student from the African Continent, who had come to study at the Camborne School of Mines. Numerous students from Namibia studied there, as the country had a wealth of diamond mines.

'Excuse me, sir, are you Mr Matthew Trembath?'

The stout bearded man sitting on a tractor turned to look at him. 'Who wants to know?' he grunted in broad Cornish.

Guthrie was about to offer his hand, but changed his mind. 'I'm a student at Camborne School of Mines, and I'm researching bees surviving in tin mines. It's for my dissertation.'

'Bit old aren't 'ee, boy? Should get yourself a proper job,' the man said, wiping his nose on his sleeve. 'Never 'erd of a bee going down a tin mine.'

'I wonder, would you mind if I took a quick look around, perhaps take some photos for my dissertation. It would be a good advert for your honey.'

'I used to be a miner, and my faither before me, and I can say that none of we ever saw a bee down a mine shaft.'

'Oh, really? They're a big thing in Botswana's diamond mines, replacing the old canary.' Guthrie had sunk.

So, he was more than surprised, when the man said, 'Matthew Trembath be on holiday in Spain with his missus, he's the owner. But, I suppose he wouldn't mind 'ee taking photos. Long as 'ee don't touch anything.'

Taking out a small notepad and pen to feign that his was writing notes, he began to inspect the hives.

Over on the far side of the field stood a plush white farmhouse. Guthrie presumed that honey must have a far higher turnover than he had previously imagined.

When he was certain the tractor was far enough away, he headed towards the farmhouse. As he drew near, it turned from a farmhouse into a white mansion with a double garage.

He wondered about security as he approached the front door and rang the bell. Having waited about 7 minutes he turned to leave. Just then the door opened, a young woman stood inside wearing a white cap and apron, obviously the maid.

'Oh, hello, sorry to bother you, but I'm doing a dissertation on bees.'

'Sorry, Mr Trembart' is away. Do you want to leave your card?' The maid was extremely pretty with auburn hair and a figure to die for. She spoke in a strong Irish brogue.

'My name is Gu. . .Gumtree.'

'Oh, yeah, and oi'm Mrs Trembart'.'

'Gumtree. That was my father's tribe, an African tribe. Haven't you heard of the Gumtrees?' he feigned to be incredulous.

'There's CCTV all around, you know. And also oi would take a bet that you're the only black man in the woods.'

'Are you being racist?' he raised his brows.

'No, sir, oi don't be racing nowhere, oi only walk.' She suddenly softened and smiled. 'Well, you'll be wanting a cup of tea or something stronger oi expect, so you might as well come in.'

Following her across the vestibule, they passed a large staircase that had a replica marble statue of a naked boy standing at the bottom.

She led him into the kitchen, where they perched on stools by the coffee bar. A copy of The Tatler lay open beside an empty cup.

Dropping the African voice, he asked, 'what's your name?'

'Kat'leen O'Brien. Direct descendent from the great Brian Boru, King of Ireland,' she smiled. 'You can call me Katie.'

'Brian Boru, eh? I've heard the tune, Brian Boru's march.'

'That's who the O'Briens' are named after.' She offered him a biscuit. 'Homemade. Tea or coffee?'

'Is it Typhoo?'

'Co-ops own brand.'

'Coffee please,' he said, biting into the buttery, sugary shortbread. It was just what he needed to give him an energy boost. 'So Tehidy Wood backs onto this land, then?'

'Yes, that's why there's security, to stop kids climbing t'rough the fence. One got badly stung once.'

'Did a security alarm tell you I was in the grounds?'

'No. The security is broken. Someone's coming to fix it around tea time,' she raised her brows. The maid placed the coffee percolator in front of him, and then sat on the stool opposite.

'You work hard,' he remarked, pouring her coffee first.

'You can say that again, bloody slave drivers.'

'I take it you don't like them.'

'Hate them. But it's a job.'

'So where are your freckles?'

'My what?' she giggled.

'Your freckles, all natural redheads have freckles on their face.'

'Well, oi must be an anomaly.'

'Do you have kids?'

'Why, you going marry me?'

'You've got lovely green eyes, Katie.'

'Same colour as yours, perhaps we're related.'

'Comedienne, I like it. Actually, I had a friend who lived around the Tehidy area, I wonder if you've heard of her?'

'What's her name?'

'Stella Johnson.'

'No, sorry.'

'She died.'

'Oi'm sorry to hear that, heart attack?'

'No, she got stung by a bee. I wonder, have you heard of any bee infestations or rogue bees in the area. Or anyone who has died from a bee sting?'

'None that oi can think of. Although, oi have known some rogue men in my time,' she laughed.

'She died in Antwerp. It's in Belgium,' he explained, his eyes wandering about the room. 'This is a huge house.'

'It's only got 5 bedrooms. Come and take a look at the library, you might find what you're looking for in there.'

A large framed photograph hung on the library wall, between the huge mahogany bookcases.

'Boss and his family,' she said, handing him a couple of books about bee stings.

'Very attractive family,' he commented.

She led him through another door into the lounge.

It was a huge room, decorated in gold and black. Its centrepiece was a white baby grand piano. In the far corner was a small cocktail bar, beside French doors that opened out to the swimming pool.

'Do you play?'

'Me? Oi can't even whistle in tune. No, it's the daughter-in-law of the house, she plays. She can paint too.' Katie pointed to a painting above the large fireplace. It was Paris, the Eiffel Tower stood in the background.

'Looks professional to me, she's very good.' Observing the painting more closely, he spotted the signature - *Suzette Trembath.*

'She's also a classically trained musician. Mrs Trembat' is a very clever woman.' Suddenly the phone rang. Katie ran back to the kitchen to answer it.

Needing a cigarette he strolled over to the cocktail bar to find an ashtray. There was a bottle opener beside the ashtray. It was a novelty opener in the shape of the Manneken Pis, the Brussels tourist attraction. Now realising that the statue at the bottom of the hall staircase was this same legendary character.

After taking a couple of photos with his pen-camera, he made his way out through the French doors.

The swimming pool looked inviting. Clear blue water and a couple of floating loungers. About to lie down on one of the sunbeds and take advantage of the sunshine, he suddenly noticed a greenhouse protruding from a small allotment at the side if the house. He went to have a closer look.

Rows of potatoes, radishes and carrots greeted him, flecked with apple blossom that had fallen from the trees.

Peering into the greenhouse, he immediately noticed the violets and saffron crocus. Both flowers looked similar, small and of lilac hue.

Sneaking inside, he plucked off a couple of the flowers and stuffed them into his satchel, along with a sample of earth and some suspicious looking leaves.

In the corner of the greenhouse, a pile of cardboard boxes were stacked up against a bonsai tree. On inspection, each box had different labels: *Violet soaps, Golden Honey bath crystals, Lavender talcum powder.* At the bottom of each label was a signature, *Sweet Bee.* He was about to grab a few samples when he heard a noise, it was the tractor heading towards the house.

'Fancy coming out to dinner with me tonight?' he asked when she returned to the lounge.

'Can't tonight, got to work.'

'If you've nothing better to do now, fancy a ride to Porthtowan. I'll buy you lunch?'

They ate lunch on the terrace of a bistro overlooking Porthtowan beach, the bay just along from Portreath. The sun was blazing down, sparkling across the ocean. But, instead of soft white sand, here, the sand was wet and dark, mostly covered by shale.

From what he was able to glean from Katie, the owner of the bee farm, Matthew Trembath, was near to retirement, and both he and his wife, Janice, spent most of their time in Spain. She also mentioned that he owned a factory shop in Portreath that sold household goods, which explained the boxes in the greenhouse. But still, it was an odd place to store them.

'Ah, look!' she cried, pointing to a gull that had landed beside her on the terrace. Turning her head towards the bird, her auburn hair caught the sunshine as if it were on fire.

'You're a very beautiful woman, Katie. But I'm not telling you something you don't know, or that hasn't been said before.' Leaning across the table he gave her an impromptu peck on the cheek.

'Oi've got something for you.' She handed him a magazine. 'Recipes made with honey.'

'I'm impressed,' he lied, browsing through the glossy pages. 'Chicken with honey glaze; honey strudel, honey banaffee pie. Oh, look here, it gives all the health cures from honey. Author is Janice Trembath.'

Thinking back to the last time he had banoffee pie, it was about 20 years earlier when Piran had hosted a formal dinner in their rooms on the Exeter University campus. He could still remember how uncomfortable he felt sitting with Piran's yuppie friends from the law department, most of whom rented houses in the nearby Cowley Bridge.

'What are you thinking about?'

'Oh, nothing much, just thinking about when I last ate banaffee pie, it was at university.'

'Did you study bees at university?'

'No philosophy.'

'What bejesus is philopofy?'

Guthrie liked her strong Southern Irish accent, it was quirky, like her.

'Philosophy is really about knowledge. For example, the obvious one is the table. How do you know this table really exists?'

'Of course oi know it exists. We've just been eating our dinner off it.'

'Yes, but it's not quite as simple in philosophy.'

'What's the point to it?' She appeared totally bewildered as to why anyone would study the subject. 'If you already knew it was a table before you went to university, what was the point of going to university if you didn't learn anything that you didn't already know before you went?'

'Love your dimples,' he digressed.

'Same as yours,' there was a hint of playful sarcasm in her voice.

'If we had kids, what's the chance they'd have dimples?'

'What's the chance they'd also have green eyes?' she winked. 'What's your star sign?'

'Capricorn.'

'Oh, ruled by Saturn.'

'Actually, I'm not really into all this.'

'Doesn't matter, it's still into you. Martin Luther King was a Capricorn. And so are Rod Stewart and David Bowie. You're a sea goat.'

'Thanks. So what is your star sign?' he humoured her.

'Born 25th June, Cancer, ruled by the moon.'

'Moon goddess or crab? So what can you tell about me?'

'Capricorn is the tenth sign of the zodiac so you're very ambitious. You're also a loner and have knee problems.'

'Well I do have knee problems so that's right, had to have a knee op a couple of years ago. Is that all?'

'No, there is more.' She raised her fine arched brows. 'Capricorn is an earth sign and one of the four cardinal signs.'

'Not the cardinal sins, ha-ha. So are we compatible?'

Katie laughed, 'yes.'

'Well that's a relief.'

'Mind if oi smoke?'

'Course not, have one of mine.' He pulled out a packet from his pocket. As he lit her cigarette their eyes accidentally connected - for a second too long, and he knew that he wanted her.

'Oi could photocopy the governor's notes about the bees if you'd like.'

'That's very gracious of you. Why would you do so much for me?'

'Cos oi hate him, what better reason would oi have?'

'Bang goes my theory that you might have liked me just a little,' he grinned.

Katie also laughed, her dimples erupting like crevices of sunshine. 'Oi may do.'

Leaning across the table he kissed her full on. She did not pull away.

'Shall I pick you up after work, I could take you back to mine?'

'And have your wicked way?' she smiled. 'Oi am a good Cat'olic girl.'

'And I'm a Catholic boy, that's a match,' he teased.

'Not unless you put a ring on my finger, wedding ring that is,' she laughed. 'Oi know what you handsome men are like, wanting your wicked way with any girl who crosses your path.'

After dropping Katie back at Tehidy, he rode on to the nearby bay of Portreath.

A handful of bronzed teens with honed bodies rode the waves, their hair bleached blonde by the sun. The surfing area was restricted due to Gulls Rock, a huge black boulder that sat in the water like an obstinate sea monster. The harbour was on the other side of the bay, and cut off from the beach. It was known as the inner harbour, with houses on either side.

After a quick pint in The Waterfront Inn, he headed into the beach shop to buy cigarettes, taking the opportunity to check out the tabloids on display. It was just the usual rant about the closure of South Crofty mine and the sewage problem at Portreath.

Plastic buckets and spades hung from the ceiling, in bright red, yellow and blue.

Beach balls, swimming accessories and cheap toys and gifts filled the shelves.

A customer entered the shop and asked for an evening paper. The man was wearing RAF uniform.

Guthrie slyly glanced over. He was fairly good looking, apart from the deep scar on the side of his jaw.

'Good afternoon,' the proprietor smiled. 'Will the girls be back for the summer holidays?'

'Perhaps, we'll have to see. Probably want to go to Spain.'

'To visit granny and granddad, I presume. I won't recognise your parents when they come home, probably be as brown as ni...' he stopped himself just in time.

Keeping his head down until the officer had left, Guthrie casually sauntered over to the till.

'Don't those RAF boys look smart?'

'You mean Wing Commander Paul Trembath? Yes, he's done pretty well for himself.'

'Oh, isn't his father the bee farmer?'

'Yes, that's right. I'm not so keen on honey, prefer jam myself. Mind you, the wife likes it,' the man confessed.

'They say honey is good for you. It's natural goodness.'

'To my mind, it's jam that is natural, it's made from fruit. But honey, well, that comes from the honeybees producing nectar by regurgitation. Puts me right off, to think it's the vomit of an insect.'

'Ha-ha, I've never really thought about it like that. So what's with the sewage problem?' He glanced down at the newspaper headlines.

'Had it for years,' the man lowered his voice. 'Between you and me, it stinks here. God knows what the kids are swimming in.'

'Oh goodness, I never knew that.'

The man raised his brows. 'I don't let my kids go in. I take them to Perranporth or Newquay. But then, I suppose, it's not as bad as what happened in Camelford.'

Guthrie looked bemused.

'It's known as the Camelford water pollution scandal. Camelford is in North

Cornwall, around the Tintagel area, you know, King Arthur country?'

'Yes, the knights of the round table.'

'Well, it was the summer of '88. Someone accidentally contaminated the drinking water with aluminium sulphate.' The man shook his head. 'It was a dreadful time. A lot of people got sick, and no one knows the long term effects.'

'Perhaps it wasn't a mistake.'

'Well, you're not the first to say that and I expect you won't be the last,' the shopkeeper said, restacking the newspapers. 'Many of the parents of children born with deformities blamed the water.'

More customers entered the shop interrupting the conversation, much to Guthrie's disappointment. He paid for the newspaper and was heading out the door when the man called after him.

'Some of the Camelford folk got that Alzheimers thing that old people get, and they are only in their thirties.'

'Anyone died?'

'Only 20 so far, - that we know of.'

CHAPTER TEN

'Hello, after ammo?' the proprietor of the St. Austell gun shop asked, that following afternoon.

Guthrie handed him the list for the ammunition he needed for his Walther PPK pistol, his MP5 9mm flat nose submachine gun and his SA80 rifle. Better to be safe than sorry, his mother always said.

'How were the last bullets?' The man called out from his stock room.

'Great.'

'Did you catch the pheasant shoot in January?'

'Yes, but missed every time,' he lied, having never been on a shoot.

'Ha-ha, there are cards on my counter. Take one. It tells you the dates of the shooting seasons.'

Searching about on the dirty counter he found the cards.

'It says Partridge Sept 1 to Feb 1. But if you live in Northern Ireland it ends a day sooner,' he looked to the man bemused. 'Is there any particular reason for adding or subtracting a day?'

'Probably another yuppie conspiracy.'

'It says the grouse season is from August 12th to December 10th. Perhaps the grouse would do better to migrate in July and return in January, ha-ha.'

'Do you sell your kill, or do you eat them yourself?'

'Give them away to friends,' he lied for a second time.

'Well, if you want to sell any, I can give you the names of a couple of butchers who'll buy them from you. They are quite partial to rabbits.'

'Thanks.'

Once outside the shop, he glanced up at the sky. It threatened rain. Smokey grey clouds were overshadowing the fluffy white ones. Perhaps he should turn the Harley around, go home and have an easy day. However, The Eden Project was next on his agenda, and he would have to do this sooner or later.

Riding out of the town, he headed along a country lane, bordered by fields decorated in a patchwork of greens and yellows. In one field cows were grazing; in another they were herding together in a circle, as if undecided on the weather. Knowing his luck it would rain.

Thinking back to what the woman from Strawberry Lane had said about the Arabs, he now wondered if he should have checked them out instead of coming here. Never mind, it would have to wait until sometime in the future, if they were still around.

The woman's name was Jill, he could tell that she really liked him. Maybe he would be able to use her in the future, to get more information about the hospital and the staff, if needed. But as for Irish Katie, well, she was a stunner, he would definitely be seeing her again.

On arriving at the Eden Project, he was happily surprised to find that building had already started. Of course, there were no huge golf ball shaped biomes, as yet, only the foundations had been laid.

Hiding the Harley between a couple of large skips in a nearby yard, he returned to the barren area to take a better look.

'Can I be helping you?' A voice asked in broad Cornish. The man was elderly, wearing a brown overall and cap.

'Good afternoon. I came to St. Austell to shop and thought I'd take a look. Didn't realise it was so far out.'

'Yes, that's what a lot of people think. Want to have a look around, although there's nothing much to see?'

'Please, that's very kind of you.'

'I might as well take you around myself. Not much to do until they bring more cement. Don't know if you know anything about the site.'

Shaking his hand, Guthrie glanced around at the dusty earth.

'Well, you be standing in china clay country. It's all down to a man named William Cookworthy who discovered the clay in 1755,' the old man stepped up to the role of tour guide. 'And then pits were opened to mine the clay.'

'I'd always thought clay was the brown squashy stuff you play with at kindergarten.'

'Ha-ha, no me 'andsome, not this 'ere clay.'

'Anything else of interest in the area?'

'Well, tourists seem to like Carlyon Bay. And Charlestown is just up the road, it's famous for its shipwreck.'

'I suppose they'll use the bay to transport building materials here or stock?'

'Couldn't tell you, but it flows out into the English Channel.'

Guthrie followed the old man, as he limped over the lumps and bumps of broken earth, until he paused to rest by a pile of concrete blocks.

'When are they going to start building?'

'Not for about 18 months or more. Got a lot of legal stuff to get through, you know,' the man panted. 'Planning permission, architects that sort of thing. They're going to build kind of domes. Supposed to be like greenhouses, lighter than glass they say. They've also put 46,000 poles into store. Can you believe that?'

'That's a lot.'

'They say that if you lay the poles down end to end, they would reach all the way from St. Austell to London. That be two hundred and thirty miles? What a waste of metal.'

'Does seem a lot.'

'Foundations 'ere will contain two thousand four hundred and eighty square miles of concrete.'

'Never, wow, that's a lot of concrete.'

'It's going be fifteen hectares, can you believe that?' The man was obviously overwhelmed by it all. 'Yes. And you'll never guess where the copper that's going to cover the roof beams is coming from?'

'Sorry, can't guess, Geevor? South Crofty?' Guthrie suggested, now wondering if the mines were going to be re-opened.

'Rio Tinto's getting it from one of their mines abroad somewhere, can 'ee believe that?'

'Rio Tinto?'

'One of the business partners of the Eden Project,' the man explained.

'Personally, I blame them for the downfall of South Crofty.'

'Why?'

'Well, they were at one time the owners of the mine. They claimed its downfall was because the price of tin had dropped.' He puckered his face tight, so that it looked even more wrinkled. 'If they had the money to finance this, then surely they could have done more for the Cornish tin mines.'

'Oh, I thought it was a Canadian firm who owned the mine,' Guthrie raised his brows. 'Actually, thinking about it, I'm sure I read it was once owned by Charter Consolidated.'

'Yes, they sold out to Rio Tinto. But don't take my word for it. You ask any Cornish miner what he thinks about the closure of the mines.'

'Well, I suppose if the tin industry is going downhill, no pun intended, they'd be throwing good money after bad if they kept the mines open.'

'That's not the reason. They're buying copper from abroad, I already told 'ee about

Rio Tinto. Everything comes down to money in the end, boy.'

Guthrie nodded for the sake of politeness.

'Now they're interested in mining in Madagascar.'

'For tin?'

'For titanium dioxide,' he raised his thick, white brows. 'Anyhows, it looks like it's going to rain. Look at they there clouds.'

Following his eyes upward, he saw a ray of sunshine peeping through the grey sky.

'There's going to be plants coming here from all over the world. Well, I suppose it will be good for conservation,' the man sneered. 'But I'll be honest with 'ee. Yes, this is all very nice, but it won't bring much work to replace the mines that have closed down.'

'No, I suppose not. So, where is St. Blazey from here?'

'St. Blazey only be up the road.'

'Isn't Mevagissey somewhere near here?'

'Yes. I live there.'

'I've heard it's beautiful. I must visit there some time.' He offered the man a Marlboro, and then lit up his own. 'Incidentally, do you know what's underneath us, is it soil?'

The old man took a long drag on the cigarette before he answered. 'We be standing on a reclaimed Kaolinite pit – a china clay pit.'

'Oh, it's a wonder they want to relinquish it.'

'Yes, well it be the same with the fishing industry and the tin mines.'

Guthrie didn't want another lecture about the tragic demise of Cornwall's tin mines, so hurriedly changed the subject.

'I heard that there were going to be bees here.'

'I think they're being supplied by a bee farm.' The old man pulled out a crumpled handkerchief to wipe his runny nose. 'Take a look over there.' He pointed towards a fenced off enclosure, that housed a row of wooden sheds and a cement mixer. 'That's where I think the beehives are going. But they don't tell me anything. I'm only the skivvy here.'

'Arthur!' a voice yelled across.

'That's my supervisor. I best be going, it's nearly half past five. He gives me a lift home, you see. Nice meeting you.'

'Yeah, likewise, thanks for the tour.'

Guthrie watched patiently as Arthur limped back over the uneven terrain, climbed into the car and drove off.

Taking the opportunity to look into the enclosure, he headed towards the fence.

There were around half a dozen sheds in the area. Only one of them was open. Guthrie peered inside.

A pile of golf clubs were stacked up against the grimy wall, amongst some broken boxes and old newspapers. A few of the clubs had fallen out of the shed onto the soil.

There was only one shed that was padlocked. It took him just seconds to pick the lock and open the door.

This shed was different from the previous one. Spotlessly clean, the walls covered with wooden shelving and tube lights. Some of the shelves were filled with transparent boxes. Inside the boxes were artificial beehives.

Photographing them from different angles, he then grabbed one of the boxes containing a hive, and stuffed it into his satchel. After all, it was premature for an apiarist to be storing equipment when the project was not yet built.

Just about to head off, a hand suddenly came crashing down on his shoulder. It was biker in black leathers. He looked to be a serious body builder by the size of his biceps, and he was well over 6'. One arm bore a large tattoo of a skull. The other was stamped with the name Lucifer.

'I was just passing. Thought I'd take a look to see how this was all shaping up.'

'You weren't just casually passing. I saw you picking the fucking lock!' the man growled. 'I saw you buying ammo in the gun shop.'

Guthrie had been negligent.

Lucifer just glared.

'The bullets are for the gun club I belong to. What's the problem?'

'Gun club my arse!' he snarled. 'I heard you were snooping around Tehidy asking questions.' The man pulled out a machete. 'I think I should teach you a lesson.'

Guthrie reached for his gun.

In a flash, Lucifer had pulled Guthrie to the ground. The steel blade of the machete hovered only millimetres from his face. The man was strong. Elbowing Guthrie hard in the ribs.

'I'll fucking kill you!' Lucifer yelled.

Smack! The back of the machete struck Guthrie's nose. Blood spurted out onto the dry, lumpy earth.

Lucifer made a sudden grab for the gun.

As Guthrie battled to keep him away from the gun, he failed to notice the machete was still in his other hand.

'Ahh!' Guthrie had been cut in the arm.

Lucifer made another attempt to seize the gun.

Drenched in his own blood, Guthrie bit hard into his assailant's balding head.

'You bastard!' Lucifer roared, as they wrestled like savages. Their teeth barred like rabid dogs.

The man made another surge towards him with the machete. Guthrie grabbed at the nearest object, a golf club. He wacked Lucifer hard, knocking his legs from under him.

Waiting for a further onslaught, Guthrie was surprised when Lucifer failed to move. Perhaps it was a ploy, feigning to be unconscious. But, when he saw the blood oozing down into the earth, the truth hit him full on. Lucifer had fallen onto his own machete. It was an accident.

Ripping the shirt off the corpse, he used the material to bandage his own bleeding arm, and then proceeded to search the man's trouser pockets.

All he found was a wallet, a passport and around £50.

The passport showed that Lucifer's real name was William Martin Jackson, DOB 22.8.1957. The passport had been stamped only once — Belgium.

Guthrie could not phone the police and incriminate himself, but the corpse was at least 143 kilos, too big to bury on site. There was only one option, and that was to chop up the body.

Reaching inside his shirt for his crucifix, Guthrie kissed it, and then made the sign of the cross.

'Our Father in heaven,' he prayed over the body. 'Forgive us our sins. Jesus Christ, forgive me my sins. Hail, Mary, full of grace, the Lord is with thee, blessed art thou amongst women. And blessed is the fruit of thy womb, Jesus. Holy Mary, Mother of God, pray for us sinners, William Martin Jackson and me, now, and at the hour of our death. Amen.'

Kissing his crucifix, he made the sign of the cross over the corpse. 'In the name of the Father, the Son and the Holy Ghost, forgive him his sins and let him rest in everlasting peace. Amen.'

Opening up the remaining sheds, he found an axe, a pair of pliers and a pair of heavy duty rubber gloves. In the last shed he discovered a roll of giant, black plastic sacks and a tarpaulin.

Making an apron out of a plastic sack, he put on the rubber gloves. Carefully laying out the tarpaulin, he pulled the heavy corpse onto it. Luckily his nose had stopped bleeding. As for his arm, although the bandage was soaked, the blood had clotted.

Raising the axe above his head with both arms, he brought it back down with a mighty thrust. The blood gushed out onto the tarpaulin as the torso split in two.

The head had come off easily, they usually did. The neck, even on a body builder, was one of the smallest parts of the upper torso.

CHOP. The blood spurted and then died. The arm had come off the socket - CHOP and now the other arm. Legs, thick, muscular, which meant he would now have to saw and chop, so difficult slicing through bone. There were so many sinews, and muscles.

'*Whoever fights monsters,*' Nietzsche's words suddenly came to mind. '*... should* *see to it that in the process he does not become a monster.'* But Guthrie knew, that for him, the warning was already too late.

Using pliers, he proceeded to remove the penis, testicles, eyes, fingers and toes. Although he was not squeamish he found it exhausting, and by the time he had removed the tongue and teeth he was near collapse.

Sitting down on top of a stray boulder he glanced down at the mess he had made, wondering what on earth he was going to do with it all. It was then he spotted a van hidden behind some trees. Perhaps it belonged to his victim.

Chopping up the rest of the body as finely as possible, he threw the deposits into a wheelbarrow. The jelly and fluids leaking everywhere.

Once the wheelbarrow was filled, he tipped the contents into five plastic sacks, and then dug up the earth to cover any remaining traces of blood and guts.

Perhaps it would have been easier if he had been killed instead, he thought. At least with physical torture there was an end in sight. As he had told the prison shrink after Stella's funeral, *'My brain is still safely floating in the CSF waters. But it's my mind that has drowned.'*

In a garage forecourt overlooking the ocean near Portreath, Guthrie sat in the van toying with the idea of dropping the sacks over Hells Mouth, the spot between Godrevy and Portreath where the suicides jumped. He even considered driving to the Lizard or Land's End where the currents would be stronger.

The sacks were piled on top of each other in a large dingy that he had found in the back of the van, no doubt belonging to the man's children. The only other items he had found in the van, was a fishing rod and a tin of maggots.

The dissected corpse was already causing a stench.

Winding down the windows, the sea air wafted in. It smelt good, salty and fresh. He had never caused an accidental death before. Although it was not his fault the man fell on his own knife, even so, it had been careless.

Driving down into Portreath harbour he noticed the tide was ebbing. It was all so silent, only the sounds of the ocean could be heard pounding the shoreline.

Dragging the empty dingy across the sand towards the water's edge, he wondered what Stella would have done, had she been there.

Returning to the van to collect the sacks, one at a time, he tipped out their contents into the dingy. Covering each load with some of the maggots.

When all the sacks were empty, he pushed the dingy out into the sea.

Once it had floated out for about half a mile, he took his handgun and attached the silencer. Aiming towards the dingy, he pulled the trigger. The dingy burst.

It was gone 3 o'clock by the time he got back to the Eden Project.

After parking the van, he sprayed it with one of his old MOD issue aerosols, to remove all fingerprints and traces of DNA.

By 3.45 Guthrie was able to climb back on his bike and head for home. Exhausted, traumatised and bruised, he vowed never to be so foolhardy again. In future it would be bullets only.

But despite it all, he was feeling positive. He was getting closer to the man who had killed Stella, and more than anything he wanted to see him die.

CHAPTER ELEVEN

Blankenberge was miserable early that morning. The rain pounded against the café window where Paul Trembath sat overlooking the marina.

Children were running alongside their mothers, carrying small umbrellas, and wearing bright yellow or red plastic coats to match their boots. These were the locals. The tourists lacked the sense to realise it might rain, they were soaked to the skin. But, the back streets of Blankenberge were full of gift shops, confectioners and patisseries that would cheer them.

The statues seemed to be the main attraction for the tourists in bad weather. They particularly admired the statue of Hendrik Conscience, and the one of the fisherman.

Trembath's favourite statue was the one of the woman with big breasts. He liked big breasts, but sadly his wife had fairly small ones. Not that he was getting to see her as often as he would have liked these days, what with work and other commitments.

Suzette would like to move to Belgium, and he would not mind too much; as his favourite attraction here was, of course, the casino. Although he had lost more than he had won, but, that was the name of the game. Trembath considered it a good night out, especially if he got to take a pretty croupier back to his hotel.

Blankenberge beach was far superior to most English beaches, he thought. Well, it used to be when they had the quaint hotels with verandas on the front. Now they had ginormous high rises lining the promenade, packed to the hilt, which meant the beach was chock-a-block with bodies. At least the gift shops still sold good quality products, nothing like the cheap tat you would get back home. Here was craftsmanship.

'Bonjour, my friend, glad you're not standing in the rain,' the tall, black haired Maxime laughed, showing a perfect set of white teeth.

Trembath laughed, standing up to kiss his friend on the cheek.

'Do you want a refill?' Maxime offered.

'Yes, please.'

When Maxime returned with the coffees Trembath was still looking out at the rain.

'You're deep in thought.'

'Just thinking what your uncle would have done if he were still alive.'

'Sebastian Dubois the Koning Bij, that's what they called him.'

'Yes, King Bee. There'll never be another king like him.'

'When are they making the drop?'

'Tonight. Your English is very good, they taught you well at Eton College.'

'Leadership qualities and Received Pronunciation, sadly I learnt neither.'

'Mm, sounds ominous.' Trembath laughed. Apart from the scar on his chin he was good looking when he smiled, it gave him a boyish look. Yet, his looks were not only an attraction for girls. He had succumbed to one other outside his usual comfort zone, and that was Maxime. He wondered if it was on offer again tonight.

'Anyway, we're here to talk business, so let's get started.' Maxime pulled out the documents from the attaché case and placed them on the table. 'You'll need to sign this one, and this one,' he pointed to the relevant pages. 'You don't need to bother signing that page.'

Trembath signed in the designated places, and then, with a strange look in his eyes, he whispered, 'we've got to eliminate him, Maxime. We've got to kill that bastard before he blows us all out of the water.'

Maxime looked quizzically.

'Our Mr Henry Guthrie OBE, worked for Intelligence.'

'Whose intelligence?'

'British Intelligence of course. And, he also worked for Interpol.'

'Never.'

'Think he was just a mercenary,' Trembath grimaced. 'Anyway, I don't know what everyone is waiting for, we should just kill him.'

'Shh, keep your voice down.' Maxime glanced round, to catch any eavesdroppers. 'I think first we need to go back to my apartment and have a nice lunch. A little wine, some music, and see what else there is on offer.'

Trembath did not like the term bi-sexual, and never had been until he met Maxime. Although, he still preferred women, he had to admit it had been a rather delightful experience. Maxime was quite beautiful, his body muscular and honed. Void of body hair like a woman, and yet not a woman. It was just a bit of fun, no depth of feeling, no commitment of the heart, not like he had with Suzette.

*****

As the Hercules C-130 flew towards the Indian Ocean, it was still undecided where they would make the drop.

'It will be too foggy, I'd take a bet on it.' Corporal Rob Mylor took a bite of the Mars bar, as he sat in the dark fuselage. 'But, it's too late to change the plans.'

'Never too late!' the pilot called out from the cockpit to the aircrew of two, Rob and a teenager, Andrew Morrish.

Andrew looked surprised after hearing the pilot's voice.

'I thought the Wing Commander would be flying this. Who's the pilot?'

'A thing of great beauty,' Rob whispered.

'Where are the others?'

'This is just a small drop today, don't need them.'

Andrew returned to his game of patience, using a pack of grubby cards. Rob finished cleaning his rifle that was lying in bits on the floor.

'Rob, did you know the King Bee?'

'Me? No. But I've heard all the stories, he was a legend.'

'Why do they call him, Koning Bij?'

'That was his nickname, I think it means king bee in Dutch or in Belgium lingo, somewhere like that. His real name was Sebastian Dubois.'

'I've been reading the books you gave me,' Andrew boasted. 'I didn't realise that the United States used 21 million gallons of Agent Orange over Vietnam.'

'Yes, to defoliate the jungle in order to kill the people. But it wasn't only the fucking U.S., Andrew. We did similar.'

'Why was it called that, was the gas orange?'

'Ha-ha, you silly arse. It was shipped in drums that had an orange stripe, nothing more exotic than that, I'm afraid,' he laughed, exposing the chewed up Mars bar in his mouth. 'They sprayed over three thousand villages, and it gave the residents cancer.'

'Various types of cancer the book says, and birth defects.'

'Yep, over 400,000 Vietnamese people died. But that's what war is like. It's either you or them, as you'll be finding out yourself,' Rob warned. 'You see, the U.S. is renowned for this sort of thing. Once, they even experimented on their own people, what a bunch of fucking morons, ha-ha.'

'What do you mean?'

'Well, you'll never believe this,' Rob's eyes opened wide. 'The US released swarms, and when I say swarms I mean swarms of mosquitoes. Their stock of quinine must have run out, ha-ha.'

'Where did they release them, New York?'

'Ha no, daftie, they'd never do that. No they released them over Georgia and Florida.'

'Wonder why they did that.' Andrew placed his last card down. He had lost.

Rob paused to eat the rest of the Mars bar. When he had finished he wiped his chocolate stained hands on his overalls.

They were quiet for a while.

The teenager helped himself to some water and then dealt out fresh cards.

'Not far now!' the pilot shouted back. 'About 15 to 20 minutes.'

Andrew looked nervous.

'You'll be fine, son, nothing to it,' Rob reassured him, slotting the pieces of rifle back together. 'The mosquitoes I was telling you about, well, it was part of an experiment to see if insects, you know, those that carry diseases, like the mosquitoes carry Malaria, could be used to carry biological weapons.'

Rob poured himself a mug of weak tea from the flask, and then lifted up the flask to the teenager.

'No thanks. What happened to the people in Georgia?'

'Dunno, probably died. That's where you get your Aids from, the Yanks dropping their lethal chemical gases over the jungle.'

'I thought it was from chimps.'

'Monkeys have been around since the beginning of time. So, the question is, why would they suddenly give the blacks this disease in the jungle?'

Andrew shrugged his shoulders.

'No doubt the Brits or the Yanks were testing it in the jungle, or dumping their chemical waste there. But, it obviously backfired.'

'Or they wanted to decrease the black population there for some reason,' Andrew suggested. 'What about Hiroshima? But I suppose they wouldn't do that now.'

'Ha, don't be too sure. It was only. . . now when was it? It was only about 2 years ago when there was that incident in Tokyo.'

'You mean the subway attack? Oh, my God. So when we drop the waste we're really like murderers.'

'No, you can't look at it like that, son. As the Wing Commander always says, these Somalis are not like us.' He paused to take a sip of tea. 'But the world is a bad place when chemical weapons get into the wrong hands.'

'So, once we make the drop we're going straight home?'

'No, the pilot will drop us off in Belgium, and then fly the plane back.' Rob reached out for the bag of sugar, crumpled up near the biscuits. 'A Sea King will be waiting for us. We have to fly some gold bullion back to Cornwall.'

'Won't it be recognised?'

'It's been sprayed black.'

'How do they sell the gold once it's back in Cornwall?'

'You ask too many fucking questions, I'm exhausted.'

'Oh, sorry.'

'Forget it. We'll be dropping soon anyhow.'

'I suppose local jewellers buy it.'

'No.' Rob lowered his voice. 'Don't repeat this to anyone. You've heard of the Gold Centre, haven't you?'

'You don't mean the Cornish Gold Centre at Tolgus Mill, do you?'

'That's the one, on the road to Portreath.' Rob now dropped his voice to a whisper. 'The deputy manager made a deal with the Wing Commander.' He paused to spoon the sugar into his mug of tea and began to stir. 'He takes a cut of the profits in exchange for putting it through their system.'

The plane suddenly slowed down.

'Right boys, get ready to drop!' the pilot called out from the cockpit.

Rob gulped down the tea, throwing the empty mug to the floor.

Both men grabbed hold of the large, black container which occupied a third of the fuselage, and dragged it towards the open door.

'Best open the lock and throw out the contents separately,' the pilot called out. 'As the container might float. Wear your gloves.'

'Okay, ma'am.' Rob opened the container, now wondering in what direction he should throw.

*****

Standing on the side of Blankenberge's vast marina, Maxime was pacing up and down. 'He's late,' he complained, lighting his fifth Turkish cigarette.

'No, he's not. He told us it would be between 1.30 to 2 a.m. depending on the tide.' Paul Trembath was agitated, constantly glancing down at his watch, 2.15.

Then, suddenly they saw her, the tug was heading into the harbour.

They both ran along the wharf to meet the vessel, waving frantically.

'What is the cargo this time?' the skipper asked tentatively, as they jumped on board.

'Only gold bars,' Trembath replied.

Maxime waited until the skipper had gone to tie up the boat, before he turned to his friend. 'What about the sweet bee, Sheik

Amir will be expecting it if he's sent all this bullion? What did you tell the courier when he asked for the suitcase?'

'Nothing.'

'Well, what happens when he returns to Dubai empty handed?'

'He won't.'

'But I don't understand.'

'There was no courier, the sheik is dead.'

Maxime shrugged. 'Please spare me the gory details. Is that why we're collecting the bullion ourselves this time?'

'Don't worry, you worry too much.'

They spent the following half hour lifting the crates from the boat, and stacking them on the wharf. When they had finished, Trembath went to collect the lorry from the adjacent car park, and reversed it down to the marina.

They had only completed half the load when the skipper shouted, 'gendarme!'

'It's too late to move the vehicle,' he whispered to Maxime, pulling out his automatic.

'What's going on here? You can't load at this time of night!' the gendarme called out.

'The boat was late in,' Maxime explained.

'Yes,' the skipper concurred, 'I was held up at Ostend.'

'I'm going to phone the station to ask for advice.'

Trembath put his gun to the gendarme's head. 'Drop the phone.'

The gendarme obeyed.

'Sorry,' he said, and then shot him dead.

The skipper gave a gasp.

'Had no choice,' he explained, as Maxime helped him lift the body into the back of the lorry.

They finished loading up, and then the skipper got back into the trawler. Maxime pressed a wad of money into his hand.

'That's for your silence, okay?'

The skipper nodded, and then steered the tug back out of the harbour.

Rob and Andrew were already at the small airfield when Trembath and Maxime arrived in the lorry.

'We made the drop, sir. Everything go okay with you, sir?' Rob asked, about to help unload the vehicle.

'No.'

'Why, what's happened, sir?'

'He shot a gendarme,' Maxime volunteered, handing around cigarettes from his packet.

'How is he?'

'He's dead,' Trembath confessed.

Rob looked horrified. 'What have you done with the body, sir?'

Maxime silently pointed to the lorry.

'It's flying home with you, Rob.'

'Oh, my God!' Rob shouted. 'Why the fuck didn't you ditch it at sea? We'll all be fucking incriminated now. I never agreed to participate in cold blooded murder.'

'Watch your mouth, Corporal Mylor. You were happy enough to participate in the drop, I don't recall you voicing any objections. And remember, you're easily replaceable.'

'Yeah, good, 'cos after this job I'm off, sir.'

'You can fuck off now!' Trembath smacked the Corporal across the face. Rob fell backwards and then steadied himself. Now lunging forward, he punched Trembath in the stomach. Suddenly fists were flying, boots kicking and blood was being spilled. The scuffle seemed to go on forever, until Maxime had had enough.

BANG!

'Whew, what did you kill him for? I could have handled it,' Trembath said, wiping himself down.

'Well, we were getting rid of him after the last drop. It may as well be sooner than later.'

'Yeah, but I needed him to help load up and fly her back. Now I'll have to fly her myself, and loading will take twice as long.'

Andrew hid behind the lorry, he was in shock. But no one had even noticed him standing in the shadows. Trembath was bleeding, his lip and eye cut. Maxime was busy mopping the blood from his face.

'A touch of a friend is worth two in a bush.' Maxime kissed him on the lips, the blood transferring onto his own mouth.

*****

It was dawn when the Sea King eventually took off, piloted by Trembath. Maxime had remained in Belgium and Andrew had disappeared. The two corpses were sitting upright next to him in the cockpit, as if they were co-pilots. They were wrapped in blankets and polythene sheets, to help stop the blood and body fluids from leaking all over the helicopter.

'Okay there, Alexandre Mertens, okay there Rob Mylor? I hope you're both comfortable,' he jested macabrely. 'Alexandre, the photo on your identity badge doesn't do you justice. You look much better dead.' Trembath threw the badge to the floor. 'Have you always been a cop, Alex? I'd once toyed with the idea of becoming a cop. You don't mind me calling you Alex, do you?'

The aircraft was over the North Sea when it went onto automatic pilot. Trembath climbed into the fuselage. He began to prepare the two corpses, wrapping them up in tarpaulin and rope, and then tied them to a large, hydraulic jack.

Moving the bundles to the edge of the open door, he said, 'I hope your families don't miss you too much. Parting is such sweet sorrow. . . so fuck off!'

Thrashing out with his foot, he kicked both the corpses off the helicopter.

The mummified bodies fell down through the clouds like bombs. The Belgian police would search high and low for the gendarme, but they would never find him. The hydraulic jack would ensure that Alexandre Mertens and Rob Mylor would sink to the very bottom of the ocean bed. Their only mourners — a few jelly fish and an anemone.

CHAPTER TWELVE

It was a five-hour journey back from Paddington. Luckily the evenings were light, so that Guthrie could enjoy the scenery through the grubby, second class carriage windows.

A woman and her three noisy brats were sitting across the aisle; shouting, crying, and spilling their drinks everywhere. He was glad he did not have children at times like this. Perhaps he had more in common with those unmarried philosophers like Immanuel Kant, Søren Kierkegaard and Friedrich Nietzsche, than he cared to admit.

It was less than a week since the Eden Project disaster, but, when his elderly friend, Solly Stein, had phoned to say that he had arranged a meeting with a professor of Egyptology in London, Guthrie had no choice but to go. Although, the meeting had been all too brief, and it was a long journey back to Cornwall.

He had first met Solly 15 years earlier in the Congo during one of his clandestine missions. They had both been staying at the same hostel with agents from Mossad, they were in search of a Nazi war criminal. The old man had known the inside of Bergen-Belson, and retained not only an East European accent, but also a number tattooed on his arm.

The meeting with the professor had taken place at the British Museum in Great Russell Street. The professor, surrounded by a variety of Egyptian mummies and artefacts, had briefly mentioned both the mythological and Biblical links to the bee. This had included an explanation about the prophetess Deborah from the Book of Judges, whose name meant Bee in Hebrew, and Apis, a Mesopotamian bee-god.

He also told them about a group of German scientists who had discovered traces of cocaine, hashish and nicotine inside an Egyptian mummy, Henut Taui. The professor had explained that cocaine was used in ancient Egypt and was somehow linked to their bee-god. Apparently cocaine affected the passage of octopamine, a neurochemical in the brain of the honey bee. But, it was when the professor had mentioned that bee venom was used to treat arthritis and Parkinson's disease, that Guthrie wondered if that was why Treliske was involved.

It was around 9 o'clock when he arrived back at Redruth, already regretting not calling on his mother when he had been in London. After all, she only lived in Ilford, 30 minutes on the train from Liverpool Street. How he longed for the taste of her cooking; jerk chicken, rice and peas, followed by homemade ginger cake. Never mind, it was still early enough for a pint.

The London Inn was thick with smoke. A sardine can of bodies were focussed on a third rate rock band playing at full volume. After ordering a lager he tried to find a seat, but they were all taken.

'Sit on this, mate, if you want.' An orange haired biker wearing shabby leathers offered him a stool that had been hidden in the corner.

'Thanks.' Guthrie gave a nod and sat down. The biker was with his orange plaited girlfriend. Both had teeth missing.

'I've seen you before, don't you live near the chippy?'

Guthrie nodded, busy sipping his drink.

'You're the guy who's just out of nick. I recognise you from the photo in the paper. I've been inside a couple of times for scoring and selling,' he confessed. 'But I have to say I felt sorry for you, mate, when I read about it. I mean, you were innocent.' The man stretched out his hand, 'Name's Chas.'

Guthrie obliged and shook his hand, 'Guthrie. I doubt I'm the first they've done it to, but thankfully we no longer have capital punishment or there'd be many more miscarriages of justice. So what do you do now?'

'Got a part-time job with Kerrier Council cleaning the streets.'

'Sounds like a dream,' Guthrie laughed, holding out his packet of Marlboro to them.

'I could get you a job if you're looking, always want street cleaners.'

'No. Thanks anyway.'

'Well, it's better than nothing,' Chas shrugged. 'I'm saving up at the minute, going to see my sick old ma in East Ham when I get the dosh for the fare. Jo wanted to hitch, but I don't think it's safe for chicks these days, do you?'

'Thanks for the fag,' the girl offered a gummy grin.

'So what happened to your teeth?'

'You know what happened, mate, but that's all in the past,' Chas jumped to her defence. 'I promised Jo if we win the lottery we'll go to a good dentist and get implants. She used to be a model, you know.'

Guthrie turned to look at her.

'It's true,' she replied. 'I did loads of covers for magazines, not sleazy ones, but the expensive ones.'

'Trouble is to keep you skinny they start dishing out speed like they are Smarties, and Jo was only a kid knowing no better at the time. Well, when you're a kid you do as you're told, don't you?'

Guthrie had heard similar stories for years, vile dealers who never took drugs themselves, merely contaminated the innocent.

'Do you get many dealers come in here?'

'See that kid over there.' Chas pointed to a bronze skinned boy with black hair. 'That's Kareem, he's an idiot dealing in broad daylight.'

'What does he deal?'

'Just coke and shit, you know, cannabis.'

'You don't buy?'

'No, gave up five years ago when Jo got pregnant, our only vice now is baccy.'

'Kareem rolls the spliffs himself to make them look bigger,' Jo laughed. 'He mixes the cannabis with crushed violet petals.'

'Where does he live?'

'St. Ives.'

Chas opened a tin and looked inside, poking his nicotine stained fingers around the stringy strands of brown tobacco.'

'Well, it will last us to Tuesday,' Jo said, trying to reassure him.

By now Guthrie had finished his lager. 'What are you both drinking?'

'No, it's okay, mate, we only came in to hear the band,' Chas winked. 'Anyway, we've got to go soon 'cos of the babysitter. She earns more an hour than I do.'

'Well, nice meeting you.'

'Listen, if you ever want to pop over to ours you'll be welcome. You know, for a cuppa and a natter. We live in the cottage with a pink door next to the launderette in Chapel Street.'

Guthrie, who was usually unsympathetic to sob stories,found himself dipping into his pocket.

'This might help you with the fare to visit your mum.' He handed Chas three £20 notes.

Strolling along Green Lane, he suddenly remembered a letter that Solly had given to him in London. Perhaps he'd read it over a fish supper, but there again, he needed to lose some weight. He was still debating whether to buy a fish supper when he reached his front door. About to put the key into the lock he suddenly noticed that the door was slightly ajar.

Racing up the stairs with his gun prepped he entered the flat. The chaos winded him. The contents from the chest of drawers were emptied out onto the bedroom floor, and the bedding was piled up on the kitchen table. Across the mirror someone had written in red lipstick, *YOU'RE DEAD!*

The police officer observed Guthrie suspiciously. Everything he said the officer made him repeat twice. But he was used to this sort of interrogation by the police.

'You should stop them letting these places to emmets!' a Cornish voice shouted out from the window of a nearby house. 'All these bloody farn'ers, we never used to have this trouble.'

'Wallis! Go and take a statement,' the officer shouted across to a younger man. 'Also ask her why she failed to report the incident when it happened. Now, Mr Guthrie, can you tell me again why you were in London, have you anyone to confirm you were there?'

'A professor of Egyptology.'

'Don't get smart with me!'

And so the questioning went on. From what Guthrie was led to understand nothing had been broken or damaged, just cupboards and drawers thrown about giving the impression that the burglar was looking for something in particular.

At last, having convinced the policeman that he had indeed been in London, Guthrie left them to get on with taking fingerprints, and went off to find himself a bed for the night.

CHAPTER THIRTEEN

It was a few days later when Guthrie found himself back at Treliske, hiding on the roof of a building called *The Mermaid Centre*, after receiving a tip-off.

The sky was black with no sign of a moon. Even so, he still risked being spotted on the hospital CCTV, and so he had taken precautions and disguised himself with a rubber Mickey Mouse head. Whilst training with MI6 they had mentioned the name Dudley Clarke. He was a Lieutenant Colonel and worked for British Intelligence during World War 11, and occasionally cross dressed. They had suggested that agents could do the same if a mission deemed it beneficial, but so far he had managed to avoid it.

He had only been on surveillance for around two hours, and yet, he was already exhausted. Not only due to the late hour, or the stress of his flat being burgled, but mainly from having spent the day with Katie at Flambards Theme Park. Although she was stunning to look at she was not really his type, still unable to say philosophy, and came out with other foolish remarks. But there was something about her that fascinated him apart from her beauty, something that he just could not put his finger on.

For the past ten minutes he had focussed his infra-red goggles on the air ambulance helicopter parked in a field beside the hospital, a BOLKOW 105 DBS. It was based at RAF St. Mawgan. Although the pilots, who were currently occupied with unloading boxes from the boot of a BMW and re-loading them onto the aircraft, were not dressed in RAF uniform.

The noise of the rotors were giving him a headache. Perhaps the patients slept on the other side of the hospital, or else were heavily medicated. At least he had managed to install four security cameras that night, and had tapped into their CCTV system. He had even managed to clamber up onto the roof of Mullions Restaurant to install one there, and then connected all the cameras to his laptop. It was lucky for him that he was still in contact with Jill, the nurse, as she had agreed to open up the security room for him. It was inside that room where the CCTV monitoring system was housed.

Three cars were now driving along Penventinnie Lane, a narrow road leading to the back of the hospital.

A man wearing a long overcoat and balaclava climbed out of the BMW, the number plate covered with a cloth. Around 10 minutes later he got back into the driver's seat, accompanied by another man in uniform.

Guthrie was about to climb down from the roof and jump onto his Harley in order to follow the car, when he saw that the vehicle had driven towards a complex of buildings only a hundred or so yards away, on the other side of the lane. Perhaps it was the nurses' home, he thought, now following on foot.

When they reached a large portacabin the man removed his balaclava. Guthrie was immediately taken aback by the man's identity. He had never suspected him of being involved. Hurriedly he took some photographs.

While they were loading boxes and several attaché cases from the portacabin into the car boot, Guthrie peered in through the barred window. It was a small laboratory, with sinks and cupboards, and other equipment. Odd, why would a scientist or doctor want to work in a portacabin when there were state of the art labs inside the hospital?

Suddenly, something caught his eye. On the grey vinyl floor were the shrivelled bodies of two dead honeybees. Turning his head to check that no one had seen him, he noticed the building behind.

'Well, well, well, who'd have thought it?' he mumbled to himself, peering up at the sign on the building:

DUCHY PRIVATE HOSPITAL

As the men drove off towards the helicopter, Guthrie took the opportunity to make a grab for the insects. He would get them analysed, although he could guess the results.

It was around 3 a.m. when the haulage trucks arrived at RAF Portreath.

Lying on the damp grass behind a bunker out of sight, Guthrie was busy clicking his pen-camera. Irritated by the crickets and other wild life, that were playing unmelodious croaking noises in his ear. He was gasping for a cigarette, but dared not risk it.

As the trucks drove past, he heard a voice ask: 'Who's the buyer?'

No one answered.

'What time are we finished?'

'When the last fucking gun is unloaded and re-loaded!' a voice shouted back.

A motorbike raced towards the group of men and stopped by a haulage truck. The rider ran towards one of the men.

'Think he's here, sir,'

'Who?'

'Henry Guthrie, sir. We saw him near Treliske as we flew out. Think he followed us here.'

'Great, why didn't you lose him, then, idiot?'

'We thought of backtracking, but you said to get the cargo here urgently.'

'Kill him on sight, is that understood?'

Looking through his infra-red goggles, Guthrie was able to see the distant floodlights around the airfield. The trucks were heading that way.

He watched as they drove onto the airfield. Men wearing combat gear began to unload the large wooden crates from the trucks. They were packed with RAF issue rifles and AK47's, along with handguns and grenades.

A Hercules C-130 was parked outside one of the hangars, partially hidden by a truck. Surely they weren't going to fly it at this time of night, he thought to himself. It would wake the whole of Portreath.

Once the trucks had been unloaded, the men reloaded the crates into the fuselage of the aircraft, confirming his fears.

Suddenly, a figure ran across the tarmac towards the Hercules C-130, and climbed up into the pilot's seat.

The engine started. The plane moved along the runway gathering speed, and then took off.

'Good job done,' a voice said, near to where he lay in the grass.

'Yes, she flies well. Right, we're finished, let's go home.'

Guthrie remained hidden until the men had left the airfield, deliberating over what had been said. '*She flies well.*' Of course, aeroplanes like boats and cars were known in the feminine, that must be all there was to it – or was it?

CHAPTER FOURTEEN

That following day Guthrie decided it was time to leave Redruth.

Riding his Harley over the bumps in Drump Road heading towards the A30, he wondered if he should trade in his bike for a car. The fact that he had never taken a driving test was of no consequence, perhaps he would get round to it someday. Apart from problems with the weather and bumps in the road, he loved his bike, loved to feel the throb between his legs. As if it was a woman sitting astride her, stroking her gently, his penis throbbing with the engine. A form of escapism, his brother had said, racing away from reality into oblivion. Of course, he was right, Guthrie conceded, as he weaved in and out of the traffic, changing lanes at whim. Danger was everywhere. But the worst danger lay in memories. The constant memories of Stella, her smile, her beautiful eyes, even her touch.

There were even memories racing about in his head of the philosophers he had read at university. Were they really seekers of truth, or just rambling fools? One of Hume's famed achievements was for awakening Kant from his dogmatic slumbers. Guthrie wished someone would do the same for him.

Hume, what was it that he had said about cause and effect? *'One event follows another; but we never can observe any tie between them. They seem conjoined but never connected.'* He had argued, that just because one might have only ever seen white swans, does not prove that there are no black swans in existence.

Guthrie hoped that Hume was wrong. He had to find the tie, the necessary connection, or, at the very least, find the black swan amongst the herd of white ones.

*****

In the distance he could see blue and mauve fields rising up to the skyline, violets ready for picking. It must be prophetic, he thought, as the next item listed on his agenda were, '*violets*'.

Fifteen minutes later he had reached Hayle estuary, a refuge to a multitude of birds. Looking down into shallow waters he could see herring gulls and a few green sandpipers wading through the debris of the outgoing tide. During the winter as many as 18,000 birds sheltered there. Guthrie hated birds, and thought it a waste of such a beautiful area. After all, Hayle had everything, the dunes, the three miles of white beach stretching from the river to Godrevy lighthouse, Lelant Saltings, Copperhouse Creek and Carnsew Basin. All it needed was better night life, perhaps a classy casino and a few upmarket clubs; and maybe a theme park like Piran had suggested.

Instead of continuing on to Penzance, he turned off at Nut Lane and rode down into the village of Lelant. Careful not to skid on the blossoms that covered the road, he glanced across at the garden centre and then at the children's fun park, *Merlin's Magic Land.* It was at times like this when he wished he had children. It would be nice to take them to places like theme parks, be a normal man, a family man. Perhaps it was too late, after all, he was almost forty.

St. Ives was a jewel in Cornwall's crown. Officially a town but more like a large village, its centre point being the harbour. A place where pilchards were once fished in abundance, the mainstay of the populace. And, like the Scots and the Welsh, the locals had considered themselves an independent country, Cornish not English. Times had changed in St. Ives over the past decade, here the Cornish had almost stopped using the word *emmets* (ants) to refer to those they deemed to be *foreigners*, mainly the English. Not due to any deep sense of altruism, but merely because the emmets were threatening to become the majority. Now the fishing boats had been replaced by speedboats and surf boards. Long gone were the bearded old men singing sea shanties whilst mending their fishing nets on the wharf, or telling their tales of the ocean whilst smoking their pipes. Even the Great Unwashed, the pot smoking hippies, had vacated the harbour wall decades earlier. Now there were only tourists, seagulls and dogs. Yet, there was one thing that remained consistent, and that was the colony of artists. St. Ives was overwhelmed by artistic creativity. Potters, painters and candlestick makers paraded their craft in seafront studios, hoping to get enough sales to feed themselves throughout the winter.

A *No Parking* sign greeted Guthrie on the slipway of Western Pier. Surrounded by billboards advertising boat trips to Seal Island, motor boat hire and shark fishing, it reminded him of his happy boyhood trips to Southend with his family. How he had loved the Essex coast, even with its dull, grey ocean and bingo pods. Here in Cornwall there were no *Kiss Me Quick hats*, no pie and mash stalls or jellied eels.

Walking onto the wharf he stared down over the railings into the ebbing harbour waters. An aquatic palette of Mediterranean blue shadowed with turquoise green, he was blown away by its beauty.

Two men suddenly appeared by the billboards, they were watching him. He could see the bulges in their jacket pockets.

There was no way of getting past them as they blocked any escape route. At the other end of the pier was the ocean.

As the men moved in his direction Guthrie ran towards a queue of tourists, and followed them down the slippery harbour steps into a waiting boat, which looked more like a large dingy.

The other passengers seemed to be over-excited, he thought it a little odd, after all, it was only a boat ride.

Wearing his sunglasses, he waved up to the men who were glaring down at him from the wharf. His other hand was firmly on his pistol.

Just as they reached for their weapons the dingy pulled away from the steps and began to thrash about in the water.

'Ouch!' he jumped. The pain soared through his back. Reaching out to grab something before he was bounced out into the ocean, he found to his dismay, that there was nothing to hold onto.

Like a speed boat programmed with a pogo stick, it crashed over the swell towards Porthminster beach. Crash, crash,

crash, the vessel hit the water head on, as it proceeded towards Gwithian lighthouse.

Looking for an opportunity to disembark, Guthrie soon realised that it was impossible. Even when this nightmare ended, he had no doubt the two men would still be waiting for him.

Although the scenery around him was magnificent, he failed to notice. His coccyx was breaking, his brain was rolling about in his head, and his knees were almost bouncing off his chin. Yet, to his dismay, the other passengers were shrieking with laughter, holding their arms up above their heads as if they were on a novelty ride at a theme park. Unable to share their enthusiasm, he grabbed hold of someone's leg for dear life, as the dingy thrashed about the shoreline.

'Right me 'andsums, we're now off to Seal Island. It's also known as the Western Carracks,' the skipper informed them. The others in the dingy all clapped, but Guthrie just wanted to go home, except for the fact that he no longer had a home.

Screams of delight continued to echo in his ear, as, with each bounce of the dingy, they were soaked by the salty sea-spray. How their eyes gleamed with excitement, despite the fact their hair and feet were drenched. Yet, all Guthrie could do was pray.

Eventually, they arrived at Seal Island, a small rocky isle just over 3 miles from the shore giving refuge to a colony of grey, blubber-cushioned seals that lazed around all day under the Cornish sun.

'No, this isn't a dingy it's called a rib, this is a rib-ride,' a passenger explained to him.

'A rib? A rib breaker more like. It feels like my ribs are broken. When did all this catch on, then? I thought we were just going for a nice cruise.'

'Ha-ha, poor you.'

'Yes, poor me,' he groaned. 'I know that three miles is only the same distance from Redruth to Camborne, but it's like travelling there on a toy space hopper.'

'I doubt if anyone has ever fallen overboard.' The man then turned away to take photographs of a huge grey seal.

When it was time for the tour to end, Guthrie's heart was in his mouth knowing there was no escape route, the men would be waiting for him back at the wharf. Yet, to his surprise, instead of the dingy sailing back into the harbour it headed towards a small group of rocks near Porthgwidden beach. Only then he realised that the tide had gone out. Breathing a sigh of relief, he knew that the men would be waiting for him - in the wrong place.

After booking into a guest house he made his way towards The Digey, a narrow, cobbled lane that lead away from the harbour towards Porthmeor beach. Packed with tumble-down, granite cottages that had been built in times past when pilchards were the livelihood of the residents.

Some were bordered by large stones at the front, others used seashells, reminding the passer-by of the verse from a nursery rhyme - *With silver bells and cockle shells, and pretty maids all in a row.*

The cottages were painted in a variety of colours, although, a few still retained their original granite. All nestling in on one another, on either side of the cobbles.

Feeling somewhat peckish, he bought a morning newspaper and entered a café. He ordered bacon and eggs fried sunny side up, fried bread, mushrooms, tomatoes and a pot of tea - he would start his diet tomorrow.

Whilst chewing on a thick, sizzling piece of bacon, he glanced at the headlines:

TIGER WOODS WINS MASTERS
AT 21 YEARS OF AGE

Noticing the proprietor looking at him, he lifted the paper towards her and pointed at the page, unable to stop grinning.

'First black player to win a major golf championship!'

But the woman pretended not to hear, obviously thinking him an over excitable nutcase.

It was still only 11.30 by the time he left the café. Trying to look nonchalant, he glanced across at the semi-detached house at the end of The Digey. It was much larger than its neighbouring cottages, with a high stone wall enclosing a spacious garden. The bronze plate on the front gate read: *Lyonesse Lodge.*

A tabby cat suddenly ran over and rubbed up against his legs, and then ran back to the house and jumped up onto the gate.

Guthrie walked over to the cat and tickled it under the chin. Security alarms were not unusual, or barbed wire. Still, the ones around this garden were a little excessive.

Peering over the wall, a blue and lilac haze greeted him. Violets covered about half of the garden, another quarter was saffron crocus and the other lavender.

The occupant obviously grew the flowers for a living. Of course, Cornish violets and saffron were a big commodity in the South-West.

Slyly taking photos with his pen-camera, he was suddenly interrupted by a husky East London voice.

'Can I help you?'

He turned round to see a woman standing there. She was in her forties, dyed yellow hair and wearing dirty dungarees. The cat moved towards her purring, she stroked it.

'I just noticed your flowers. I want to buy my mother a gift from here and was thinking of violet perfume.' Guthrie gave a huge smile.

'To be honest, I don't like strangers looking over my wall,' she said brusquely. 'If you wish to purchase any violet products you'll need to go to the shop on the Island.' The woman picked up the cat and returned to her house, failing to notice Guthrie's nod of thanks. He had no doubt that she was the person he had been looking for.

Heading up the road he noticed the postman had dropped some letters. Guthrie rushed forward to pick them up and handed them back to him, except for two.

The Island was the diamond in St. Ives mystical crown. A small grassy hill overlooking Porthmeor beach, attached to the mainland by an isthmus that hosted a car park. Originally a fort, its correct name was Pendinas, fortified headland. On the summit stood a small granite chapel that had once been a haven for smugglers. A few benches were positioned outside the chapel for the fatigued climber.

The Coastguards station was situated on the other side of the Island. Guthrie had read in a travel guide that during the Napoleonic Wars the Island gave refuge to a battery that accommodated several cannons. At night the chapel was illuminated by a golden glow, like a magical castle in the sky that could be seen for miles around.

Just along from the car park were several gift shops. He was looking for one particular shop, The Beehive. Eventually he found it, situated between a surfing shop and gift shop. The Beehive was not very original as a name, he thought, recalling the Beehive pub in Ilford's Beehive Lane. Whether the pub was named after the road or vice versa, he never knew.

It was only a tiny shop, painted in lilac and pink with transfers of bees stuck on the walls.

Soaps, bubble baths, gels and face creams filled the shelves. They were labelled, *ST. IVES PURE HONEY & VIOLET SKINCARE.*

There were two display stands, one hosting an assortment of honey in locally made clay pots, the other small bags of dried lavender.

Guthrie placed a couple of soaps and honey pots into a basket, followed by two bags of lavender tied with a blue ribbon. He would post them as gifts to his mother and aunt.

'Where does the honey come from?' he asked the girl at the till.

'A bee farm, I think.'

'Cornish honey, then,' he smiled.

'Yes. The lavender is also grown locally, and the violets.'

'I just saw a garden full of violets round the corner.'

'Oh, that's Mrs Kaleel's house, she owns this shop,' she replied, adding up the bill. 'The total comes to twenty-five pounds and 40 pence, please. Do you want them gift wrapped?'

'May as well,' Guthrie replied, opening up his wallet.

The girl began to wrap the items individually in pretty floral paper.

'Kaleel, not a Cornish name.'

'No, her husband's called Mustopher, although he was born here. My aunty knows him from school.'

*****

Below the Island lay Porthmeor's magnificent surfing beach, where white-kissed, barrelling waves, rolled towards the shore. No mermaids here, although seals could be seen and the occasional shark or whale.

Removing his shoes and socks, Guthrie headed across Porthmeor's soft white beach towards the sea. The sun was shining down, catching the waves, turning the sea from turquoise to gold before his eyes.

Dipping his toes into the water, he found that it was much colder than it looked.

Not far from where he paddled, a group of teenagers wearing black wetsuits and carrying fibreglass boards, raced down to the water's edge. Guthrie watched as they ran fearless into the ocean, eager to ride the highest wave.

Further along the beach were a row of blue beach huts, reminding him of childhood holidays in Butlins.

Overlooking the beach huts stood St. Ives' pride and joy, The Tate Modern. The local artists claimed that it was the natural white light, unique to St. Ives, that drew them there. The townsfolk still boasted of the late Bernard Leach and Barbara Hepworth, their work exhibited in the enormous white building near Barnoon Cemetery. That was where he would like to be buried. He reasoned, that if his tortured soul never found rest, at least he would have a wonderful view of the ocean.

Deciding that a swim could wait for another day, he sat down on the warm sand and lit a cigarette.

After a few drags he retrieved the stolen letters from his satchel.

The first envelope contained an electoral roll renewal form. The next letter was addressed to V. & M. Kaleel at Lyonesse Lodge. It was postmarked Blankenberge, Belgium.

Taking another long drag on his cigarette, he wondered if there was any post for him back in Redruth. Suddenly, he remembered the letter that Solly had handed to him when they had met up in London. He had forgotten all about it, it was still in his satchel.

'My dear Guthrie,' the letter began. 'Just a few notes I've put together for you. You mentioned Somalia to me, so I photocopied this for you:

'UNITED NATIONS

Reference: C.N.299.2013.TREATIES-XXVI.3 (Depositary Notification)

CONVENTION ON THE PROHIBITION OF THE DEVELOPMENT, PRODUCTION, STOCKPILING AND USE OF CHEMICAL WEAPONS AND ON THEIR DESTRUCTION GENEVA, 3 SEPTEMBER 1992

SOMALIA: ACCESSION'

Guthrie studied the photocopy, and then, returned to the letter.

'But the rule against stockpiling won't come into play for years, son. Anyway, here is a little information I found for you. As you know, the Federal Republic of Somalia resides in the horn of Africa. Bordered to the north by the Gulf of Aden, Kenya to the south-west, and Ethiopia to the west. Along its eastern border lies the Indian Ocean. In 1991 it became a country of great tragedy when the controversial Marxist leader, Mohamed Siad Barre, was replaced by the opposition, and the country was taken over by warlords and clans.'

Guthrie had not anticipated a lesson in history or geography.

'At the end of 1991 there were fierce battles in Mogadishu during a bad drought. So, by the following year, over half the population were facing starvation and at the very least 300,000 men, women and children died.'

Well, he already knew all this, it had been in every tabloid at the time.

'Apart from the famine resulting from the civil war, there was far greater evil afoot. For many years Europe has been dumping their chemical and medical waste on the country causing untold misery. Most of the waste was dumped on the beach in broken containers and leaking barrels. The Swiss and Italians were the greatest culprits highlighted by the Italian newspaper Famiglia Cristiana. Of course, the local warlords were also to blame when Barre had been forced out of office in 1991 and his replacement, Ali Mahdi Mohamed, took over for a year. He was paid £60 million in exchange for allowing 10 million tonnes of toxic waste to be dropped on the country. But, that was merely a minute piece of icing on the very lucrative but deadly cake.

Britain withdrew from British Somaliland in 1960, so that it could join up with Italian Somaliland, and become Somalia. Just over 20 years later Greenpeace proved that there had been the dumping of chemical waste there, they claimed it began in the late 1980's, but it probably began much earlier. Greenpeace exposed Italian and Swiss companies and others, of being involved with this transportation of waste, including the Mafia. And this might interest you, Guthrie, it also included Nancekuke. The company who shipped the waste was owned by the Somali Government. Around 35 million tons of waste was exported to Somalia. Puntland has only just declared autonomy.'

So Nancekuke had been active during the 80s, yet how could that have been possible? Guthrie asked himself, seeing as the men from RAF St. Mawgan who would usually oversee Nancekuke had been sent to the Falklands and Yugoslavia, and possibly even to Ireland. So, who were those left behind? Well, he already knew from Tom Smith's coded letter, that one of those left behind was a very young pilot, who later became a Wing Commander, based at RAF Portreath.

CHAPTER FIFTEEN

Miller's, Lanhams and Laity's estate agents had offered Guthrie a brief list of available properties in the town. They had all said the same thing - that he had chosen the wrong time of year to flat hunt in the area.

The first home he looked at was described as an 'Apartment'. It was halfway up The Stennack, a steep hill leading away from the harbour towards the council estate and Halsetown. By the time he had puffed his way up the hill, he had little energy left to climb the three flights of stairs to the bedsit. The room consisted of single bed, wardrobe, and wash basin.

'There is a TV room you can use, but there is a no smoking policy,' the sour faced landlady told him. 'For another £5 I can change the bed every fortnight. There's a shower room and toilet on the floor below. If you're on the dole, I expect the money weekly.'

'Um, I don't think...'

'If you're working you can pay monthly if that's easier. But I want a month in advance. Also you'll need to give me 2 references.'

The second apartment he viewed was an attic on Penbeagle Estate. The accommodation looked more the size of a large toilet than a flat. The third viewing was a tiny, but lovely, bedsit near the harbour. To view it had meant him walking back down The Stennack and cutting along Fore Street, a long cobbled street that ran parallel with the wharf. Starting at Market Place it terminated just before the Sloop Inn, depending from which end you came in by. The stonework on the frontage of many of the shops, along with the cobbled road, ensured an ambiance of times past. Catering mainly for tourists, it included shops selling Cornish pasties, fish and chips, Cornish Fudge, gifts and surfing equipment. There was also a public house, Methodist church, and a large black and white shell shop that had been there for donkeys' years. Most of the gift shops were getting ready for the tourist season.

Windows were being washed and painted, iron grilles taken down, and new stock filling the shelves.

Taking a quick look at the façade of the vacant bedsit above the fish and chip shop, Guthrie thought better of it and headed back the way he came.

The bells rang out from the Parish Church of St. Ia on the hour, like a timeworn old grandfather watching over his town.

Guthrie followed the line of tourists inside the church, although, they somehow reduced the aura of spirituality, packing out the aisles with their beach bags and constantly flashing their cameras.

Standing below the rood beam, he peered up at the effigy of Jesus, Mary and John. They appeared to be looking down on the Jacobean pulpit, although no one was preaching.

Although the rood screen had long gone, destroyed by the Puritans in 1647, the church was still extravagantly decorated. Everywhere he looked there were carvings, even on the ends of the pews, where examples of ornate 15th century craftsmanship could be seen.

Entering the Lady Chapel to the right of the altar, he sat down on one of the small wooden seats and focussed on Barbara Hepworth's Madonna and child. The plaque below the sculpture revealed that she had carved it in honour of her son, killed whilst serving in the RAF. Suddenly, he was overcome by a feeling of remorse. All those heroes in the Royal Air Force who had sacrificed their lives for their country, and there was he, about to destroy their good name.

Placing a few coins in the tin, he removed a thin, white candle from the box. Putting the wick to one of the other lighted candles, he watched it catch the flame, and then placed it into the candle holder.

Falling down onto his knees he crossed himself.

'I confess to Almighty God, that I have sinned through my own fault, in thought, word and deed. In what I have done and in what I have failed to do. And I ask blessed Mary, ever virgin, all the angels and saints, to pray for me to the Lord our God. In the name of the Father and of the Son...' He paused to cross himself. 'And of the Holy Spirit. Amen.'

Leaving the church by the side door, Guthrie made his way to the Blue Haven teashop along Pednolva Walk. In the summer there would not be an empty seat in the place, but now he was the only customer.

'Pot of tea and...' he glanced down at the cakes on the counter. 'A piece of lemon meringue, please.'

'Clotted cream?' the waitress asked.

'Please.'

He found himself a seat by the panoramic window overlooking the ocean. Two small children were playing with their buckets and spades on the patch of beach opposite the tea shop. Using their spades, they dug into the soft sand, watched over by their mother who was holding a baby in a sling. He wondered what it would be like to be a father. To kick a ball about with a son, or walk a daughter down the aisle. Odd, that he had never discussed having children with Stella, the subject had never crossed their minds. Work had dominated his life since he was twenty-one. Sometimes he had wondered how his life would have turned out if he had followed his university peers into law or medicine.

The waitress placed the tray down on the table. His eyes focussed on the enormous slice of pie and cream.

'Thank you. I love clotted cream,' he said, tucking in.

'Yes, so do I, legend says that it was brought here from the Middle East. I think it was the Babylonians, or maybe it was the Hebrews.'

'Wonder who stole the recipe?' he laughed.

'This cream is now made in Redruth, a firm called Roddas, they're in Scorrier.'

Guthrie was astounded that the town he could not wait to leave, had produced this pièce de résistance.

'Well, who would have believed it, but it's yummy, that's for certain.'

'Are you here on holiday?'

'No, I'm actually thinking of moving here,' he replied, with a mouthful of pie.

'Oh, you'll love it. My husband and I moved down from Essex.'

Guthrie's heart missed a beat. Too many Essex people were moving here. One day he would be spotted and the game would be over. He knew she was waiting for him to say where he came from, as he still retained his London/Essex accent.

'Clacton-on-Sea,' he lied.

'No, well what a small world. We went to Clacton for our anniversary. Used to go to Jaywick as a kid, loved it.'

'What part of Essex do you come from?' he just prayed she wasn't going to say 'Ilford'.

'Harold Wood.'

Guthrie smiled, yet felt sad at his deception. It would be nice, just for once, to tell the truth. Perhaps he was getting old.

A blue and white paper napkin beside the plate caught his attention, embossed with Cornish words and pictures. The picture of a head read Pen, a house was Chy and a fish, Pysk. It reminded him of the Latin word for fish, and the astrological sign, Pisces. A Cornishman had told him that the Cornish used the word Piskie for Pixie. But he could not see any obvious connection between a fish and a fairy-like creature.

*****

After he had left the teashop he decided to give MI6 a call. Although, of course, it was no longer called MI6 but SIS. They had even changed their headquarters from Century House in Lambeth to 85 Albert Embankment at Vauxhall Cross. If they agreed to his request then he would continue with this investigation, if not, then he would have no choice but to pull out and return to his home in Sussex. But that would mean he had failed Stella, and he knew that he would rather die than do that. He also knew that if he continued in his search for her killer, it might actually come to that.

Just along from the café was a lane called The Warren, a fairly narrow, cobbled lane with houses on both sides. One of those houses was named, LOBSTER ROCK. It was a lighthouse shaped building, four floors high. The front door was at the back of the property.

Guthrie opened the door, and found himself inside the kitchen. In the centre of the room was a spiral staircase. A small table stood in the corner, covered in a red and white gingham table cloth, matching the curtains.

A small bedroom led off from the kitchen, he decided that would suit him fine. He would just need to buy a bed.

Climbing up the stairs he came to the next level, the sitting room. Nicely decorated in Wedgewood Jasper print wallpaper of light blue and white, with a matching blue and white striped suite. A drop leaf dining table stood in the corner, under a Keith English print of the harbour. But, the first thing that caught his eye was the panoramic window and French doors.

Guthrie headed straight through the doors onto the veranda.

The view across the bay took his breath away. Tranquil blue waters stretched in every direction across the panorama. He could even see the Western pier and the harbour, like a painting on a chocolate box, almost too perfect.

Below the veranda the tide ebbed and flowed gently onto the granite and blue Elvin rocks. Lumpy stone with patches of greys and browns resembling a crocodile's tail, as it jutted out from the foundations, seeping down into the ocean.

On one side of Lobster Rock was a large house, Crab Rock, it had been converted into flats. On the other side was a hotel.

After inhaling a few deep breaths of salty air, Guthrie felt refreshed enough to climb some more.

On the next floor was a small, all white shower room and toilet with washbasin. A box room stood opposite. Inside were bunk beds and a broken wardrobe. The spiral staircase rose up another flight and terminated in the centre of the top floor bedroom. It overlooked The Warren, a good post for a CCTV camera.

Perhaps he would invite his family to come and stay once this was all over. It was very good of the MOD to agree to buy Lobster Rock for him, but of course, there had been conditions.

Katie joined him early that evening, over a bottle of chilled Muscat Blanc on the veranda.

'Oi would love to live in a place like this.'

'Yes, it does have lovely views,' he conceded, looking out over the sun-spangled ocean.

'Oi'd get myself a boat, a small yacht and sail over to the Scillies.'

'Sounds nice, am I invited?'

'We'll see,' she laughed. 'Have you seen any dolphins?'

'No, not yet,' he confessed, his hand stroking her slender arm. 'Perhaps we could swim with the dolphins if we ever find any.'

'Oi wish oi could stay here forever and ever...with you.' Katie lowered her head and rested it on his lap, lulled by the sunshine.

'What's so special about me?'

She did not reply, just snuggled up closer.

The gulls swarmed overhead, some landing on the balcony of the neighbouring hotel, hoping for rich pickings from empty plates. Guthrie watched them, greedy yet beautiful as they glided past, their white wings gently flapping their way up into the heavens.

As he stroked her hair, he wondered if Our Lady was watching them, and if she approved.

An hour or so later they decided to go for a walk on nearby Porthminster beach. Holding hands, as if glued together, they headed down the black slippery rocks that led to the beach.

'Be careful,' he warned, helping her step down from one boulder onto another, carefully avoiding the seaweed.

'Should have worn my bikini.'

'It will be dark soon, wear it next time. You could even stay over when you get time off work.'

'What are your swimming trunks like, bet they are woollen?' she laughed.

'Think we should go skinny dipping,' he joked, helping her down the final boulder onto the sand.

The beach was empty apart from a small crowd on the far side.

'What's happening over there, Gut?'

'Private party by the looks of things.'

Katie giggled, 'shall we take a look?'

The air was still warm, the sky azure blue, as hand in hand they skipped barefoot across the beach like teenagers.

The group of people were all dressed in 60s paraphernalia. They were listening to man play Rod Stewart's, 'Maggie May', on his guitar.

'Hi, sit down and join us, we're having a reunion,' a woman wearing a flowery dress and headband called over.

They both sat down on the cold sand, observing their surroundings. Only one man had long hair, the rest had short back and sides or were bald. The women also had strains of conventionality streaking across their middle aged faces.

'What reunion, school or university?' Guthrie asked.

'A hippy reunion. We were lived here in '73 and slept on this very beach. I was only 16 at the time.'

'That sounds wonderful,' Katie smiled. 'Oi wish my teenage years had been like that.'

'Donovan was a dosser here in the '60s, before our time. We used to sit on the harbour wall after we were booted out of the woods. We weren't even allowed to sit on the beach in those days.'

Guthrie looked bemused.

'In '73 the St. Ives town council employed a security force with dogs to get rid of us, and poured lime all over our belongings. I was at work at the time and lost all my stuff.'

'Where did you work?'

'The Golden Egg, that was. This was where the scene was at in '73. Until the security force appeared. With help from some of the locals and police, they drove most of the dossers out of town.'

A man wearing a kaftan walked over and joined the conversation. 'Looking back, I don't totally blame the council. After all, some of us did look scruffy, and there were a couple of thefts of milk bottles. They needed the tourists, you see, that's their livelihood.'

'Well, oi doubt anyone would mind you sleeping on the beach tonight,' Katie suggested.

'We've all grown up now, too old to sleep rough, ha-ha.'

'So, do you all live in Cornwall?' Katie asked, wiping the grains of sand from her hands.

'No, I live in Portugal. Colin lives in France, but most of the others live around Britain. Francesca over there is a neurosurgeon,' she pointed to a tall slim woman wearing an afghan coat.

Their chat was suddenly interrupted when the guitarist began to sing Donavan's 'Colours'.

'Yellow is the colour of my true love's hair,' they all joined in. 'In the morning, when we rise, in the morning, when we rise, that's the time, that's the time, I love the best.'

It was during the last verse when Katie leant her head against Guthrie's chest; curling her body up like a foetus, inviting protection from his strong arms. They remained in this position as the musician sang his way through the list of Donavan songs, and then, moved on to the albums of Simon and Garfunkel.

Guthrie began to regret having missed the hippy experience, wondering how his own life would have turned out if he had joined them. Spending the days of his youth smoking dope with the hairies, making love. Talking of peace, while watching the gentle turquoise waters of the harbour ebb and flow under the summer sun. Instead, he had spent the years murdering whoever was on the hit list.

It was during, 'The Sound of Silence', when Katie turned her head towards him and kissed him full on the lips.

'Oi love you, you know, never meant it to happen,' she whispered. 'Oi prayed to

Our Lady today, asked her what she thought.'

'She knows me well, so hope she gave me a good reference,' he smiled, and then gently kissed her. 'So what is this love you have for me, Kathleen O'Brien? Is it eternal or just for now? Is it soul-deep, or is it physical, name your love?'

'Love is love. You can't diminish it or define it. It is just love – from the heart.'

'Hey, who is the philosopher here, me or you?' he laughed. 'A guy called Moore said something like that about the word good.' Looking into her sparkling, temptress eyes, he asked, 'Can I invite you to stay over tonight with me at the guest house?'

'Oi've told you, oi have to be at work at midnight. My employers are throwing a party, and oi've got to go and help clean up?'

'Wonder they didn't make you stay and help.'

'Oi had to help prepare it all, that's why oi couldn't come over this afternoon. Oi wish oi could stay, oi am so happy when oi'm with you, Gut.'

'Likewise,' he smiled, pressing his lips onto hers.

By now, the air was chilly, the large white sun had turned orange. This could be anywhere in the world, Guthrie thought, as he observed the horizontal lines of reds, blues, and oranges, swimming through the fluffy white clouds as the sun slowly fell into the sea and drowned.

CHAPTER SIXTEEN

A dozen or so men wearing combat gear and balaclavas sat in the back of a haulage truck, loaded with grenades, AK47s and M4 Carbine, as it drove up to RAF Portreath in the early hours of the morning. Once they arrived on the base the men jumped out of the truck, and began to load the weapons into another vehicle.

Guthrie was lying down on his stomach in the tall damp grass watching the scene play out. He was glad that he had decided to take a look at the airbase after dropping Katie off at Tehidy.

Along with the infra-red goggles, he had also packed his SIG SSG550 sniper rifle. Shoot first ask questions later was his motto, it was the only reason he was still alive.

'He's fucking been here, left tracks,' a man spoke softly into his mobile phone. 'Yes, we've got the tools... What? Export of course... Shall we finish him off? — Okay, whatever you say.'

'What did he say?' someone asked.

'The boss said we have to wait until after the last shipment of Sweet Bee has gone, and then we fucking kill him,' the man gobbed onto the earth. 'But, I'm not listening to the boss over this one, if I see him, or even smell him, he's dead, and that's a fucking promise.'

Guthrie was relieved that the trail he had left had been spotted, the more he riled them the better. Although, he doubted the majority of men there were RAF personnel.

The men made their way towards the single storey block that he had seen before. But, this time, there were no lights on or BMW parked outside. Following them across the terrain he noticed small, chimney-like objects erupting from the grass which he had not seen on his previous visit. They were the ventilation stacks for air raid shelters, each shelter had 12 external ventilation stacks which ran in two parallel lines across each side of the roof. From his research he knew there were also underground control rooms and other shelters scattered about.

As he hid out of sight behind some concrete pillars, he realised that it was all residual from the last World War. There was also an 'ops room' on the other side of the bay, once used by the military, and subsequently became The Ops Room Inn that held weekly discos. But, that had closed down in 1996.

Arriving at a thick copse of trees, instead of stopping, they headed into the woodland. Guthrie followed stealthily, feeling as if he were participating in a children's fiction, about to enter some sort of secret garden or wardrobe. Suddenly, he noticed an iron gate. Attached to the gate was a huge board:

MINISTRY OF DEFENCE CDE NANCEKUKE – RESTRICTED ENTRY – PERMITS MUST BE SHOWN – CAMERAS NOT PERMITTED

Remaining hidden in the shadows he watched them head through the gate crocodile fashion. But, he had no way of getting through the security gate. Instead, he relaxed on the grass and had a smoke.

He had only just got through half the Marlboro when the gate opened. Two men were carrying a trunk out, but failed to close the gate behind them.

Taking full advantage of the situation, Guthrie headed through the gate and followed the path.

It led to a pod shaped enclosure.

Lights were blazing everywhere; it was a large factory complex. Several fork lift trucks and a small crawler crane stood in the grounds. A glass greenhouse stood near the factory entrance, behind it was a small portacabin.

Interestingly, the literature he had read about the base failed to show the pod or factory. Now he knew the reason for the density of the trees, so that any passing aircraft would not spot the factory, safely hidden beneath the foliage. Although he was fascinated by his surroundings, he was not overwhelmed; he had seen this type of plant before in several countries, mostly involved in the manufacture of arms or drugs.

Creeping up towards the portacabin he noticed a group of men coming out of the factory. They were carrying large crates. Wearing his goggles, he could see that the crates were crammed full of jars of honey and live beehives.

Suddenly, he was bombarded by a haze of crane flies.

'Git,' he swatted the flies, only now aware of all the other insects flying about the pod, attracted to the light.

Switching on his pen-camera he decided to film the men. They reminded him of a Lowry painting, matchstalk men with no faces.

From the corner of his eye he noticed a figure running into the pod. Guthrie watched closely, bemused why he was dressed in black and not wearing combat gear like the rest of the men. The figure ran over to a man who was busy digging up some earth. After a few minutes the man dropped his spade, and followed the figure towards a jeep parked near the factory.

Guthrie wondered how the vehicle had managed to get in through the gate. He was also curious to know what they were digging for. But, he did not have to wait too long, as a large, transparent, plastic sack was hauled up out of the ground.

All eyes were focussed on the sack. Nobody noticed Guthrie crawl up behind them and peer into the sack. Inside was a body, it was fixed by rigor mortis.

'Shall we give him a funeral?' a voice asked.

'Don't be daft, we haven't got the time.'

'Very sad, he was one of us after all. It seems a pretty rotten ending getting contaminated, and not even given a funeral.'

Before they had time to continue the debate, the jeep had reversed towards them, and the corpse was lifted in.

For the next half an hour the men busily stacked up the wooden crates onto barrows. Once all the crates were in position, the men grabbed the handles of the barrows and made their way to the far side of the pod. It was only then, when

Guthrie noticed the other exit, much larger than the gate he had come through.

Guthrie wondered how he would get out of the pod without being seen. The only way possible was to go back the way he had come in.

As he made his way around the perimeter of the trees outside the pod, he recognised some of the landmarks from his previous visit, although he had never been this close before.

On reaching the other side of the copse, he caught sight of the men loading the crates onto large haulage trucks. He decided that it was time for a smoke.

Once the crates were loaded, they started to move in the direction of the airfield. Closely followed by the other vehicles, including the BMW and a Land Rover.

Also on their tail was Guthrie. He was kept company on the journey across the rough terrain by a couple of bats. They flew close to his head, as if considering him either their friend or their prey. It seemed odd that they were the only mammals that could fly, he thought. Maybe that was the reason they were used in so many horror films.

Just across the field was an object that resembled a giant TV screen cum electric circuit on wheels. It was Type 93 mobile radar.

As they moved close to the edge of the cliff, he could hear the waves crashing against the ragged rock face, and smell the salty air rising up from the sea.

Ahead of him, the trucks were rocking from side to side, it was a wind trap between Portreath and Porthtowen.

If this operation lasted all night, he would pick some mushrooms in the morning for breakfast, and perhaps catch a crab or a handful of shrimps from the rock pools below.

The area was suddenly flooded with bright lights. The haulage trucks had stopped moving. Guthrie recognised the lights from his previous visit, and knew they had arrived at the airfield. He was standing on the legendary Nancekuke Common.

There were four runways on the airfield, although only one appeared to be in use.

A giant balloon-shaped object stood within the perimeter of the runway. Looking through his goggles he saw that it was covered in plum and green pentagonal shaped cells, reminding him of the biomes he had seen in the plans for the Eden Project. It was a Kevlar radome. No doubt it housed a Type 101 radar.

Guthrie knew that its raison d'etre was to give long range observation of the coast. He began to wonder why an unmanned RAF base, under guise of being a mere Reporting Post, would require two remote radar heads.

A Hercules C-130 stood beside the runway. The men pushed the barrows towards it. The figure he had seen earlier, dressed in black, emerged from the jeep and climbed up into the cockpit of the plane.

Grabbing his Walther PPK pistol Guthrie left them to it, and ran across the uneven, spongy ground towards the nearest hangar. There was only one aircraft inside, a Canberra PR9. He knew that a Canberra PR9 detachment had been sent to Zaire that previous November, in order to establish the location of refugees in Central Africa, where Kalashnikovs were ten a penny.

There were two other hangars nearby. The second hangar contained a Harrier jet. Climbing up into the cockpit he focussed his attention on the centre stick and left hand throttle, longing to mess around with them. Although, he did not give in to temptation, he was unable to resist touching the standard flight controls. Fascinated with the lever that controlled the direction of the four vectorable nozzles.

After playing with the buttons for a few minutes he turned round to investigate the fuselage. It was empty, except for a large object covered in a black sheet.

Climbing out of the pilot's seat he struggled into the back of the aircraft and removed the sheet. Before him stood a black chest, it was padlocked.

Shooting off the lock with his handgun, he hurriedly opened the lid. It was exactly what he had anticipated, the chest was packed with RAF issue weapons. They were tied up in various bundles, each bundle was labelled: 20 x Rifles 5.56 mm L85A1; 20x Pistols Automatic 9 mm L9A1; 15x Pistols Automatic L47A1 7.65 mm; 10x Machine Guns 7.62 mm L7A1; 10x Machine Guns 5.56 mm L86A1; 20x Shotgun Automatic 12 bore L32A1.

Jumping down from the aircraft, he raced towards the third hangar. A Jaguar GRIA stood inside. It was equipped to carry 1,000 lb free fall bombs, cluster bombs and other missiles. Yet, he did not bother to board, he had already found what he had been looking for.

Desperate for a cigarette he lit up, trying to conceal the flame. It was then that he saw them, columns of round steel cylinders. They lined the walls of the hangar, their destination printed on the sides, 'GB for Somalia'.

With a heavy heart Guthrie stared at them, all too aware that they were packed with chemical waste. It was the same waste that Nancekuke was supposed to have disposed of a decade earlier. After all, GB did not mean Great Britain in this instance, GB was just another name for sarin.

Sitting down on a rock outside the hangar, he watched the first light of dawn burst through the black sky. Now he could tick off the next task on the agenda, chemical weapons.

Only a couple of months earlier, John Miller of ABC television had interviewed Osama Bin Laden. One of the topics discussed was the Mogadishu slaughter of 1993, known as Black Hawke Down, where the US forces had attacked the Somalis. Bin Laden had said that he blamed the US for the attack, and also blamed them for their crusade against the Islamic countries.

Yet, after supporting the slaughter of the Somalis, the UK had then offered aid, in exchange for a finger in the lucrative oil pie.

Flicking his cigarette ash onto the earth he watched it smoulder, a tiny red flicker of fire. Once this job was finished he would be away as fast as he could, to Kos maybe, and the MOD could go and fuck itself.

'You're dead!'

A sudden thud to his back and he went down. The pain sliced through his spine as they beat down on him, kicking at his back and head. The blood trickled down his forehead blinding him, as he fell to the ground.

'Think you've killed the fucker.'

'Yeah, he's dead. Shall we leave him here?'

'Don't be fucking stupid. What if a helicopter or some random fucking hang glider sees him in the morning?'

One of his assailants bent down to pull off his goggles. With a sudden shriek he stumbled back, as Guthrie's teeth sank into his arm.

The other assailant kicked him again in the head, aggravating the wound. Within seconds Guthrie had him in an arm-lock, and then handcuffed both of them together back to back; all three of them covered in a sea of his blood.

After wiping the blood from his eyes, he was surprised to find that they were only teenagers. He wondered why the enemy was using kids to fight their battle.

'The question is do I hide you, liberate you or kill you?' he demanded, with the little breath he had left. The pain made him nauseas. This scenario should never have happened; he had been careless for a second time.

'And you're going to tell me that this base is being used for... let me guess - Smuggling out arms and chemical weapons of mass destruction, is that right?' The blood trickled down into his mouth.

The ginger haired kid nodded.

'You see, if this had been a couple of years ago, I'd have blown your fucking heads off and asked questions later. What should I do now? If I let you live, well, then I die. If I shoot now, then you die.'

They did not answer.

'Okay, I'll make a deal.' He twirled his gun around his fingers. 'If you give me some details – I mean details that I don't already have, I might, now I'm not promising anything, but I might let you live.'

'What's the point if you might kill us anyhow?' the ginger kid asked.

'The point is, if I choose to kill you, and I haven't said that's a cert, have I?' he said breathlessly. 'I could kill you quickly and get it over with if you tell me what I need to know, or I could kill you slowly.' He was laughing, yet not inside, he was just trying his hardest to remain conscious. 'You know, like cutting out your tongue as a starter. Then chopping off your dick, then your fingers one by one and then removing an eye. You know the sort of thing. There again, I could be merciful and let you go.'

He would have killed them either way if he was still under contract. But, it was difficult now, and his head was bleeding. Even so, he was under no illusion, he knew that his chopping days were well and truly over.

'So your name is Kareem Kaleel,' he read from the driving license belonging to the other teenager. 'I've seen you in the London Inn, drug dealer extraordinaire. You wouldn't be the son of Vivienne and Mustopher Kaleel would you?'

Turning to the ginger boy he then read from his driving license. 'And your name is...' he stopped short. The name he was reading was, William Jackson. Was this kid the son of the man whose body parts he had blown up?

Suddenly the noise from a Sea King grabbed his attention, they were looking for him. Its searchlight scanned the area, highlighting the airfield and the numerous mounds of earth that bordered it. On seeing the mounds, he suddenly remembered the document that he had read: 'But they lied! Not all the buildings were destroyed. Nancekuke produced 20 tons of the nerve gas sarin during 1951 to 1976 and 35 tons more after'.

Guthrie knew instinctively that the mounds highlighted by the aircraft, were the dumping areas of the deadly nerve gas, sarin.

CHAPTER SEVENTEEN

Falmouth was a more upmarket town than Redruth or Camborne. Large Georgian houses that had been converted into guest houses, overlooked the beach. There was also the harbour and its tributaries full of yachts, ships and seals. It was the third deepest natural harbour in the world.

Wing Commander Paul Trembath owned a newsagent on the corner of Dracaena Avenue and Killigrew Street. He wanted to buy a string of them all across the South-West, and had already put in a bid for several more.

'Good morning, Susan,' he smiled at the grey haired manageress behind the counter. She only lived down the road from the shop, which was the main reason he had picked her from the numerous applicants.

'Good morning, Mr Trembath, it's a bit nippy out today.'

The newspapers were placed in neat piles on the shelves, alongside the magazines. The confectionery spread out on the opposite side of the shop, beside the fridge hosting ready-made sandwiches and cold drinks.

'A lighter and Mars bar were lifted. He's on camera but I didn't see him do it. Sorry.'

'It doesn't matter, Susan, these things happen. Although, I have been thinking of moving the sweets nearer to the till.'

'Yes, that would be a great help. I could keep an eye on what's going on then, especially with the children after school.'

'Have you sold any violet soaps or perfumes yet?'

'Oh, I meant to tell you,' the woman said excitedly. 'The customers who bought them said they were wonderful. We've sold at least a dozen soaps, and 5 perfumes.'

'That's great news.'

'I remember my own mother always put a few drops of Cornish violets behind her ears before she went to chapel.'

'I'm actually thinking of bringing out a violet wine when I retire. Maybe even a lavender wine.'

'Oh, what a good idea, I don't think it's ever been done before. Reminds me of that song, what was it now - violet wine?'

'You're thinking of lilac wine – Elkie Brooks.'

'Yes, that's right. My husband, Denzel, he's clever like you.'

'How is Denzel these days?'

'Yes, getting better. They said the cancer's in remission which is good,' she smiled, blinking her eyes. 'Reckon he got it from Geevor. You know, that radon gas in the mines gets into the lungs.'

'Yes, I had heard.'

'The papers say the government wouldn't give South Crofty four point seven million pounds to help the mine stay open. My Denzel's raging mad about it.'

'Yes. But the rescue package was around twelve million. Never mind, there's worse troubles at sea.'

Falmouth harbour was packed with tourists that day, although it was still only 10.30 in the morning. The sky looked fairly bright, just a few grey clouds. The weather forecast had said dull but not much else. A speed boat suddenly bolted across the waves catching his attention.

These days the harbour was chock-a-block with speed boats and water skiers coming over from Swanpool and St. Mawes. Even the sheltered inlets were packed with catamarans.

At times like this Trembath wished he had a son, just to do the normal father and son things like fishing or diving. Well, there was still time.

One of the boats anchored in the harbour was a trawler. Trembath climbed down the harbour steps onto the boat and entered the wheelhouse. Just as he started the engine, a swarthy, heavily built man, jumped onto the deck.

Trembath went over and gave him a hug.

'Good to see you.' They had been best friends since childhood. Mustopher was closer to him than a brother.

'Likewise, by the way, thanks for the extra cash.'

'You're a good man, Mustopher, and you've been a great friend to me. I couldn't have done this without you.'

'And my daughter wouldn't be alive without you.' He placed an arm around Trembath's shoulders.

'How is Sfiyah doing?'

'Yes, Sfiyah is doing well. Are your own kids home for the summer?'

'No, my girls are staying at their boarding school. Suzette and I hope to be taking them away on holiday in September,' he revealed.

'That's a good way to bring up your children, see them as little as possible,' Mustopher laughed.

'Incidentally, we're trying out a different route to Dubai today. Just to see if we really need to stop at Belgium.'

'I thought you'd ended the deal with Sheik Amir.'

'Doesn't mean I don't have a more powerful buyer in the Emirates, does it?' Trembath winked. 'Admittedly, I don't like taking the risk of carrying the load myself, but, if it means getting paid twice, I'll take my chances.'

'Twice?'

'Well, Amir already paid for it once, ha-ha,' Trembath laughed, even though he was still unhappy with the way the boss had gone about ending the contract.

Mustopher failed to understand, but, just laughed along with him.

Glancing at his watch, Trembath said, 'We'd better set off now, catch the tide.'

'What's the distance we're sailing?'

'I'm not quite certain to be honest. It's about 130 nautical miles to the Bay of Biscay from Cornwall.'

'Would have brought my dvds if I'd known,' Mustopher laughed, shaking his friend's hand warmly. Then he headed down into the galley to stocktake the cache of firearms and explosives that awaited him.

*****

It was as dawn broke the following morning, when the trawler reached the Bay of Biscay. A few dolphins and a whale had been spotted along the way, but the journey had been uneventful. Now it was the turn of the gannets, their long pointed wings flapping around the mast before diving headfirst into the water.

The two men were sitting on deck in their vests, smoking Turkish cigarettes and drinking mugs of hot tea, as they looked out at the distant French coastline.

'What are the white boxes you've put in the fridge?' Mustopher asked.

'Syringes, they contain sarin and cocaine in liquid form.' Trembath yawned and stretched. 'Soon we'll be into our final leg of the journey.'

'Shame we couldn't go faster.'

'Well, 7 knots is fast enough for a trawler, and we had to avoid the Ushant.'

Trembath turned away from the coastline and focussed his gaze on the horizon. Sometimes he wished that he could bring Suzette and the girls on one of his sea missions, how they'd love to swim with the dolphins. A gannet suddenly caught his attention as it nosedived into the sea like a white dart.

Suddenly, the wind whipped up. The dark grey clouds overhead looked ominous. The trawler began to bounce.

'Ten knots!' Trembath shouted, throwing his cigarette over the side of the boat, that was now dipping spoon-like into the ocean. There had been no warning, it had gone from a smooth glide to a rib in a second. Gigantic waves now swept towards them like aprons of foam, the noise getting progressively louder with each breaker.

Entering the wheelhouse, he took hold of the wheel. The swell had risen to 20 feet, along with gale force winds. He could see Mustopher throwing up over the port side, as the billowing waves covered the deck with white foam. He knew they must be at the 100-fathom curve.

Switching on to automatic pilot, he went to help his friend, who had by now slid on his back along the deck. Hanging onto the stern, he grabbed Mustopher's arm. Their legs wriggling frog-like through the rising water, the whole vessel now covered in a white snowstorm of froth.

He knew it was his fault for taking this route, he should have known better. His hands now red and sore like his eyes, from the harsh, salty spray.

By now Mustopher was gasping for air.

'Make a run for the galley, I'll turn her round and we'll head home!'

Like a drowned rat, Mustopher clawed his way across the deck, and descended the slippery steps into the galley.

Making a dash for the wheelhouse, Trembath grabbed the wheel. Using all his strength he tried to turn it. But, it would not budge. The waves came crashing down onto the wheelhouse, drowning the trawler. Again he tried to turn the wheel as the vessel bounced up and down.

Eventually, after several failed attempts, he managed to turn the boat round, and then set it back on automatic pilot.

Soaked to the skin he made his way down into the galley, securing the door behind him. Heading straight for the stove he warmed himself, changed his clothes, and then grabbed a bottle of whisky and two glasses.

They had only just started on their second glass when the phone rang. Trembath answered it.

'Hi, how are you...What?' He moved away from the table where they sat, in order to speak in private. 'What do you mean?... Don't be fucking ridiculous. No I won't... Oh, don't be insane... Yes, I am calling you insane if you can suggest this... Yes, I do mean it!' he raged. 'Not only the obvious, best friends since time began... No, he's never put a foot wrong and as loyal as I could wish for... I don't fucking care! No!... I just paid for his kid's op... No. No I won't! Never! Do you understand, NEVER!'

But, after 20 minutes of rants he found himself saying, 'Okay, okay. Okay I said. You're the boss as you keep reminding me.'

Turning off the phone he poured himself another drink, and then one after that.

The rain pelted down hard on the galley's wooden ceiling as if raining pebbles.

'The noise is making me want to piss,' Mustopher laughed, heading towards the toilet. He failed to notice Trembath remove a knife from one of the drawers. Quick as a flash he grabbed Mustopher from behind, holding the blade to his throat.

'Why are you doing this, is this a joke?' Mustopher gasped, struggling to get away.

'No joke I'm afraid. The boss just said you know too much. And now that your son's in custody...'

'But, we're friends, we are business partners. What have I ever done to you?'

'No, you're right, Mustopher, you've been a good friend, better than a brother.'

'I don't understand,' Mustopher wept. 'What about the children. Sfiyah's only just had surgery. And... And what about my son and Vivienne?'

Trembath did not reply, as if he might be having second thoughts.

'I love you, my brother,' Mustopher cried. 'You know my boy won't talk.'

'But, the boss said this must end, and I never argue with the boss.'

'Why not just end our contract, friendship even? Why do you have to kill me?' Mustopher sobbed, tears were streaming down his face. He knew that Trembath was the stronger and fitter of the two of them, there was no way he could break free, as the knife hovered by his throat.

'Who is this boss you are always speaking of; why don't you say his name?'

'Sorry.' And in a second he had slit Mustopher's throat.

Trembath's hands were now covered in blood as he stood astride his friend, who now lay dead on the floor.

'Good God, what have I done?' he screamed, falling to his knees. 'I love you, Mustopher, my brother,' he wept, holding the corpse against his chest.

Trembath found it hard to get the body up the steps of the galley, and out onto the deck. The problem was made worse now that thunder and lightning raged across the skies.

The inclement weather also caused the blood from the body to flow around the deck. It was everywhere, even on his clothing, causing him to wonder why he had been so foolish. A bullet would have been better.

After wrapping the body in polythene, he dragged it into the wheelhouse, and then, spent the evening drinking himself into oblivion.

Trembath did not wake until the next morning. Racing up on deck, he breathed a sigh of relief to find the body still there in the wheelhouse.

Grabbing some old dumbbells from under a bunk in the cabin, he attached them to the corpse.

Checking to see that he was still outside the seven miles limit from the UK coastline, he pulled the body across the deck. With all the energy that he could muster, he lifted the corpse up onto the side of the trawler and tipped it over into the sea.

'Goodbye you foolish, adorable Arab. I love you, my dearest friend and brother.'

Trembath turned the trawler around and headed back towards Falmouth weeping.

CHAPTER EIGHTEEN

The gulls were already squawking as the sun rose that Monday morning. Bread was being baked, pasties were in the ovens, and the milkman had left the bottles of milk outside nearly every cottage in the town. He had already delivered to the High Street, Fore Street, and by now had reached The Digey.

Ada Beckerleg was looking through her net curtains waiting for the milkman, when she noticed the tabby cat lying dead in the road.

'Vivienne! Vivienne!' Ada cried, as she rang her neighbour's doorbell.

A curtain slightly moved in the upstairs bedroom. A few moments later a woman opened the front door in her dressing gown.

'Vivienne,' the old lady began. 'It's Marmaduke,' she pointed to the cat.

The woman, Vivienne, raced out to the road and picked up the dead animal, cradling it in her arms.

'Was it run over, dear?' Ada asked.

Vivienne failed to reply as she rushed back into the house.

A moment later the milk float came around the corner.

'Mornin', Ada, just a pint today? Hey, what be the matter, me 'andsome?'

Ada sniffed back the tears. 'Just found next door's cat, Marmaduke, dead in the road.'

'Now don't you go upsetting yourself. Here, have some of this 'ere cream on the house. Go nice with a bit of bread and jam.' The milkman handed her the pint of milk and a tub of Roddas clotted cream, and then continued with his deliveries.

Ada popped the milk and cream into her fridge, and then picked up the phone.

'Hello, my dear, and how are you?'

'Aunty Ada. Lovely to hear from you,' a groggy voice answered. 'It's only 8 o'clock, are you alright?'

'I just witnessed the most terrible thing. Marmaduke was lying dead in the road.' Ada wiped her eyes with a cotton handkerchief.

‘Oh, dear, how awful. Aunty, would you like me to pop over, I’m not doing anything much today?’

‘Would you, dear,’ Ada suddenly stopped snivelling. ‘See you about lunchtime then?’

She had only just put down the telephone receiver when she heard a motor vehicle pull up outside. Looking through the net curtains she saw a Land Rover parked outside her front gate.

The driver got out, a stocky man in his late sixties, dressed in green Wellington boots and a wax Barbour. He headed towards Vivienne’s front door. Ada had seen him there before, Vivienne had told her he was a bee farmer.

Turning up her hearing aid she listened by the window. But all she could make out were murmurings of an argument.

‘We’re waiting for the soaps.’

‘I’ve only got one pair of hands!’

‘Your memory must be playing you up, Vivienne. We had an agreement.’ The man walked into the house uninvited.

She could hear Vivienne shouting through the granite walls, the row continuing into the back garden.

Ada hurried as best she could to get to the back door, although she was a martyr to her swollen ankles, that bulged over the edge of her pink slippers.

'We've got people wanting to buy and there is nothing left to sell, do you understand?'

'Too fucking bad! So you've come all the way back from Spain just to cause me more grief?' Vivienne yelled. Then her voice calmed down, 'I don't want all the neighbours hearing. The old gel next door is always nosing around.'

Ada pursed her lips with irritation. Ada Beckerleg nosy? Of course she was not nosy, just caring of her neighbours, that was all.

It was 12.30 when the doorbell rang.

'How lovely to see you, dear, do come in.' Ada welcomed her bespectacled niece into the cottage, having changed into her grey dress, enhanced by a silver broach.

'Oh my dear how slim you are, you've lost so much weight,' the old lady stared at her niece. 'You look wonderful, darling.'

'So do you, Aunty.'

After kissing each other, Olivia hung her coat on the rail in the narrow passage. She loved her aunt's tiny cottage, it was so quaint and olde worlde.

'How is Polly?' Ada asked, when they entered the sitting room.

'She is still hanging about with that awful friend of hers, the council house boy.'

'Well, there have been some great men originating from council houses, you know.' Ada replied reassuringly. 'Have you seen your father recently, is he keeping well?'

Olivia knew how much her aunt disliked her father for the way he had treated her sister, Olivia's mother.

'As you know, he's like a cat that has got the cream since the new wing at Treliske was built.' She handed her aunt a small bouquet of pink and lilac tulips.

'Oh, what beautiful flowers, the smell, mmm,' she said, putting them to her nose.

'Thank you so much, my dear. I'll put them in a vase.'

As Ada hurried through to the kitchen, Olivia took the opportunity to examine the familiar surroundings. The same three-piece cottage suite and walnut bureau, the same beige wallpaper that she had since the seventies; even though Olivia's mother, Phyllis, had offered to pay for new decoration and furnishings. The family photos were still displayed on the small mantelpiece over the fireplace. Olivia felt sorry for her aunt having never married.

'Would you like some help in the kitchen?'

'No thank you. It is chicken and dumplings, used to be your favourite,' Ada laughed.

Olivia would have preferred salad, as dumplings were not on Weightwatchers list of diet food.

'So what's been going on next door?' Olivia asked, once they were both sitting down with their lunch.

'Do you know dear, Vivienne and her husband have had some very strange visitors calling? I'm frightened to leave my windows open.'

'You're sounding like Miss Marple. By the way, this chicken is delicious.'

'Vivienne Kaleel and I used to be so close. I helped her a great deal when her daughter had the kidney transplant.'

'You're too soft-hearted, that's your problem. People take advantage of you.'

'I found Vivienne's cat, Marmaduke, dead in the road today.'

'Yes, you told me over the phone. It's such a shame. Was it run over?'

'No, it was just dead in the road. And, do you know something?' she said, her mouth puckering. 'I also saw a funny looking bee.'

'I always tell Polly not to go near bees. But, if you tell her not to do something she'll do it.'

'This bee was in Marmaduke's mouth.'

'Oh dear, maybe the poor cat died of a bee sting.'

Ada lowered her voice and moved her head nearer to her niece.

'I don't want this going any further, but I saw your friend Mr Guthrie speaking with Vivienne not so long ago, but she gave him short shrift.'

'Perhaps he called to see you, and thought you weren't in.'

'Why would he want to see me? He must know something's going on next door.'

'I don't think so; he was probably just asking the way. He's recently moved to St. Ives, you know,' Olivia smiled reassuringly. 'Piran said he had been working at Treliske as a courier or something, but for some reason packed it in. Piran wasn't too happy I can tell you, after the trouble my father went to, to get him the job.'

'Well, my love, you know what I think of your father after the way he treated your poor mother. But, this Guthrie is obviously a layabout. I mean, didn't you once tell me that he hadn't had a career since leaving university?' the old lady scorned. 'You and Piran are too gullible, after all, wasn't he charged with murder?'

'Of course he's not a layabout, Aunty. I'm sure there's much more to him than meets the eye. I've always fancied him you know,' she giggled. 'In fact, if I wasn't married to Piran I could see myself...'

'Oh, don't say such things, Olivia.'

'Okay then, but I still think he was innocent,' she reiterated. 'By the way, did you leave the dead bee with the cat, Aunty?'

'No, I took it out of Marmaduke's mouth hoping he would wake up. I've thrown it in the bin. Do you want to see it?'

'I'll give it to my father, he can get it analysed.'

The Aga took up most of the kitchen, Olivia had no idea how her aunt still cooked on it.

'I've wrapped the dead bee in some tissue paper for you.' The old lady handed her niece the tiny parcel.

After putting the dirty dishes into the sink, Olivia left her aunt to dish up the dessert and returned to her chair.

'I brought you today's paper, Aunty,' Olivia called out from the sitting room.

'I'm just dishing up afters. Would you be so kind as to read the front page to me?'

Olivia took the newspaper from her bag and glanced at the headlines.

'Interest rates are soaring. It just goes on about share index and the financial state of things. I know Daddy has shares here, there and everywhere, but, I've only got a few.'

'Yes, I have a few shares and bonds that I'm leaving to you.'

'Don't talk like that, Aunty. Oh, there's something here about a man who was holidaying in Redruth found washed up on a beach in Belgium.'

'Not another death, that's all there is in the news these days, all doom and gloom,' Ada muttered, as she shuffled into the room and placed the dishes of apple crumble and clotted cream onto the table. 'I'll just get my specs.'

Ada reached above the walnut bureau and retrieved her glasses. Her old, wrinkled hands were shaky as she took the paper from her niece and began to read.

'Body washed up on Belgium shores. How sad. It says he stayed in the Penventon Hotel. Actually the hotel is very nice, dear, I went to a wedding there a few years ago,' Ada digressed. 'It says that he drowned. What a shame.'

'Perhaps that was where he was from, Belgium, think there's a photo of him, Aunty.'

Ada took a glance at the small photograph beside the article. 'Oh, goodness gracious!'

'What on earth?' Olivia coughed, almost choking on a piece of crumble.

'I know this man. I saw him going into Vivienne's a few months back, he was with two other men.' Ada was visibly shaken by what she had read. 'I don't think he was Cornish. He looked Asian or from the Middle East, something like that. Definitely not Cornish.'

'Might be a different man you saw.'

'No, this is definitely him. They were with that farmer.'

'What farmer?'

'The same man who called there this morning in a Land Rover, soon after Vivienne took poor Marmaduke indoors.'

'How can you tell this man in the paper is the same one that visited Vivienne?'

'Oh, my dear, I fear something rather unpleasant is going on.'

'Please stop upsetting yourself, and eat this wonderful apple crumble. I'm sure you're worrying over nothing.'

Ada obeyed, and laid the newspaper down on the tablecloth beside her.

'I've made you a batch of saffron buns to take home with you.'

'Thank you, Aunty, but you shouldn't have gone to so much trouble.'

'No trouble, dear, not much else to do with my time.'

'That's probably it, you have too much time on your hands. You should go to the WI meetings like you used to.'

'I think the farmer's name is Trembath,' the old lady said, oblivious to her niece's comments. 'Yes it's Matthew Trembath. Married to that woman who wrote the cookery book.' Ada was now on a roll. 'Do you think I should phone the police? What do you think, dear?'

'Aunty, I think you should stop reading those crime novels,' Olivia scolded light-heartedly.

'The newspaper article suggests that he might have been murdered.'

'Okay I'll mention it to daddy,' she acquiesced. 'I'll see what he thinks. He's a friend of the police superintendent of Cornwall, they play golf together.'

'Thank you, dear. It's been such an upsetting day, what with Marmaduke and now this.'

'I do think you're worrying over nothing, Aunty. By the way, this crumble is moreish.'

CHAPTER NINETEEN

Guthrie had overslept that Monday morning. Sleeping soundly as the dustbin men threw the bins along The Warren. He even failed to hear the milkman jingle past his window.

It was around lunchtime, with eyes half closed, when he dragged himself out of bed and into the kitchen. After lighting up a Marlboro he filled the kettle, and then prepared a mug with milk, sugar and a teabag. Perhaps Typhoo was the only constant in his life, he considered.

Once the tea was made he headed up the stairs.

Opening the French doors in the lounge of his new home, Guthrie was immediately deafened by the nose of the gulls threatening to land on the veranda. Rushing out to shoo them away, he was overcome by the salty smells from the ocean.

He watched as the gulls flew up into the azure sky, tinged with a white haze from the midday sun. It reflected down onto the waters of the bay, and traced the waves across to Hayle Towans and Godrevy lighthouse in the distance.

The unread post still lay on the table. He opened one of the letters. It contained the results from the specimens he had purloined from the greenhouse at the bee farm. Most of the results he found unintelligible, but three things stood out. Firstly, the violets were contaminated with an insecticide. The report suggested that it might be Malathion, although the results were inconclusive. Secondly, the leaves were coca leaves. Lastly, the saffron crocus contained cocaine. Now he knew for certain that Tehidy bee farm was somehow mixed up with cultivating cocaine. But, for Guthrie, the big question was, what else were they cultivating?

Suddenly there was a knock on the door.

'Mr Guthrie...'

'Just Guthrie.'

'Okay, Guthrie. We've spoken on the phone, head of CID, Detective Inspector Brian Pendeen,' the man introduced himself, thrusting his hand forward. He was in his late forties, over 6ft, smartly dressed in a fitted suit and highly polished shoes.

Guthrie shook his hand and invited him inside. 'You'll have to excuse the state of me, but I was working late last night.'

'No need to apologise, I only come over on the off chance you would be in. I got a call this morning from the MOD.'

'So hopefully they filled you in. Go up to the lounge, I'll bring up some coffee and biscuits, or do you fancy cake, I've got some scones?'

'No thanks, a biscuit will be fine.'

After settling down with their refreshments, Guthrie filled him in on the details of his arrest and subsequent incarceration. Then he showed him the letter that he had received in prison from Tom Smith.

'It's pretty obvious, Guthrie, that you moved here to be the bait so to speak,' Brian Pendeen said, as if he had only just realised.

'I knew I'd stick out like a sore thumb. If I wanted to be hidden, I'd have camped at the Lizard or somewhere.'

'I expect you've wondered why we've done nothing about the shenanigans up at the airbase.'

'It had crossed my mind.'

'Well, as you will appreciate, we aren't allowed to march up there and make arrests without a nod from the top brass, as it is MOD territory. And of course, most of their history of manufacturing weapons of mass destruction was legal.'

'Yes, I understand,' Guthrie nodded, lighting up a Marlboro. 'This is why I can investigate in areas where you can't. I'm my own boss.'

'Well, if you sign this,' the officer produced a document and pen. 'We can say that you're helping us with our on-going investigations, and in return we can offer you extra protection.'

'Thanks, but I don't need protection.'

'I know your history and it's very impressive if I might say. I know you can handle yourself, but, I can't disobey my boss.' Brian Pendeen gave Guthrie a friendly pat on the back. 'With your permission we will put our own security system in place around this house. By the way, your own alarm system needed a battery.'

'I didn't realise I was helping you. And thanks anyway but...'

He was suddenly interrupted by someone coming up the stairs.

'Oh, I see your protection has just arrived.' Brian Pendeen focussed on a middle aged policewoman standing in the doorway. Her uniformed figure gave the impression of being a solid square, rather than feminine curves. She was accompanied by a large, shaggy sheep dog.

'Wow, what amazing views,' the woman headed for the window.

'I'm not sure if I'm allowed dogs here,' Guthrie mumbled, suddenly feeling that his life was being taken over.

Her name was Abigail, a detective with the CID, married to a fisherman in Penzance. He found himself telling her about Katie over a pasty lunch. They were constantly interrupted by the sheepdog, MacKenzie, who barked futilely at the seagulls through the panoramic window.

'She sounds like a sweet girl.'

'Yes she is, but...' he failed to finish the sentence.

'I hope I won't be in your way when she comes, you know what I mean. So what is your Katie like?'

Guthrie just smiled, there was nothing she could get in the way of, Katie was a chastity belt Catholic.

'Um, pretty, slim, Irish.' He did not know what else to say, that about summed her up.

'My father was of Irish stock,' she revealed. 'The grandson of an Irishman to be exact, the family came from County Cork. They were in a boat that set sail for America and got shipwrecked, and ended up in Penzance.'

'So I presume your mother was a local girl?'

'Yes, her family came from Mousehole.'

'But you don't speak with a Cornish accent, if you don't mind my saying.'

'No, I went to boarding school as a child, my father was in the forces. Anyhow, where am I to sleep?'

Guthrie looked at her mystified.

'I have to stay here, they are my orders.'

'Ok. Well, you have the room on the top floor, it's really nice.' If Katie stayed over again he would give her the box room with bunk-beds, perhaps it would entice her into his bed.

'I'll use the lounge when no one else's here, if that's okay with you?'

'Course you can. Use it all the time when we are here if you want. I'll be glad of the company.' He smiled at Abigail, wondering if he could trust her.

That afternoon the workmen arrived to secure the house. By the time they left his head was throbbing from all the banging. Then his mother phoned, followed by a call from the insurance company who insured the house, asking him to pop in at his convenience to sign a few forms due to the nature of his business.

He had only just put the phone down when it rang again.

'Hi, Guthrie, Brian Pendeen here. I thought I should let you know they've agreed to exhume the bodies of Colin Brodie and Stella Johnson.'

'Well, we know what they're gonna find, but thanks for letting me know,' his voice was choked, trying to hold back the tears.

He was just about to take a sip of coffee when the phone rang for the umpteenth time.

'Guthrie here,' he almost groaned.

'Hi, Gut,' the Irish voice greeted him. 'Just phoning to see how you are as oi hadn't heard from you. Oi wondered if oi could come over and stay for a few days.'

'I'll come and pick you up.'

'No, it's fine. My friend Demelza is dropping me off at St. Ives train station. She lives in Hayle.'

After they had said their goodbyes he put the mug of coffee to his lips.

'Did you say you wanted to watch some cricket?' Abigail asked, turning up the sound on the TV.

'No point, but thanks anyway. Katie's on her way here.'

'Oh, that will be nice for you. By the way, have you checked how to use the alarms and CCTV?'

'No,' he sighed, 'I'd best do that now.'

Soon after Abigail had left the house to take MacKenzie for a walk, Guthrie took the opportunity to go to her room.

On the bed was a holdall. He carefully removed the clothes and toiletries. It all looked pretty normal, although the waist length knickers were not to his taste.

Then suddenly he saw it. Wrapped in a striped towel was an automatic pistol - L47A1 7.65 mm, it was only issued by the RAF.

Through the bedroom window he could see Katie, she was descending the stone steps that led from the train station down into The Warren. She looked beautiful, wearing a pink dress and fluffy white mohair bolero. Her hair was tied back in a ponytail.

'Gut'rie! Gut'rie!' she called out, waving her slim arm trying to get his attention. As he ran out to help her with her bags she flung her arms about his neck.

Guthrie pulled her tight against his chest and stroked her hair, wondering if this was the woman who could help him forget Stella.

Early that following morning they visited Tintagel, North Cornwall's tourist attraction. It was Arthurian territory, or so the rumours had it, Camelot. The castle was in ruins, but beautiful nonetheless. It stood in two halves, one on the mainland, and the other on the island, accessed only by a wooden bridge that hung precariously over the ocean.

Abigail had insisted on accompanying them as bodyguard, no matter how Guthrie had argued against it.

It had been a hard climb to the top of the steep staircases built into the cliffside, resembling giant cobwebs stretching up to the summit. From there they had scanned the turquoise blue seas of the Atlantic, and the white sands below, in search of Merlin's cave and the Lady of Shalott.

By midday they found themselves on a pony trek; sitting on the backs of what had been advertised as Bodmin Moor ponies, yet large enough to be termed horses.

Galloping across the rough terrain, on the back of a 19+ hand dapple grey filly, Guthrie's strong thighs gripped tight against the animal's sides.

Katie galloped beside him on a smaller brown mare, looking divine in only a pair a white shorts and a pink top.

Guthrie slyly gazed at her slim figure sitting tall like a professional show jumper, her long flowing hair catching the rays of sunshine and turning them into pure gold.

'We're heading to Jamaica Inn!' the guide, a man of around 50 who constantly chewed gum, called out to the stragglers at the back of the dozen or so riders. 'Daphne du Maurier territory.'

'Thank God,' Guthrie mumbled, he needed a pint.

'Isn't that book popular with your people?' Katie asked, as they slowed down to a trot. 'It must make them homesick.'

'What book?'

'Jamaica Inn.'

He wondered if she was purposely acting the fool, even joking. Could she really be this naïve - ignorant?

By now they had joined the route known as Smugglers Way. Although the whole of the moor only covered 10 miles, it seemed more like a hundred to the three riders. The terrain looked bare, with few trees. Just a vast, empty plain overshadowed by several high granite tors. The occasional plant or bush would pop up here and there, mostly yellow gorse or purple heather, and white puffs of cotton grass resembling dandelions. There were so many smells, fresh smells like new mown grass, and as they neared the marshland there were earthier, more pungent smells, reminding him of the White Musk perfume that Stella had occasionally used.

'Get off!' Katie shouted at the swarm of flying ants that bombarded her as she galloped through the bog, with Guthrie following close behind.

'Where did you learn to ride so well?' he shouted over to her.

'A children's home back in Ireland. Where did you learn?'

'Jamaica.'

A flock of lapwings and a few warblers flew about the marshland, a couple of them landed amongst the shrubs.

Grabbing the reins of Katie's pony, he brought both horses to a halt beside a stream.

'Wonder how Abigail is doing?'

'Think she's walking it from what I can see,' Katie laughed, looking through binoculars at the other riders on the trek who were about a quarter of a mile behind.

They sat on a rough stone bridge, as the horses drank from the soft clear waters of the stream. The birds were more abundant here, as were the brightly coloured butterflies winging their way down the stream.

There were flowers near the stream amongst the ferns and rushes, brightly coloured petals flourishing under the blazing heat. They reminded him of his student days, when he and his fellow philosophers had discussed the refraction of light, prisms and colour. Like the masters, trying to differentiate reality from illusion. They had concluded that everything was an illusion, apart from God.

Lighting up a Marlboro, he watched Katie feed a finger of Kit-Kat to a couple of skylarks and a goldfinch. The colour of the goldfinch was more yellow than gold. It was only Katie's hair that shone gold.

'It's too hot to ride,' he said, removing his damp shirt, leaving his chest bare.

'I'll rub some sun protector onto your back if you like,' she offered, removing a tube of cream from her bum-bag.

He was not going to refuse a massage.

'Thanks, much appreciated.' He stubbed out his cigarette.

How soft her hands were, smoothing the white cream over his back. The cream felt cold, erotic, soothing his skin, burning his loins.

By the time she had finished, the rest of the party had joined them.

Abigail looked the worse for wear, limping along in bare feet, as were a few of the other riders. They were leading their ponies by the reins.

'Are you both okay?' Abigail wheezed, perching on the bridge.

A herd of wild ponies suddenly appeared downstream.

'Most of the moor ponies live wild,' the guide said, noticing the object of their gaze. 'They have to fend for themselves, and around September they are taken to be sold at Hallworthy Livestock Market.'

'What, for cat meat?' someone asked.

'Talking about cats,' one of the men interrupted. 'What about this big cat, it's been in all the papers? There have been numerous sightings, they call it the Beast of Bodmin Moor. Some say it's a panther.'

'It won't attack us, will it?' a woman looked fearful.

'No, it doesn't come out during the day, that is, if it exists at all,' the guide replied.

After riding a few more miles, the guide stopped, and pointed across the moor to a granite hill rising up in the distance.

'The Tor you see now is the highest point in Cornwall, 1,378 ft. It's called Brown Willy.'

All eyes looked to the hill.

'You got one of them, mate?' a man joked to Guthrie.

'Mine's much bigger than that,' he laughed back.

'In the Cornish language,' the guide explained, 'Bronn Wennili means, the hill of swallows.'

Half hour and just over three miles later the guide reined in his pony.

'Right folks, we're here at Jamaica Inn. You have about forty minutes to get something to eat and have a rest.'

The signpost above them showed a pirate with a parrot on his shoulder. Yet, it was not an olde worlde inn as Guthrie had anticipated, nothing like the original inn built in 1750. From the outside it looked like any other country pub or grey manor house. Just beside the building was the A30.

The riders climbed down from their mounts, stretching their aching legs.

Guthrie removed his feet from the stirrups. His back was throbbing, his bum was bruised and his legs were cramping.

'We have to return the horses to the stables near Fowey. There'll be a minibus waiting to drive you back to Camelford.'

'Well, at least we don't have to trot back,' a young woman giggled to her friend.

'I couldn't do it,' Abigail admitted. 'Every bone in my body feels broken.'

The guide smiled to her, he had heard it all too often before.

'Now before you all go in I have to tell you, the inn was the haunt of smugglers and it is indeed known to be haunted. Those of you who have read Jamaica Inn, the author got the idea to write the book having ridden here and got lost in the fog and discovered the inn.'

'Have you any dates for this?' a woman asked.

'Plenty of books inside to buy about the subject, and various free leaflets. And, of course, books by Daphne Du Maurier.' He spat his chewing gum into the palm of his hand. 'There is also a smugglers museum inside, and a gift shop.'

'Thank you.'

'Oh, by the way, remember when we spoke about Brown Willy, well, there are caves below Brown Willy that were once used by smugglers.'

His audience looked adequately impressed, chatting their way into the inn. Guthrie let Abigail go ahead, so that he could stay close to Katie.

When they re-emerged from the inn the weather had dramatically changed. The blue skies and sunshine were nowhere to be seen, replaced by a damp, grey mist.

Waiting behind to light up a cigarette, Guthrie watched the others mount their ponies and trot off. After a few drags he climbed onto the large dapple grey.

In the near distance he could hear the trotting of hoofs, but it was too foggy to catch them up.

Cantering was also proving hard work, as the sky began to spit rain.

The clip clop of hoofs disappeared into the mist.

A sudden gunshot. His horse reared up.

'Whoa!' Grabbing the reins tight with one hand, he tried to reach for his gun. The horse reared up again on its hind legs.

Above them, the haunting whistle of a buzzard filtered through the fog, bringing with it a torrent of rain.

Another shot rang out. It just missed the animal's head.

Now he was being bumped up and down out of the saddle like a bucking bronco. Unable to hang on any longer Guthrie was thrown to the ground. The horse bolted.

Lying on the soggy wet ground he held his gun close, ready to shoot.

'Guthrie, are you okay?' the voice belonged to Abigail. 'I heard those shots. I think they're hunting rabbits or deer.'

'I'll live,' he replied curtly, struggling up onto his feet. He did not trust her. After all, she was supposed to be his protection, and yet, had conveniently failed to spot the gunman. Interestingly, she had also been the first person there after he fell. Had she in fact, been the one shooting the bullets?

As he stood on the puddled earth, pounded by the heavy rain, he knew that this had not been a real attempt on his life, this was just a warning.

CHAPTER TWENTY

The Meadery was a large granite building next to Redruth library. There were a few of these themed restaurants around Cornwall. The interior was designed as a medieval castle with an upstairs balcony area.

A pretty young wench wearing medieval costume comprising of a white off the shoulder blouse, and a long, rust coloured skirt with a small apron, escorted Guthrie across the ground floor of the restaurant and up the wooden stairs. Dressed in a smart grey suit he resembled a businessman rather than a biker, although the Harley was parked outside.

The pre-booked table was in one of the balcony stalls. A small lamp sat in the centre of the table flickering gently. The interior walls of the restaurant were decorated with impressive paintings of knights and shields and all things Arthurian. Even the piped music had a medieval air. This was his favourite place to chill for an evening, although the high backed wooden stalls were not too comfortable.

The waitress returned with a jug of elderberry mead. Pouring himself a small goblet full, he put it to his lips. The liquid tasted sweet and cool, ruby red, made from honey but highly potent.

Just about to take another sip his mobile rang.

'Gut'rie.'

'Oh, hi, Katie, did you get home okay last night?'

'Yes, got to work on time.'

'That's good, bet you're battered and bruised, I know I am. You should have let me pay for a taxi...'

'Where are you now?'

'I'm in Redruth having a meal with friends.'

'Oh, oi'm also in Redruth, in my flat.'

Guthrie was taken aback. He had presumed that Katie lived at the bee farm.

'Where is your flat?'

'Top of the hill. Can oi see you tonight after your meal? Oi'm a bit scared, think someone is watching my flat.'

'I'll come up now, call the police.'

'No point, he only drives here after the pubs have shut, he was watching last night. But oi took his number plate, it's an RAF truck type thing.'

'Okay, I'll come over later, what's your address?'

'Oi'll meet you outside the Collins Arms pub and take you there. The pub's just at the top of the hill on Fore Street?'

'I'll be there about 10.'

He felt slightly guilty for not inviting her to the Meadery, but he doubted Jonathan would be impressed. Hurriedly he made another call, cancelling a pre-existing appointment for later that same evening.

He had only just switched off the mobile when Piran arrived, shortly followed by Jonathan. Like Guthrie they were both wearing grey suits, although Jonathan had accessorised with a bow tie.

'Piran, you look awful,' Jonathan said, pouring himself some of Guthrie's elderberry mead wine from the jug.

'Got caught in the rain, I think a storm's brewing.'

'So you survived Alton Towers?' Jonathan quizzed his son-in-law.

'Polly had a wonderful time.'

'Did my daughter go?'

'No, she said she had other engagements.'

'Looks like you've been doing some digging, Jonathan.'

'Yes, Guthrie, I was gardening yesterday, and can't seem to get the earth out of my nails,' Jonathan complained, cleaning his nails with a cocktail stick.

'Olivia had me digging yesterday too. Wanted me to water the lawn and rose bushes. Anyone know of a decent gardener?'

'I'm sorry, Piran, I've no idea,' Jonathan replied. 'Incidentally Piran, I'm really not happy with Polly hanging around with that council house boy. I want you to do something about it.'

Piran stared wide eyed, his jaw visibly dropped. Even Guthrie wondered if this was the moment when his friend would stand up to his father-in-law.

Just then the waitress arrived with their drinks. Guthrie wondered if there would be an atmosphere all evening, but the waitress was young and pretty, and Piran had seemingly forgotten all about the comment.

'So how are your family, Jonathan?' Guthrie used the opportunity to digress, referring to the children from his second marriage.

'Tamsin and Charlotte, sweet girls, bit of a handful sometimes for my poor wife Gemma.'

'Polly sent you this from her holiday.' Piran handed Jonathan the gift-wrapped package.

With childlike excitement he tore open the wrapping. It was a musical carousel. As he wound the key the carousel began. The bright horses and their riders moved to the tune of *Eine Kleine Nacht Musik*.

'How beautiful. Polly knows I love horses,' he sighed, as if he might cry at any moment. 'She knows how I used to love to play this tune on my violin.' He held the musical box tight, as if it were his most treasured possession.

Guthrie took the opportunity to view his surroundings and inhale the ambiance. A jester was laughing beside him on the wall of the alcove. Vibrant colours painted so lifelike, that the jester eerily looked as if he were just another customer at the end of the table. The medieval music continued to resound about room.

Turning round to peer over the balcony, he could see the diners below on the ground floor. How happy they all looked, one table celebrating a birthday party, another just a family night out. High above them the large banners, some with diagonal cut edge, hung mid-air waving gently in time to the music.

On his own table the drinks were flowing thick and fast, although he tried to limit his alcohol intake. He and Piran had both chosen chicken in the rough for their main. Jonathan had chosen scampi in the rough. Naturally they ate with their fingers.

'Funny that mead wine comes from honey,' Guthrie could not resist saying. 'Did you know that the scientist who discovered that queen bees are inseminated by drones outside the hives, was a blind guy called Huber?'

'Can't see how he could have done that?' Jonathan said, munching through his chips.

'He couldn't see how he did it either,' Guthrie laughed, taking another sip of mead wine. 'Didn't a couple of popes use the bee symbol?'

'You're thinking of St. Ambrose. He had a fetish for bees and virginity,' Jonathan elaborated.

'Oh, I almost forgot,' Piran exclaimed. 'Olivia was telling me that her aunt thinks the man who drowned in Belgium, you know the one that was recently in the local paper who stayed in Redruth? Well, she thinks he visited her neighbour Vivienne and...'

'Oh, do me a favour, Piran, we're not going to spend the rest of the evening discussing an elderly woman's imaginings,' Jonathan protested.

Guthrie dipped his fingers in the finger bowl and wiped them with a serviette.

'You haven't let me get to the point,' Piran almost pleaded. 'Guthrie, to be honest I rarely visit Olivia's aunt, Ada Beckerleg, she's Phyllis's sister.'

'Who is Phyllis?'

'Olivia's mother.'

'Phyllis is my ex-wife,' Jonathan muttered.

'Oh, yes, of course, I've met her.'

'She's let herself go,' Jonathan scorned. 'Like her daughter.'

Guthrie looked to his friend, wondering when he would get a backbone.

'Apparently Aunt Ada found her neighbour's cat dead in the road and a bee was in its mouth, or perhaps by its side, I can't quite remember,' Piran said excitedly. 'But the interesting thing is the bee was gold and black. Jonathan, what colour was the bee that stung that Stella Johnson who used to work with Guthrie?'

'I presume yellow and black,' Jonathan replied, wiping his mouth with the serviette. 'It's of no consequence.'

'Oh, I think it is,' Guthrie smiled. 'What happened to the insect that killed the cat, did the vet take a look at it?'

'Well, actually, I've brought it with to show you, Olivia suggested it.' Piran opened a piece of tissue paper containing the gold and black striped corpse.

'Ha-ha, it looks more like an orange humbug than a bee,' Jonathan laughed.

'Perhaps it was fed saffron,' Guthrie smiled.

'Oh, don't be foolish, Guthrie, bees eat nectar and suchlike.'

'So what do you think?' Piran asked, watching Guthrie examine the insect. 'Could it be the same type of bee that killed the Johnson woman?'

'Well, depending...'

'I appreciate that you read philosophy at university, Guthrie, Jonathan interrupted. 'Perhaps that's why you go into such depths.'

'Jonathan, Guthrie needs to clear his name and prove he didn't kill that woman, surely you understand that.'

'So tell me, how's work, Jonathan?' Guthrie tried to lighten the mood. 'It must be nice working in a private hospital.'

'Yes, very nice. Not like the Royal Cornwall Hospital, the place Piran still insists on calling Treliske. That's far too overcrowded. Well, like all NHS hospitals really. Although I have to admit the new wing does look rather splendid.'

'Yes, I was very impressed,' Guthrie agreed.

'Of course, if one joined up with something like Bupa they'd send you to my hospital. Piran's with Bupa.'

'But the NHS isn't all bad, Jonathan,' Piran responded. 'My grandmother had a knee replacement at St. Michael's in Hayle and was extremely satisfied.'

'Well, all I can say, Piran, is, that you get what you pay for. At my hospital patients get clean toilets, hygienic staff, respect at all times, no libellous medical notes, afternoon tea and cakes. And no waiting lists.'

'Yes, but they pay through the nose,' Piran replied. 'Every sugar lump or painkiller goes on the bill at 100 times the going rate.'

'I believe you have left your job, Guthrie, I thought you might have stuck at it a little longer,' Jonathan digressed, as if to hit back indirectly at Piran who had been winning the debate.

'Yes, I know you both went to a lot of trouble getting it for me, but I was offered a better job with better prospects and salary.'

'Oh, really. Well, then, you were right to take it,' Jonathan conceded. 'May I ask who your new employer is?'

'I'm back working with the MOD.' Then turning towards Piran, he said, 'I have a confession to make.'

It was drizzling as Guthrie left the Meadery, now wearing his leathers. Hoping he was not too much over the limit, he lit up and then climbed onto the Harley. It was only 9.50 yet the sky was black. Slightly dizzy from his overindulgence of alcohol, he smoked his way along Bond Street, and then turned the corner into Fore Street. A group of teenagers were standing on the corner smoking. They did not seem to notice him as he revved up the road past John Oliver's, Redruth's bookshop. Both the London Inn and the Red Lion public house were full to heaving as usual. The hill got markedly steeper at Jim's Cash and Carry and Berryman's pasty shop.

It was as he neared the Collins Arms when he spotted Katie. She was peering out of an alleyway near the pub. Before he had a chance to get off the bike she ran over to him.

'There they are!' she pointed to a vehicle parked just up the road. 'That's them, Gut.'

It was an RAF wagon. The driver turned on the engine and pulled away.

'You go inside and lock the door.'

'But, Gut, don't leave me.'

'Just lock your door, call the police if anyone returns. I'll be back soon.'

The wagon continued to race along Mount Ambrose with Guthrie close behind, heading towards the A30. Perhaps he should phone Brian and get it sorted now, he thought. But it was late, Brian was probably at home with his family.

It was raining heavily by the time he reached the dual carriageway. Doing his best to keep the bike upright as he splashed through the deep puddles of uneven tarmac, he accelerated to 60 mph. But, instead of the RAF wagon increasing its speed, it slowed down, and turned off the dual carriageway heading in the direction of Portreath. But, by the time he neared the hamlet of Bridge he had lost them.

By now the sky was raging, as lightning electrified the sky followed by roars of thunder. Thinking about turning back, he slowed down at the junction. But the memories of Stella and the need to find her killer overpowered his fears.

At the top of Tolticken Hill he noticed the security gates were open. Instead of stopping, he rode directly onto the RAF base towards the airfield. It was then when the shot rang out. Guthrie had been hit, they had been waiting for him. The bullet pierced his upper arm, exploding inside. The Harley skidded along the wet road and landed in a nearby field behind a hedgerow.

'Ahh!' the pain sliced through him. The blood was thick. His chest wet from the flow bleeding through his leathers, the heavy downpour washing the blood from his body into the sodden earth.

Struggling across the rough ground like a worm, he tried to make his way to the airfield. His breathing was shallow, he knew that he did not have long. After crawling for only about thirty meters, sweating profusely, he collapsed against a tree trunk.

It was a good thirty minutes before he attempted to remove the injured arm from the sleeve of his jacket. But, by then, the blood had already coagulated and glued the skin of his arm to his shirt sleeve and jacket. A tug of the sleeve and the clot detached from his skin, Guthrie's green eyes rolled back in pain as the blood flowed. Taking his knife, he sliced through the shirt sleeve to use as a tourniquet, but the pain from the bullet made his arm feel like it was on fire, melting the flesh.

Suddenly he heard voices, struggling to steady himself he decided to have one last try to get to the airfield. As the blood leaked from the soaked tourniquet, he was regretting not having confided in Abigail, knowing that he might not even live to see this through. But he could not trust her, not after finding the L47A1 7.65 mm RAF pistol in her bag.

The sky was pitch black. The storm was howling across Nancekuke Common, small branches had blown off the trees flying through the air flying onto the runway. Then came the lightning; illuminating the hill lighting up the perpetrators, lighting up Guthrie.

'He's here!' a voice shouted through the gale. 'Let's finish him off now.'

Unable to run, Guthrie tried to drag himself away from view, but slipped on the wet leaves. His wound was weeping, his whole body now soaked in blood. Heart racing. Shaking, dizzy, he rolled into the bushes. Wriggling through the undergrowth like a dying snake. The winds rushed through his ears, the gorse stinging his flesh as they shouted his name into the air, lost in the storm. His breathing was shallow; he did not know how much longer he could remain conscious.

'Hail Mary mother of God, blessed be the fruit of thy womb...' His heart was beating oddly, like a hammer, his head ached, and his vision was blurred.

A voice rang out through the elements, 'I'll split you open from your throat to your dick, you black bastard!'

'Holy Mary Mother of God pray for me...'

With his one good arm, he struggled to reach for his mobile, and then tapped out Brian's number?

Was the face real which suddenly pressed up against his face?

'I got the fucker!' the man yelled, pointing a revolver at Guthrie. But the others did not hear through the storm. Guthrie hallucinated that he had lashed out spontaneously with a knife, knocking his assailant to the ground. Dreamt that he grabbed the revolver and pressed it to the man's temple.

'This is how it's done,' Guthrie snarled, and in the dream he shot him through the head, the blast of the bullet absorbed by the lighting.

Twenty minutes later Detective Inspector Brian Pendeen was racing along the dual carriageway with Guthrie lying on the back seat of his car unconscious. The ambulance was waiting for them on a slip road. Once Guthrie was in the ambulance he was given oxygen and his chest was covered in plastic to keep air from being sucked into the wound.

'This helps prevent the development of a collapsed lung,' the paramedic explained. 'If you get any shortness of breath I'll remove the seal.' The paramedic injected him with a pain killer, and put a cannula into his arm attached to a drip. But by now Guthrie was away with the fairies.

As he was being wheeled from the ambulance into Treliske's A & E he awoke momentarily, catching sight of a blue BMW convertible parked in front of the hospital.

CATCH THE STINGER

CHAPTER TWENTY-ONE

Sunday morning and Trembath was having a well-earned lie in. He looked up at the flaking white ceiling, it needing a good coat of paint. Maybe he should buy a four poster as his wife had suggested, and then they would not see the ceiling. A four poster was quite romantic, and he liked romance. Although his love making that night had not been much to boast of. Perhaps he was stressed from work, or burdened with guilt over the death of Mustopher. But in truth he knew the real reason. It was because of Maxime. Sex was always better when performed in forbidden territory, and Maxime was very naughty. At least he did not have to worry about what Guthrie was up to. He had been in Treliske all week bandaged up, hopefully dead by now. If not, he soon would be.

'Breakfast in bed,' Suzette called, entering the bedroom with a tray. He gazed at her tall, slender body, wearing only a T shirt. She had the best legs he had ever seen. Her long, black hair fell forward as she lowered the tray onto his lap. He loved her hair.

'Mm delicious, bacon and eggs in bed, served by the most beautiful woman in the world. What more could a man ask for?' He blew her a kiss on his palm and took the tray.

He sometimes wondered if Suzette knew about his escapades with her cousin, she had not been as physically close of late. Perhaps she had also played away. But he doubted that, she was far superior to him in every way. A graduate of the prestigious Sorbonne with film star looks, why she had ever bothered with him he had no idea.

'You make a good servant, Suzy,' he teased.

'I'm going for a swim in the pool, darling, enjoy.'

Once she had left the room, Trembath tucked into his meal and then washed it down with a mug of hot tea. This was just what the doctor had ordered, a nice relaxing day.

Taking the last few drags from his cigarette, he contemplated getting up, it was then the phone rang.

'Yes, what?' he growled.

'He's discharging himself today,' the voice said.

'What the fuck!' he cried. 'He's not fucking human; he was at death's door.'

'Yes, he's a cat it would seem.'

'Well, you sort it then. It wouldn't be the first time.'

'No, I will not. Especially not on these premises, I'm not shooting anyone.'

'Did I say anything about shooting him? You surely have numerous ways you can make it look like an accident.'

'What, with bee serum like before? I don't think so, not again.'

'Well, keep me informed I'll sort it, just make sure the next batch is ready.'

'Will you be telling the boss?'

'Not sure at this stage, I might sort it out myself.

How's he getting home?'

'Train.'

'Okay, I'll wait for him at St. Erth and put an end to him.'

*****

As the train pulled out of Truro Station Guthrie suddenly changed his mind about going straight home. Having just discharged himself from Treliske he was still in pain, but five days was long enough to be in a hospital bed without fags. At least the morphine helped.

When the train reached Redruth he disembarked, and hobbled into a taxi with his arm still in a sling. He got out at Morrisons in Pool, and headed for the nearest cashier.

'Two packets of Marlboro, please.'

'£3.36.'

Guthrie handed over the money. 'I'm a student at Camborne School of Mines,' he said, in a fake Jamaican accent. 'I don't suppose you know of an access point into South Crofty tin mine?'

She laughed. 'Actually my husband was a miner in South Crofty, the access point is just along this road and turn left at Tuckingmill. It's called the Tuckingmill Decline.'

'So did they lay your husband off?'

'Well, you've probably heard what happened. It was February of 1991 when the DTI stopped funding the mine.'

'I suppose there isn't much work round here, other than the mines.'

'Nothing, and the government don't care. They be sitting pretty down in Westminster,' she pulled a face. 'Anyway, you'll only be able to go down 250 metres due to the water. I'll draw a map for you if you like.'

Once he had obtained the information he needed from the woman, he left the shop. Outside, near the trolley bay, he struggled to light his cigarette with his good arm, and clutched the map with his redundant hand that poked out from the sling. Of course, he knew that he was acting foolishly and going against MOD guidelines, but he also knew that time was running out. On the other side of the road was an engine house, obviously no longer working, perhaps an exhibition piece. With a tall stack and large wheel, it looked impressive, hosting a balcony of sorts, reminding him of the scene from Shakespeare where Juliet appeared.

Limping all the way to Dudnance Lane Guthrie ignored the voice inside him telling him to turn back. Yet, the morphine was strong, he could hardly feel the bruises, least of all the bullet wound. On reaching his destination, marked by an asterisk on the map, he noticed that the whole area was spotted with mine shafts and buildings that lay in the shadow of Carn Brea Hill. The largest building on the site looked like a huge grey warehouse. Guthrie knew that in fact it was a tunnel, the start of the Tuckingmill Decline.

Satisfied that he now knew where it was, he was just about to turn round and head back to the train station, when suddenly he spotted the padlocks on the security fence. There was one thing that Guthrie could never resist, and that was accessing forbidden territory.

It took a while to open the padlocks and the lock on the gate. The entrance to the mine was on the far side of the compound, it backed on to the railway line and also the Red River, although Guthrie did not see any river. As he limped towards the Tuckingmill Decline he realised that the building was actually dug into the ground. This meant that the entrance descended deep into the earth. There were more heavy padlocks and chains on the main door, all the more difficult to unlock with his arm in a sling. But he had come this far, he told himself, he might as well take a peek. On opening the door, he found himself inside a dark tunnel with a markedly steep descent, supported by steel arched walls. The smell was putrid.

Wondering if this was the entrance to Dolcoath Mine, he decided that, in any event, it must be somewhere near to the Eastern Valley Shaft that the cashier had mentioned. The woman had told him that they had once mined 600 meters deep, but since its closure he would only be able to descend 250 meters above the water level.

Although, he had read somewhere that they had mined as low as 910 meters.

Sitting on the cold floor of the tunnel he lit up, and then re-read Tom Smith's cryptic letter:

This reasoned evidence law is key,
And is a high flyer with its new wing of the eagle numbered SW673455. A crown as sweet as honey on French Pancake Day, sweet as marzipan, sweet bee, the same day the star returned to heaven. Mine is the last of tin puzzles.

He hoped that he had worked out the last sentence correctly and that Mine referred to South Crofty, the last tin mine to close in Cornwall.

There was no daylight now, the only light coming from his torch, as he headed down the tunnel into the unknown. His shoulder and arm had now started to throb with each step, but he thought he would go just a little further. The stench was worse here, getting stronger the deeper he went. Ignoring the warning sign instructing him not to go further, he continued down the tunnel. Ahead of him were tram lines running into a stope. An abandoned cart stood inside the stope, empty, bar a few old tools.

The pain was hitting harder now, the drugs were wearing off. Glancing around he noticed a croust seat nearby. Sitting down he swallowed a couple of painkillers with the orange juice.

Suddenly he heard a noise. Footsteps, someone had followed him in. The Jackson boy was in custody so it could not be him. There was nowhere for him to escape now, except the way he came in, the direction of the footsteps. Grabbing his pistol, he prepared to fire.

'It's the end, Guthrie, you might as well give up!' a voice shouted.

'Show your face you fucking coward!'

There was no reply. His stalker was now running down the tunnel towards him.

'I'm coming to get you. This is the end, you're about to die!'

Guthrie decided to head in the opposite direction along the tunnel, he had no choice. But the further he walked the worse the conditions. Water was running down the walls, dripping from the tunnel ceiling, even the floor was puddled. His wound prevented him from progressing more speedily, yet the footsteps were getting closer.

Holding his pistol out in front of him ready to shoot, he turned into another tunnel. An old black telephone hung on the wet wall encased in a green tin box, it had been disconnected. In the distance a cage stood open, he headed towards it as the sweat dripped from his face.

Shining his torch onto the cage he saw a handwritten notice on the cage door:

THIS CAGE HAS BEEN CHARGED - AT LOWER LEVEL TURN RIGHT WHERE LOCO IS WAITING

Stepping into the cage he noticed the small brass plate inside the door. It read: 380 fathom level, 730 metres.

There was barely any room in the cage, as most of the space was taken by a stack of steel canisters. He guessed what they contained.

The footsteps were running now. If he pressed the button to go down, he might never see daylight again. Pulling the catch back on his gun he waited for his pray. But it was then when he heard a second set of footsteps, there were two people following him, not one. And then he saw them, black clothes and balaclavas. The smaller figure was holding an AK-47 Kalashnikov. Like a mouse in a trap he knew there was only one option, he pressed the button.

The cage rattled and shook its way down. There was no light, just a black void. By the time the cage had descended into the lower seams he was ankle deep in water, the pain throbbing through his body. Suddenly the cage started to make strange sounds, and just before it reached the 730 metres it juddered to a halt and crashed. With no idea if he would ever get back to the surface, and no power in his mobile phone, he battled with the cage door until it broke from its hinge. It had stopped about 1½ metres from the ground. Stepping to the edge of the cage he jumped out. The jump caused his body to explode in pain, falling onto his knees trying to breathe.

After a few minutes Guthrie struggled back up onto his feet and then began to inspect his surroundings.

Here the water was deeper, and he was submerged in darkness. Plato had said that a child who is afraid of the dark can be forgiven, but the real tragedy is when men are afraid of the light. Plato was wrong, Guthrie decided. The dark was everything.

Stale water dripped down onto him as he waded over the lumpy rocks, his brogues ruined, his brown cords going the same way. A mountain of earth stood inside one of the parallel stopes between the pillars. Half buried under the earth were small gas canisters. Obviously the disused mine was now being used as a dumping ground for chemical waste.

The next half hour was spent blindly feeling his way along the damp seams, with their wet, stained, craggy walls, using only a torch to guide him. The noise of the constant drips gave a decidedly eerie feel, along with a death-like stench. And of course, there was still the possibility his pursuers would find him there via another route. Perhaps he should just sit down and wait to die, he was trapped, there was no way out. What foolhardiness had caused him to enter the mine in the first place? Stella was dead nothing would bring her back.

Sweltering in the damp heat, he removed his sling and shirt, exposing his blood drenched bandaged arm. The bottle of juice was almost empty as he descended even deeper into the mine.

Now waist deep in water he was just about to turn back when he noticed a ladder. It reached up to a small narrow stope. The lower rungs were immersed in water where another batch of steel chests stood lined up against the rock. He wondered what would happen if the mine flooded and the chemical waste was flushed out into the ocean. Of course, there was little doubt that this was not the only redundant tin mine packed with sarin.

Shining his torch onto the rungs he saw a broken tin plaque that had been left hanging there. It read: *The 400-380 fathom ladderway.* Guthrie presumed that the plaque had been moved from its original post.

Climbing tentatively, careful not to slip on the wet rungs, he soon reached the top. That was when he spied a tiny flicker of light at the far end on the stope. It was just big enough for him to get inside, although not to turn around. Lying on his back in order to protect his arm, he dragged himself along the stope. The floor of the stope was covered with jagged rock and puddled with damp water aggravating the bullet wound, causing him dizziness and nausea. He wondered if he would be able to get out the other end, if not, he would be stuck there until death. Even if he did make it out, there was every chance that they would be there waiting for him. His tired, bloodshot eyes focussed only on the light as he wriggled snake-like along the rugged, excavated area. With his last bit of energy, Guthrie crawled out of the stope and jumped down to the floor below. The pain of the jump caused him to scream out, shooting through his arm and shoulder like bullets. Winded, he glanced around looking for the source of the light. His heart sank when he discovered that it was merely a lamp flickering.

Still holding his arm, he vomited his way along the seam, he'd lost all hope by now.

'Hail Mary, full of Grace, the Lord is with thee. Blessed art thou among women, and blessed is the fruit of thy womb, Jesus,' he prayed, gasping for breath between each sentence. 'Holy Mary, Mother of God, pray for us sinners now, and at the hour of death. Amen.'

His pulse was racing, his body was hot and cold intermittently; he knew this was the end. How foolish he had been.

'I believe in God, the Father almighty, creator of heaven and earth…'

Then suddenly something caught his eye. He moved closer to take a look. It was a locomotive with a cart attached. On further inspection it appeared to have been charged up. The cart contained several steel containers. He knew they were also packed with chemical waste. He pressed the button and then climbed into the cart, standing on the opposite side to the canisters.

As the locomotive began to move slowly along the track he held tightly onto his crucifix and prepared to die.

About an hour later the locomotive drew to a halt. It was the end of the track. Tired and aching he dragged himself out of the cart. Under torchlight he could see several stopes leading off from the tunnel, but by now he was near to collapse. He had already vomited numerous times along the way, almost blacking out, and knew that his blood pressure had dropped too low.

Wiping the sweat from his face he fell to his knees in prayer. 'I believe in the Holy Spirit, the holy Catholic Church, the communion of saints, the forgiveness of sins, the resurrection of the body...' A sound - it came from a nearby stope.

Struggling up onto his feet he hobbled towards the noise. Perhaps it was a bird, he knew they used canaries in mines, although he was almost certain that the last one was used in 1986. The sound was growing louder - definitely a bird, could he dare to hope that it might be a gull? Guthrie entered the stope.

There before him lay the ocean, sparkling brightly under the summer sun. Again Guthrie fell to his knees, kissed his crucifix and crossed himself as he inhaled the fresh, salty air. Only now realising that the long winding tunnel he had just struggled through, led straight from South Crofty tin mine and terminated where he stood, directly below Nancekuke, the RAF base in Portreath.

And then he spotted them, five large steel containers that stood half hidden in the shadows. Two dead bodies were draped over them.

CHAPTER TWENTY-TWO

The weather was scorching on that Saturday morning, the sea a white haze of sunshine. The gulls were in their element as a sharking trawler was sailing inland, squawking and screaming in their familiar vulgar tones.

The tide was out, leaving behind debris of shale, tiny fan shaped shells and strands of black seaweed. By 10.30 the beaches were already heaving with sun worshippers. Red and yellow plastic buckets and spades were scattered amongst the deckchairs and windshields. The sea was also packed to the hilt with motor boats and surfers.

Guthrie filled up the kettle, as he watched next door's cat stretch lazily by the doorstep of Lobster Rock. He was pleased that he had invited Katie to move in after his return from hospital. Now that she had given up work at the bee farm, this would be the first full weekend they would share together. Although he was still in slight pain, the wound had healed. Abigail had gone to the launderette up The Stennack that morning, he was glad to have a few hours free from her. The police officer needed watching more closely, after all, if she was working for Trembath then she would be reporting his every move back to the enemy. Of course, he had checked her out, but the data showed that she was as clean as a whistle.

Just as he was enjoying a cigarette and mug of tea by the kitchen table, Katie suddenly appeared in her red and black bikini.

His eyes followed the curves of her slender body, brushed lightly with a hint of a tan. Her legs long, perfect, her belly taut.

'I love your hair,' he smiled, inspecting her glossy auburn locks.

'Demelza did it for me. She used to be a hairdresser.'

'She's very good. How does she get it to shine like that?'

'Products.'

'I see. Well, I suppose I'd best put on my shorts if we're sunbathing.'

'Think you should just put on your birthday suit.'

'Doubt Abigail would approve.'

'Oh, fuck her, she's a moody old bitch,' Katie complained, following him into the bedroom.

Suddenly she pulled him towards her, pressing her soft, full lips against his. How good she smelt, her perfume filled the room. He went to undo her bikini top but this time there were no slaps. The top fell to the floor revealing her naked breasts. They were smaller than he would have liked, just a handful and no more.

Dropping his head down onto her nipples like a baby, he pushed her onto the bed and ran his tongue down her naked body until his mouth reached her bikini bottoms. Pulling them down, he sank his mouth into a bed of black hair, sucking, biting and licking.

'Oi love you,' she sighed, as she laid her head back on the pillow, her long, slim legs wide apart.

Guthrie did not reply, instead, he slithered up her body, replacing his tongue with his penis.

Nestling his face into her neck he slid in and out and in. Harder and faster, thrusting, sliding as the sweet moans came from her soft, warm lips.

*****

Afterwards, they relaxed on the rocks beside neighbouring Crab Rock. The cat had joined them, snuggling up between Katie's feet. The tide was slowly coming in, lapping gently against the lower level of the crocodile tail of rocks on which they lay. They focussed their attention on the surfers trying to catch a wave or two, arms out, legs astride, floating - flying until they crashed, the surf drowning out any hopes of a smooth ride.

Katie closed her eyes as she soaked up the sunshine, her golden hair on fire as it streamed in wisps across his stomach.

Guthrie also closed his eyes, thinking about their love making, it had been good, so good. Yet, he was curious as to why she had initiated it after all her previous Papal inflicted arguments. He had found even stranger the absence of a hymen in his virgin lover. But none of it mattered as he lay under the sun, falling into a perfect sleep.

'Bejesus, Gut, you have your 6 pack back,' Katie woke him from his slumbers ten minutes later.

'I was having a dream.'

'Were you dreaming of me?' she laughed, her fingers tracing the lines of his ribs where muscles protruded.

'No, Plato.'

'Oh, wasn't he the one in the cartoons of Popeye?'

'I wouldn't think so.'

She continued to run her finger down his chest, her long hair shading him from the sun.

'You are a beautiful man, Gut, my own Brian Boru.'

'So is that my new name?'

'Yes, it is my angel name for you, Brian Boru. You have the spirit of that great Irish hero.'

'This hero sometimes wonders why you spend more time with your friend Demelza, than here at Lobster Rock.'

'Well, take last week for example, she wanted me to go with her to church to see the priest, you know about baptising the baby,' Katie explained. 'But the priest didn't get home until the next day because he'd been to Lourdes and the plane had been delayed.'

'Maybe you have a secret lover,' he laughed.

'Yes, you're right,' she laughed back. 'Demelza and oi are having a lesbian relationship; we hide our children in the cupboard when anyone calls.'

Pulling her down on top of him, he held her tight against his chest.

'Oi wish we could stay like this forever,' Katie sighed.

'Get a bit cold.'

'No, Gut, oi mean just lay here forever and forget about the debts.'

'What debts? I can pay them for you. You really don't have to worry about anything. I'm here to look after you.'

'Oi do love you, you know. Oi've never met anyone like you before.'

'Thank you,' he kissed her not quite knowing how to respond. Love was a tiny word with huge implications; he was unable to return the sentiment.

'Gut, oi wish oi could explain it all to you, so much to tell. You see, growing up for me wasn't so easy, everything was mapped out. Oi suppose you would call it a preordained life.'

'Were you expected to join a convent or something?' He now wondered if she had been a nun, that would explain her former frigidity.

'Did you have a happy childhood?' she asked, failing to answer his question.

'Yes, very happy.'

'There was a programme on TV once, something about give me a child before they are 7 and oi'll give you the man, or something like that,' she said. 'It's true you know, parents, children's' homes, teachers, whoever raises the kid can really fuck them up for life given half a chance.'

'Were you brought up in an orphanage?'

'No, not exactly. Oi met this boy when oi was only a kid, a family friend. Daddy wanted me to marry him when oi grew up.'

'But you didn't?'

'Don't let me spoil anything,' Abigail suddenly interrupted, causing Katie to jump up. 'I've bought us all fish and chips. I'll put them on the table.'

Guthrie responded with a grunt of thanks, silently wishing she would crawl off into a pit somewhere. He had told the police he did not need protection, least of all from someone like Abigail who had seemingly moved herself in permanently. But they had insisted.

When he lay back down on the rocks to catch a couple more minutes of sun before going in, he noticed that Katie had been crying. Gently, he pulled her down on top of him.

'I wish I could kiss away your tears,' he said, kissing her forehead as she lay in his arms.

She began to play with his crucifix.

'Perhaps we should go to Mass together,' he suggested.

She shook her head, causing a storm of fiery gold to sweep across his chest.

'Oi never go to confession, too much to confess,' she whispered.

'Would you like to tell me what you were going to say before Abigail appeared, I'm a good listener?'

'Our Lady knows everything. She prays for us sinners - Now, and at the hour of our death.'

CHAPTER TWENTY-THREE

The July evening held a certain ambience, now that the tourists had returned to St. Ives like migratory birds.

Pubs were heaving, cafés and restaurants packed to the hilt, and gift shops bursting at the seams.

The bright light from the shops intermingled with the street lights, bathing Wharf Road in an orange, golden glow. Out on the harbour the sunset had submerged into the black waters.

The men met in a small harbourside wine bar near the Sloop Inn. High stools with quilted velvet seats were lined up against the bar. It had a continental feel. Pine tables with triangular cloths and small candles were scattered around the room with chaotic precision, beneath the glossy prints hanging on the pine walls.

'Have you heard about Ada Beckerleg?' Detective Inspector Brian Pendeen asked, as placed the tray of drinks down on the table where DC Gerry Brown and Guthrie sat having a smoke.

Guthrie shook his head, glancing about to check that the other diners could not overhear.

'She's been rushed to hospital with suspected sarin poisoning.'

'Oh, my God,' Guthrie's jaw dropped open.

'Yes, she's in intensive care,' Gerry added.

'It seems that Mustopher Kaleel disappeared and the wife, Vivienne, went looking for him. And while she was away the old girl saw a bird trapped in their greenhouse.'

'How could she get into the garden; the wall is too high?'

'Apparently she had a key; seems like they had once been on friendly terms.'

'Oh, I wish I'd only known, could have taken a look inside myself,' Guthrie complained.

'Anyway, the doctor at Treliske said that she appears to have accidentally spilt some contaminated water onto her skin,' Brian grimaced. 'Think it was in a jug or saucer that the bird was perched on.'

'How can she get poisoned from water?' Gerry asked.

'My sources tell me that Sarin mixes easily with water,' Brian explained. 'Food even.'

'So you mean she drank it?' Gerry asked incredulously.

'No, of course not, but according to the doctor, even if it just got onto her skin or clothes she would have got sick or probably died. Lucky for her it was diluted to a miniscule amount.'

'Who found her?' Guthrie asked.

'Interestingly it was the Kaleels' daughter. She'd found the bird dead outside the greenhouse, and luckily noticed the old girl inside on the floor.'

'So what are her chances of survival?'

'Actually, very good,' Brian tried to lift the mood. 'I've done a bit of research, and it seems that all nerve agents can be chemically deactivated with a strong alkali, such as sodium hydroxide.'

A waiter suddenly approached them to take their order. They stopped talking about

Ada Beckerleg and concentrated on the menu.

Outside on the wharf tourists were milling about thick and furious, buying up the merchandise like ravenous seagulls. Others were standing outside the Sloop Inn glued to their pints, smoking, laughing, and watching the pretty girls go by. The tide was going out, the harbour chock-a-block with small boats tied up for the night, caressed by the moonlight dancing over their wooden decks.

Suddenly, a figure appeared from the shadows of the wharf. Clad in Wellington boots and hooded jacket, the figure pulled out a handgun, and then entered the shallow waters heading towards a tugboat.

'Abigail okay?' Gerry enquired, after they'd finished their pasta.

'She's fine. But Katie wanted a break from her tonight. She's gone to see a friend in Hayle.'

'Will she be safe?'

'She took a taxi.' Guthrie recalled how he had offered to drive her but she'd declined. 'She goes there quite a lot to help out, it's hard having new-born, I suppose.'

'Doesn't sound like a great romance,' Gerry teased.

Of course, Guthrie knew Gerry was right. It did not make for a great romance but he wasn't complaining, he needed his space. The last thing he wanted was a whining woman asking where he was going and when he would be back.

They chatted some more as Guthrie confided a little of what he knew. He would save the best for the finale.

A loud bang could be heard in the distance, except no one heard it, not really. The lifeboat might be out training, or a ship was in distress letting off a flare, but more likely a motorbike's exhaust.

'I fancy a latte and a slice of gateau,' Gerry confessed to the waiter. 'Anyone else fancy a dessert?'

'Wouldn't mind an ice cream or something,' Brian replied. 'What about you, Guthrie?'

Guthrie scanned the menu. 'A clotted cream trifle looks good; think I'll have that.'

The waiter wrote down their order and then hurried off to the kitchen.

'Do any of you remember that old song, went something like - Eifle trifle o diddle eyeful, trifle, trifle o diddle dee?' Brian asked.

'No, but you were born long before us,' Gerry teased. 'I remember going to see the Stones when I was 17, my mum went mad.'

'My mother wouldn't even let me grow my hair to my neck, always had to have a crew-cut. What about you, Guthrie, did you have lenient parents?'

'Depended on what my mother's mood was that day, I suppose. But I got away at 18 when I went to university, so it wasn't so bad, could do what I liked then.'

'What about, say when you were 17 or even 15?' Brian quizzed.

Gerry laughed, 'Brian, are you training to be a shrink or something?'

Guthrie grinned. 'Well, it was during the early 70s, T Rex and rock concerts were around, so I nagged my mother to let me go, and she did.'

'Oh, you were lucky, my mother wouldn't have let me go,' Brian complained.

'In my first year at uni I took Piran with me to the rock festivals, you know, so he could mix with the plebs for the first time, ha-ha.'

'Have you seen him much since you've moved down here?'

'No, sadly we've both been too busy,' he said guiltily. 'I did meet up with Olivia a couple of times. I'm Godfather to their daughter.'

But before they could continue prying into his private life their desserts arrived.

It was getting nippy as Guthrie made his way back home, passing the Lifeboat pub that was full to heaving. As he glanced across at the harbour he noticed that the tide had gone out. His gaze suddenly hit on several police officers standing below one of the boats. Lighting up a cigarette he decided to take a stroll down the slipway into the harbour. The seaweed deposits on the wet sand reminded him of his childhood holidays in Clacton, sitting on the beach below the pier popping the blisters with his brother and sisters. He had no memory of his father.

'We're waiting for our governor and an ambulance,' one of the officers told him after seeing his identification.

'Who's up on deck?'

'A corpse. Someone's blown his brains out, we've been told to wait here to show them which boat.'

'Can I go on board?'

'Suppose so, just don't touch anything.'

Guthrie climbed up the slippery rungs onto the deck. He did not have to look far. Slumped over the wheel was the skipper, his skull was shattered. Pieces of bone and brain tissue were splattered around the helm, like some Tate Modern horror show. The blood slowly seeping away from the corpse and along the deck towards the starboard.

CHAPTER TWENTY-FOUR

It was raining heavily by the time he arrived back at Lobster Rock late that following evening. He had spent most of the day with Katie in Plymouth. On their way back across the Tamar Bridge he had suggested her spending the night with him, but she had replied that Demelza was expecting her. Unimpressed, he had driven home in a bad mood.

'Odd that she stays out so much,' Abigail mumbled with a mouth full of chocolate, as she lay sprawled out on the couch. She had read him the riot act the moment he had entered the house, for sneaking out that morning without telling her. Guthrie resented her being there at all, so the last thing he wanted was to have her tagging along with them around Plymouth.

'Perhaps she is seeing another man.'

'Thanks for that. So what have you been up to today?'

'Well, I took MacKenzie for a walk on the beach and then a couple of colleagues popped round for lunch, and then I watched some TV.'

Now he was infuriated. How dared she invite her cronies into his home? The very least she should have done was to ask if she could invite guests. They had probably gone through his belongings, passed round his photos of Stella and goodness knows what else.

'Anyway, I got a gift today.'

'Yes, the chocolates, I noticed.'

'No, they are just from my husband,' she grinned up at him like a Cheshire cat who had got the cream. 'But an anonymous admirer sent me a lovely box of toiletries – talc, soaps, bath salts, that sort of thing.'

'Nice for you, think I'll go and take a bath,' Guthrie grunted, heading towards the door.

'Help yourself to one of my new soaps if you want. Funnily enough, the picture on the box is of violets, isn't that a coincidence?' she giggled. 'Yet I've no idea who sent them. Came special delivery by the Royal Mail.'

Suddenly, Guthrie turned to face Abigail.

'Where are they?' he demanded, his voice dropping an octave.

'In my bedroom, why?'

'What sort of fucking protection did you think you could you offer me?' he yelled. 'Firstly, you know there is no delivery on a fucking Sunday, so weren't you a bit fucking suspicious?' He banged his fist hard against the wall. 'And you know we are investing contamination of fucking violets!' Within a flash, Guthrie charged up to her room and removed the offending box.

Racing back downstairs to the kitchen, he grabbed a can of coke from the fridge, and almost ran out of the house before he throttled her.

After giving Brian a call on his mobile, he dropped off the offending toiletries at the local police station for collection, and then jumped on the back of his Harley.

By the time he reached the roundabout at Lelant he was soaked. Suddenly he changed his mind about joining the A30 dual carriageway, and instead, rode onto the back road, the B3301. It was difficult to see through the torrents, although he could vaguely outline the estuary now empty of birds. They were probably sheltering nearby, he surmised, glimpsing across at the river. The boats were securely moored as if hibernating, whilst being barraged by the weather.

As he rode further along, the sea was no longer visible, hidden behind the shops that lined Hayle's main thoroughfare. He had read that the entrepreneur, Peter de Savary, had proposed to develop Hayle some years earlier, but from what he understood the man had failed to attract funding. Now thinking back to what Piran had said when they had met for lunch, about how Cornwall needed a Cornish version of Disneyland, perhaps he was right after all.

The further he rode the rougher the road became. The black tarmac, invaded by holes and large puddles, resulted in frequent drowning. It was not until he reached Gwithian when the rain stopped. Parking up near a wooden bench that overlooked the wet, seaweed strewn beach, Guthrie lit up a cigarette. There was no one else in the vicinity, but it was gone midnight after all. Retrieving the night vision goggles from the pocket of his leather jacket, he placed them in front of his eyes.

St. Ives looked tranquil through the goggles. The wet puddled streets were now mostly empty. Everything was so still, like a musical box that had suddenly been unwound. Only a couple of boats out at sea, probably fishing boats, he conjectured.

Now his attention had moved away from St. Ives and onto Godrevy lighthouse. Three and a half miles across the bay from St. Ives, it stood on Godrevy Island resembling a white goddess. Perhaps he should have been a lighthouse keeper, he considered. An easy life, living on a tiny piece of rock in the sea, with no neighbours to annoy you. It had to be better than a career where so many people to want to kill you.

Once he had finished his soggy fag, he climbed back onto the bike and continued his journey along the cliff top.

Now that the fog was clearing he could see the white waves rolling towards the shore, exploding onto the cliffs below. It was not long before he came to the lethal precipice of Hell's Mouth and Deadman's Cove. In daylight, the jagged cliffside looked quite beautiful, covered in yellow gorse and purple heather. Here the sea was the deepest blue, laced with patches of white surf dancing around the craggy rocks where suicides jumped.

It was as he neared Portreath when he suddenly spotted the BMW. Turning off his headlight, he followed from a safe distance, as the car drove down the steep hill towards the beach and car park. But instead of stopping, the car continued round the bend in the road that led back up towards the airbase.

*****

'This is a nice surprise, Professor Trevithick-Bray.' Guthrie was perched on the bonnet of the BMW now parked in Tolticken Hill, pointing his Walther PPK pistol directly at the windscreen, as the wipers went back and forth. Sliding himself across the wet bonnet towards the driver's door he shot off a wiper.

'Aren't you going to invite me into your car on a night like this, Professor Trevithick-Bray, or should I just call you Jonathan?'

Jonathan stared blankly. He went to turn on the ignition, but Guthrie was too fast, the gun now pressed hard against Jonathan's temple. Jonathan put his hands up and got out of the car.

'Aren't you going to ask me why I'm here?' Guthrie said, leading him towards the bushes out of sight. 'You see, when we first met, I'd never heard of Duchy Hospital. And then, when I did learn about it, idiot that I am thought it was some posh place way out, like St. Mawes. Who would believe that it is merely a house or two, virtually backing onto Treliske like a garden shed? You even have your own isolated sleaze-bin in the grounds.' Guthrie spat his gob a millimetre away from Jonathan's foot.

'So tell me, who was the mole in the MOD, because I know I was being set up in Belgium, it had to be an inside job?'

When there was no reply he shot a bullet at the gob, startling a small bird nearby.

'Of course, the reason why you were so eager to help me get a job at Treliske was to keep tabs on me, feign you were a good guy. While all the time you were feeding back information to the puppet master.' Guthrie shot another bullet, killing the bird.

Jonathan flinched. He was pale and clammy.

'You don't understand,' he stuttered. 'They offered to pay for a new laboratory and give me funding for my research, it would save millions of lives.'

'And in exchange you'd help them kill millions.'

'You don't understand,' Jonathan pleaded, his grey hair now drenched from the wet bushes. 'It wasn't just for my research. How do you think we got the money to build the new wing in Treliske? It was me who donated a big chunk of that money, me!'

The rain had started again with a vengeance, pelting down hard.

'They did head hunt me after graduation, did you know that?' Guthrie said almost casually, trying to light up a cigarette, as if they were having a pleasant chat over coffee. 'MI6, it is SIS now, but a name change doesn't really change anything, does it?' he laughed, wiping the rain from his face. 'And Interpol too, they wanted me to be a special agent - that's a sophisticated name for an assassin. There really is no other name for it. That was my job. And even though I say so myself, I was very good at it.'

After 4 attempts the cigarette caught the flame, he inhaled slowly.

Jonathan watched him like a frightened rat caught in one of his laboratory cages.

'Although, of course, they didn't say to me, Mr Guthrie, you are going to be a contract killer.' He made a funny face pretending to be downcast. 'I've done some of the most amazing things, working mainly in the Gulf, the Congo, Argentina, Yugoslavia. Some of my exploits have even been on TV news bulletins, but you wouldn't know it to meet me, would you? Plebby Guthrie, that's me.'

'I never thought you a fool, never!'

'Of course you did. Although you knew from the start that I was an agent for the MOD, you never thought that a working class black boy would be so damn good at the job,' Guthrie almost spat out the words. 'You see, it would be so easy for me to kill you — except I won't, only because you happen to be the father-in-law of my best friend. But I assure you, that is the only reason.'

'Thank...thank you. I am ashamed...' Jonathan dropped his rain savaged head.

'Not interested,' Guthrie sneered, exhaling the smoke in small foggy rings into Jonathan's face, causing him to cough. 'So who is the leader of this cock-up, RAF Wing Commander Paul Trembath?'

'He just takes orders.'

'So, is someone in the MOD behind all this then, do they want me dead?'

'No, this has nothing to do with the MOD. Trembath just has access to sensitive information. I don't know much about that side of things; in fact, I don't know much about anything.' Jonathan was breathless, visibly shaking. But Guthrie did not care, the only person on his list worthy of compassion was Stella.

'So, you didn't know anything about anything, yet you are so involved it beggars belief.'

'I told you, I'm not involved, I just mixed up some chemicals, that is all.'

'That's all – you're having a laugh. You administer them to, now what is it? Bees, violets, people. Even children.'

'I was trying to help...' Jonathan paused to sneeze, his expensive grey suit now soaking wet and grubby from sitting on the ground.

'So murder doesn't taint your middle class conscience.'

'I had nothing to do...'

'Who put the contract out on Stella?'

'It wasn't Trembath, and it definitely wasn't me.'

Guthrie offered him a cigarette, but Jonathan shook his head.

'I don't smoke.'

'Well, it might help if you start, it eases the time away in jail. I should know, I went through enough packets during my year inside.'

'Please, don't stop my work. Look, I think I may have found a cure for MRSA,' Jonathan begged. 'It's in the honey you see. Scientists in the Emirates gave me the idea, in Dubai they are researching…'

Lightning bolted across the grey skies, highlighting Jonathan's face. He was weeping. Guthrie pushed him out of the bushes.

'Give me your mobile and get into the car, and I'll follow you on the bike. Make one wrong move and I'll blow your fucking brains out!' Guthrie threatened.

'I won't, I give you my word. Where are we going?'

'Camborne Police Station, I'll leave you there until Detective Inspector Pendeen can come and question you.'

'Does the Chief Super have to know?'

'This is reality, Greg.'

As they neared the car, Guthrie said, 'Don't worry about your research, they let prisoners study for degrees nowadays, so I'm certain they'll be able to accommodate you. Keys.'

Jonathan handed him the car keys and watched Guthrie unlock the door.

'Life is usually about 10 to 20, so you'll have ample time to complete your research. I mean, look what the Birdman of Alcatraz achieved,' Guthrie mocked, as he pushed the doctor into the drivers' seat.

CHAPTER TWENTY-FIVE

It was gone three a.m. by the time Guthrie got back to St. Ives. Soaked to the skin, his long black curls dripping rainwater down his cheeks and neck; he was looking forward to a nice hot shower. Just as he put the key in the lock the kitchen door opened. Katie stood before him dressed in a hooded, red plastic mac and wellington boots holding an umbrella.

'Oh, I thought you were at Demelza's, what a nice surprise to see you back.' He leaned forward to kiss her, and then entered the kitchen dripping water everywhere.

'You know Demelza wasn't well, which was why I said I had to go over,' she explained. 'Well, the doctor was called and she's been taken to hospital. It's okay though, as her boyfriend's gone with her.'

'You should have phoned,' he said, removing his helmet. 'I could have picked you up.'

'Let's go for a walk,' Katie said excitedly.

'A walk? It's a hurricane out there. I'm tired, Katie. Can't we get into a nice warm bed?' he suggested, removing his leather jacket almost flooding the kitchen.

'No, Gut, my darling, oi've got a surprise to show you.'

'What surprise?'

'A shooting star and a possible eclipse, it only happens once every 500 years, didn't you read about it in the papers?'

Guthrie shook his head, accidentally spraying water over the table.

'Abigail's sleeping so she won't miss us. We must go, please say yes.'

'No, sorry. I'm too exhausted, and I'm soaked to the skin.'

'Dry off first, and put some waterproofs on.'

'Look at the weather, Katie, we'll get pneumonia.'

'The forecast said the rain will stop, it's only going to be like this for another 20 minutes.'

'Oh God. Okay then, if we must,' he groaned, too tired to argue. 'But why would you be interested in astronomy; you've never mentioned it before?'

'You know I read my star sign daily in the paper.'

Walking towards the bathroom, he wondered if Stella was turning in her grave, to know that she had been replaced by someone who did not even know the difference between astrology and astronomy.

After a pee he dried his hair and changed his coat and boots for a pair of Doc Martins and a thick MOD issue coat, and then searched about for a suitable hat to no avail. Grabbing hold of his bike helmet he decided that would have to do.

They walked arm in arm along the harbourside, as the lightning flashed across Smeaton's Pier like novelty rides at a funfair. Fishing tugs and motor boats bounced manically in the water, as if they would rip from their moorings. The angry waves lashed up against the harbour wall with even greater force by the time they reached the Sloop, flooding the walkway.

But still Katie insisted on continuing the journey.

Dustbins had fallen over in the wind, litter was blowing around, flying off in various directions. The umbrella blew inside out so often that Guthrie threw it into a nearby bin.

Splashing their way along The Digey's cobbled lane, he wondered if there was anyone else awake in the town. There were no lights on in the cottages or café, not even a sighting of a cat or tourist.

'So where's this star?'

'Ha-ha, just a bit further. Where have you been this evening, oi missed you, my Brian Boru?' she shouted above the thunder.

'I had a meeting. It would have bored you if you'd come along!'

'You look like a Martian in that helmet,' she laughed, snuggling her drenched body up against him. 'Oi wish we could just run away and be together for always.'

'Who said we can't?'

'Sometimes freewill and choices aren't always available to all.'

'I see my philosophy is rubbing off on you,' he laughed, the rain targeting his mouth.

The Island and Porthmeor Beach were also empty of souls, windier here than on the harbour.

'How beautiful the moon is, and look how clear the sky, you can see the stars,' she smiled. 'Look at the moon's reflection in the sea.' Then she began jumping over the puddles, stretching out her arms as if she were flying, dancing, twirling. He was unable to resist her, removing the helmet he pulled her close. He could smell her perfume wafting across his face, her smell. He wanted to have her now, right there, with the rain pelting on their naked bodies.

'I'm tired now; can we go home?' His lips touched her lips, hands reaching for her breasts.

'Not here, not yet, first oi have to take you to see the star.'

'I want you, now. Here, right here.' Guthrie pushed his body against hers, the weight had gone. He was honed, strong, like in the old days.

'No, wait until we get home and snuggle up in bed.' She suddenly sneezed.

'See, now you've got a cold. This is foolish, standing out here in this weather.'

'Please...'

'We won't even be able to see a shooting star in this sky. Let's go home.' He started to turn back, but she tugged him by the hand.

'No, Gut, please, this is a once in a lifetime event. Look, the sky is clear now, it's just a bit of thunder,' she went to kiss him on the lips. 'Oi was t'inking, you and me can pay a visit to Eire soon, and oi can tell them that Brian Boru has come home to get the six counties back.'

'Don't think I look much like Brian Boru,' he laughed.

Replacing his helmet, he conceded to continue the journey, it was easier than arguing.

Watching the breakers pound savagely onto Porthmeor Beach, he realised that they were heading towards the high, rugged cliffs of Clodgy.

Pitch black with only the moon and stars for company, they stood on Clodgy Point listening to the roar of the sea, as the wind whipped against their legs and stung their faces. In the daylight he could see right across to Lizard Point from here. But now, there was nothing, only darkness. Freezing, he pulled up the collar of his coat. But Katie did not seem to feel anything, as she led him by the hand, across the terrain to a bench near the cliffside.

'Oi dream, you know. Oi have strange dreams, some are with you. We are together in a house with children running around. Like normal people. But we aren't just normal people are we, Gut?'

They did not speak as they rested on the bench, just cuddled up close like two lovers getting soaked. The only light was from a distant trawler, it seemed to be the only vessel out in the storm.

'So where is this shooting star and eclipse? I can't see any other people here as mad as us looking for them, are you sure you got the date right?'

'Oi t'ink we're just early. The others must be sheltering somewhere.'

'That sounds more sensible than us sitting here.'

'The Tate might have opened up for the event.'

'You said the forecast was the rain would stop.' he responded, angry with her for dragging him there.

'It will soon, oi promise. The BB...the BBC are covering it, they'll be down soon, probably setting up their equipment.'

'Oh, you're crying. Why are you crying?' he asked, wiping away her tears with his hand.

'Oi wish we could...I wish...' she failed to complete the sentence.

Over towards Godrevy lighthouse a Sea King was flying inland. Its light resembled a giant star flickering its way along the coast, until it came almost in line with the trawler. Perhaps there had been an accident out at sea. Guthrie peered out to see if there was a vessel in distress. But it was too dark to see anything. The helicopter was now flying away from the trawler towards the cliffs.

Katie moved away from him slightly, not far, but just a few inches too many.

'I love you,' he confessed, and then yanked her onto his lap and held her there so tight that she could not move. The bullets began to rain down from the Sea King, they were meant for him, but they only pierced his shield, Katie.

Overhead, the light from the helicopter was beaming down, illuminating the plateau. By the time the aircraft landed on the grass she was riddled with holes. Her beautiful face was lifeless, her skin waxen — like an angel. Guthrie hurriedly removed his helmet throwing it down on the wet ground. Bending forward he gently kissed her bloodstained head as the tears rolled down his cheeks.

'Hail Mary, full of grace, the Lord is with thee. Blessed art thou among women,' he sobbed. 'Blessed is the fruit of thy womb, Jesus. Forgive us our sins. Have mercy on her soul.' He kissed his crucifix and then made the sign of the cross, avoiding looking down at her lifeless body weeping with blood.

Nearby, the blades of the Sea King started up, he knew his time was short. They would know by now that it was not him they had killed but her. They would be looking for him, wanting his blood.

Guthrie raced across the terrain towards the coastal footpath that trailed above the cliff top.

The mud along the footpath was thick and wet from the springs that flowed down the hillside, causing him to slip and slide. Suddenly he tripped over large invisible stepping stones, falling flat on his face. The blood trickled down his cheek. By now the Sea King was whizzing overhead, its bright searchlight sweeping across the plain like an apparition.

Wing Commander Paul Trembath wailed in the cockpit. There was no one else there with him to share his grief, except for the corpse perched on the seat beside him.

Switching onto automatic pilot, Trembath rose from his seat and went into the fuselage. The missiles were still there, originally meant for Sheik Amir, he would have no use for them now. He opened the side door. The winds were strong as the rain pelted down, causing turbulence to the aircraft. But he hardly noticed as he grabbed the machine gun.

By now Guthrie was crawling along the summit of Zawn Quoits, the two sided cleft of rock that rose above the roaring black ocean. The beam from the Sea King drew closer. The noise was worse here with the repetitive crashing of the breakers. His wet, sore hands grabbed hold of the jagged rocks to stop him flying off into oblivion. And then the lightning flashed, shadowed by a great blast of thunder echoing across the peninsular. There was nowhere to hide. The Sea King swayed dangerously overhead, its searchlight scanning the rock. Guthrie reached into his pocket to find the gun, but to his great dismay he realised that he had changed his coat back at Lobster Rock.

About to descend the cliffside, a massive wave exploded into the deep, black chasm below. Unable to reach the edge of the cliff after several attempts, he tried to lower himself down into a small alcove at the top of the chasm. But the treacherous waves reared up from the sea like demonic talons. The beam from the aircraft came nearer. The ledge was slippery from the water. His hands were sodden and numb, as he tried to avoid falling onto the hazardous rocks below. His arms now so tired. Raw bloody fingers slicing, slipping away. Guthrie fell down into the hungry seas below.

The Sea King began firing into the water, scouring further along the terrain around Hor Point and Pen Enys, as the trawler searched the rocks below Zawn Quoits.

Trembath had witnessed Guthrie falling into the ocean through his binoculars, and now there was no trace of him. He laughed out loud. Henry Guthrie was dead at last.

CHAPTER TWENTY-SIX

The white globe floated lazily across a backdrop of deep blue sky. Hovering over St. Ives bay, it turned from white to gold, casting diamonds over the waves.

Hotel guests had been breakfasted and children were already on the beach, spades in hands. Fathers were battling with their new dinghies and surfboards in the shallow waters, while their stressed out wives rubbed cream into the backs and faces of their children.

Along Wharf Road the dustmen and street cleaners were busy washing the roads and pavements, and clearing up litter, making space for more litter. The shops were setting up for the day; sweet shops, gifts shops, restaurants, cafes and a pub. Front entrances washed, window displays re-stocked and radios switched on.

In the harbour, below the Western Pier, tourist boats were in the process of being cleaned and re-fuelled, besieged by herring gulls doing their morning rounds painting the town white.

A queue had started to form for a place on the Cornish lugger, Dolly Pentreath, named after the last person known to speak the Cornish language. It was still in the process of being hosed down after a fishing trip.

The men in the boats glanced up, knowing they only had 15 minutes to get it ready.

The commotion of the previous night had gone unnoticed, and everyone was enjoying the weather, everyone other than Abigail.

'They went out late last night and haven't returned,' she wailed to Brian over the phone from Lobster Rock.

'Why did you let them go out alone?'

'You can't blame me; you have no idea what it has been like trying to protect him. He refuses to let me do my job.'

'Okay. Well, give them another hour or so,' he sighed. 'If you still haven't heard by then, let me know. I mean, he's probably fine, just gone somewhere for the night and forgotten to make contact.'

'His bike is still here, Brian.'

'He might have booked into a local b and b for some privacy,' he suggested.

'At that time of night?'

'What about the campsite, have you checked with them?'

'Camping, on a night like that? You must be joking.'

After the call ended, she made herself a mug of tea and took it back upstairs to the lounge.

The French windows were wide open, casting shadows across the room. She headed out onto the veranda. One of the striped deckchairs had Katie's bikini draped over it.

Looking out to sea, Abigail could not stop thinking about the helicopter she had heard that previous night. What if it had been going to Guthrie's aid? Or perhaps Katie had drowned and he was in a state of shock? She would give the coastguard station a ring soon, they might have some news.

*****

Guthrie did not wake up until around 10 a.m. feeling the worse for wear. Covered in cuts and bruises, his body felt like it had been ripped apart. Dried blood was everywhere. Perhaps he was dead. Or maybe, this was the meadow, where Plato claimed the souls of the dead hung around. Waiting for some judge to decide who would go up and who would go down, and who would be unlucky enough to be reincarnated.

Unable to move his numb shivering body, he slowly turned his head to ascertain his whereabouts.

Squinting through his bloody, swollen eyes, he noticed a black head suddenly pop up out of the water. It resembled a dog, with beautiful black eyes, almost human. It even had a black snout-like nose and long white whiskers. Halfway between fish and mammal, wanting to run but could only swim, as if the peculiar shaped back flippers had not fully developed into limbs. Endothermic vertebrates that suckled their young. Cursed to slither snake-like over the rocks, or play ball at an open air theme park.

He was even more bemused by the 30 or so creatures that suddenly came into view, lazily spreading out over the rock. It was only then that he realised he was not dead at all, he was lying on the Western Carracks, a group of ragged islets known as Seal Island.

Now he could see clearly, the white fluffy pups snuggled up to their mothers, crying for some breakfast. The cow seals, some with dark grey skin, others with patchy charcoal and brown skin, slithered across the jagged rocks like shiny giant snails. The males, larger and darker than the females, flopped into the sea as if bored, watched over by the noisy cormorants and gulls. All were enjoying the morning sunshine.

Not so far from land, he thought, probably near Zennor. He could see the cliffs, almost touch them, but too weak to swim the short distance ashore.

A large cow seal moved closer to him and flopped down, as if she somehow knew he must be kept warm. Mesmerised by its odd shaped hind legs. Yet even on this desert isle there was no peace to be had, what with the constant barks of the seals and squawks from the birds.

And now the memories came flooding back. She was dead. The beautiful, quirky Katie was dead. Bursting into deep heartfelt sobs, the tears ran down his battle worn face. Her voice whispering into his brain like a sea nymph or banshee. Calling to him across the waves in an Irish lilt, carried by the morning breeze.

'Lady Metamorphosis,' he whispered under his breath. 'Sweetest and most beautiful of butterflies.'

His breathing was shallow; Guthrie knew he had to get to a hospital sooner rather than later.

The waters were lapping near his head giving him the urge to pee. But he could not feel his body parts. Drowning in and out of consciousness, comforted only by the warmth of the sun and the wet blubbery bodies nearby.

It was another 30 minutes of seal bonding before the Dolly Pentreath sailed towards him.

CHAPTER TWENTY-SEVEN

The Heron Inn was a long blue and white building that resembled a hotel rather than a pub. It overlooked the banks of the Malpas Estuary. In the distance, small boats could be seen gliding across the sun-spangled waters.

Brian and Abigail led the way to a corner table by the panoramic window, followed by Guthrie and Gerry. Most of the other diners were outside on the terrace enjoying the sunshine.

'You've lost weight, look like a film star.' Brian said to Guthrie as they took their seats.

'Yep, none of my clothes fit.'

'A male model cum body builder more like,' Abigail teased. 'I think you must be related to Katie, what with those big green eyes and dimples, perhaps you had an Irish ancestor. By the way, you missed the post this morning when you were in the shower.' She handed him a sealed envelope. 'It was registered, I signed for it.' She looked more feminine than usual, wearing a blue summer dress and a little make-up. The men also wore casual summer clothes due to the scorching weather.

Guthrie gave a nod of thanks, placing the envelope unopened in his satchel.

Gerry looked bemused. 'If you don't mind my asking, Abigail, why are you still living at Lobster Rock?'

'I'm not. I just went over to give Guthrie a lift here; he's still not strong enough to ride the bike.'

'I was in the shower when the post arrived,' Guthrie added.

'And I forgot to give it to him before we left...anymore questions?'

'That's all for now,' Gerry teased.

'And before you ask, yes, I've still got the ribs bandaged up,' Guthrie laughed. 'By the way, Brian, how is Mrs Beckerleg?'

'As well as can be expected, she seemed quite comfortable when I last visited her.'

They continued to make small talk, until their meal was served.

'The papers are full of it, you know, about what happened with the RAF,' Abigail sighed, as she played with her spaghetti. 'Odd though, don't you think, that an air force should involve itself in chemical warfare during peace time?'

Guthrie shook his head. 'It wasn't peace time when Portreath first initiated the manufacture of chemical weapons. It basically started on May 11th 1941, when the airfield was used for raids on France.'

Gerry nodded in agreement. 'I read somewhere that it was a base for both British and American bombers.'

'After the war the MOD had a huge stockpile of nerve agents they'd captured from the Germans,' Brian joined in with the explanation. 'So they decided to make Nancekuke the area for a sarin production plant.' He paused to dissect his lobster.

'What about the connection between the Emirates and this Sebastian fellow?' Abigail asked.

Guthrie failed to answer, focusing on the lobster and the long legs of a waitress heading towards the kitchens.

'Let him eat in peace,' Brian said.

They continued to eat their food, almost in silence, until they had finished their main course.

'It's okay, mate,' Guthrie said belatedly to Brian. Then he turned to face the policewoman. 'Sebastian Dubois's interest in the country of Somalia began some years ago. Dubai had an inadequate sewage system. It was inundated with human waste, and still is from all accounts.'

Abigail turned up her nose. 'Well, I shan't be going there for my hols.'

'Sebastian Dubois took a large fee for taking tons of the sewage away. After that contract he was contracted by RAF Portreath, and that was when the Trembaths' joined forces with him.'

Guthrie paused for a few moments to pour a glass of water from the jug. A slice of lemon fell into the glass, but he did not have the energy to fish it out.

'What was the contract?'

'He was contracted to assist the RAF in transporting chemical waste from Nancekuke and dropping it on Somalia.'

'Let me get this straight,' Abigail said, putting down her glass of wine. 'The base in Portreath started off as an RAF joint, then became Nancekuke, a chemical weapons plant, and then went back to being an RAF post?'

'Yes. But even when it went back to the RAF they still continued to produce the sarin.'

'I thought the United Nations, or some other overseeing body, had banned it,' Brian said.

'In 1993 the United Nations Chemical Weapons Convention was signed by 162 member countries,' Guthrie grinned to the detective. 'They banned the production and the stockpiling of certain chemical weapons, one was sarin.'

'When did it go into effect?'

'Ha, good question. Not until last year, 29th April 1997,' he laughed. 'Which means that the RAF continued the production of chemical weapons after Nancekuke gave the base back to them. Although, the UN had called for the complete destruction of the stockpiles of chemical weapons, that was supposed to go into effect by 1997,' he emphasised. 'But the end date for the complete destruction of all the stockpiles isn't until April 2007. That's 9 years away. And I would imagine that it will continue long after that.'

'Best not go for a swim in Portreath then,' Gerry sniggered.

'Before I go into deeper territory I just need to explain, that after Sebastian Dubois's death a few years ago, Trembath must have been in a dilemma as what to do with the remaining chemical waste that Dubois had been contracted to dispose of.

'Couldn't he sell it or just dump it?' Gerry quizzed. 'And why would the MOD want to produce more if they still had the stockpiles?'

'Firstly, Sarin degrades after a couple of weeks, or, at a stretch a couple of months. The stockpiles most likely were, at least in part, some of the old batch they had confiscated from the Germans during the Second World War. It was the same gas that they had used to exterminate Jews.'

'No!' Abagail gasped. 'And they kept it here, right by the seaside where children play?'

'Maybe it was past its sell-by date. But to be honest I have no idea why they needed to produce so much more, unless they had numerous buyers,' Guthrie admitted. 'But don't get the old stockpiles confused with their on-going new production of sarin.'

'Hope you've put all this in your report,' Brian said.

'You'll have to wait and see.'

'So, is this what you hinted at over the phone about Camelford?' Brian lit a cigarette, and then placed the rest of the packet in the centre of the table for the others to help themselves.

'To be honest I'm fucking knackered, Brian,' Guthrie sighed.

'I know, sorry mate, but needs must.'

'Well, let's have a fag first.' He helped himself to one of Brian's cigarettes and took a few drags.

Glancing through the window onto the terrace, he watched as some diners fought off an offending gull that had invaded their table. Perhaps they should have left this to a cooler day, or maybe met on the beach so he could have gone for a dip. What more could he tell them, what more did any of them need to know?

'Okay,' he sighed. 'I'll tell you this little tale. On the 6th July 1988, a relief tanker went to Lowermoor Water Treatment Works – it's in Camelford on the edge of Bodmin Moor. The driver discovered it was unmanned.' Raising his brows towards the others, it was obvious where he was going with this. 'The driver accidentally poured 20 tonnes of aluminium sulphate into the wrong tank. This contaminated the drinking water for around 30,000 people. When the water was tested, they not only found the aluminium sulphate but other noxious substances.'

'Ha-ha, so now you're going to tell us that after Trembath discovered what had happened in Camelford around 9 years earlier, he went and dumped some waste there too,' Brian laughed.

'Not sarin, it's 500 times more toxic than cyanide. But I'd guess a little of the other waste was put into the tank, and I bet some of it was also dumped into the drinking water tank.'

Abigail looked horrified. 'So are you saying that some of the other noxious substances in the Camelford water was chemical waste?'

'Only a fraction of it, Abigail.'

'If this is true,' Gerry began suspiciously, 'then why weren't the RAF boys up at the base contaminated from the waste and the sarin?'

'Who said they weren't? From what I've discovered some did become very ill. Actually, some died,' he replied. 'So far, the total number of deaths is 41, and they are only the ones we know of.'

Abigail looked bemused. 'So how wasn't this Sebastian Dubois arrested for his transportation of sarin?'

'Dubois made money legally, Abigail, it was legal to drop waste on Somalia,' Guthrie emphasised the point. 'All the governments of Europe were at it.'

'Oh, my God. So this was with the full knowledge of the British Government?'

'MOD sanctioned, Abigail. They were also fully aware of Trembath's involvement.'

'The poor Somalis, how badly we've treated them because they're black. No offence, Guthrie.'

'Abigail, did you know that the company that shipped the waste from some European countries over to Somalia, was owned by the Somali Government?'

'Oh, my God, that's dreadful.'

Brian re-filled all the glasses with wine. They paused for a moment to drink and reflect.

'This has to be my last glass, I'm driving,' Abigail sighed.

'We could sit out on the terrace if you want, there's an empty table,' Gerry suggested, looking through the window.

'Good idea,' Brian conceded. 'We can have our dessert out there. Just let Guthrie finish the story about the sarin.'

'Okay,' Guthrie took the hint. 'It was after the MOD was exposed for what they were doing to the Somalis, and these drops over Somalia were no longer viable, when Dubois extended his own business.'

'What, manufacturing sarin?' Abigail asked.

'No. By taking RAF Portreath's unwanted chemical waste and initially making the drops himself over Somalia, as an independent courier service so to speak.'

'Oh, my God.'

'And then he progressed to selling it. But don't ask me who were his buyers as I've no idea.'

Abigail continued to look perplexed. 'Can you just go back over a couple of points, please?'

Guthrie nodded.

'The chemical waste that RAF Portreath confiscated from the Germans, was separate from the chemical weapons produced by Nancekuke, when they took over the RAF base?'

'Exactly. Nancekuke was a Chemical Defence Establishment in its own right, producing sarin and a small amount of VX.'

'Wonder the people who live in Portreath didn't get ill.'

'Some did. Locals complained of numerous ailments and even deaths, and pointed their finger at the base.' Guthrie recalled what the shopkeeper in Portreath had told him. 'As I mentioned earlier, Nancekuke claimed to have stopped the production of chemical weapons. But of course they weren't telling the truth.' He turned to Brian. 'But you probably know all this anyhow, it was fairly well publicised by the media at the time.'

Brian nodded.

'Eventually they made a half-hearted admission,' Guthrie continued. 'And it was accepted that they had stopped production in the 1980s, that's when Nancekuke officially handed the area back to RAF Portreath.'

'But, didn't you say before that...'

'You must never presume that a government or security force will tell the truth,' Guthrie interrupted. If they did, it would put the country in grave danger.'

'So they developed weapons of mass destruction to protect their own, whilst poisoning their own.'

'Yes. But you already know we work on a sort of backhanded utilitarian philosophy, that it's okay to sacrifice the few for the greater good of the majority.'

The waitress returned to their table with the dessert menu. They remained silent for a while, as they selected their choice and placed the order. It had been a long road, more painful than most. There were still so many questions that would have to remain unanswered.

CHAPTER TWENTY-EIGHT

That afternoon Olivia and three workmen were busy redecorating Ada Beckerleg's home in The Digey. Although her aunt had declined past offers of decoration, Olivia resolved to make the decision for her, while she was still in hospital. A new look to the cottage would also help her forget the trauma. What Ada Beckerleg also did not know was, that since her neighbour Vivienne had gone AWOL, the large semi-detached house next door was up for sale, and Olivia had bought it. Although, for now, she had booked into a hotel until the house was ready.

It had been an easy decision to seek a divorce from Piran, Olivia reflected. Mainly due to his constant womanizing and adultery. Their old home was up for sale, and Piran could look for a new sugar mummy. Although, she had to admit, his heartfelt pleas of love and adoration were Oscar worthy, and his onion filled tears were a sight to behold.

Apart from putting up new wallpaper and laying carpets, the workmen had also knocked down the high garden wall which separated the two gardens. Exquisitely landscaped with several water features and rockeries, it bore no resemblance to its former life.

'Meow.' The sound came from a tiny tabby kitten that she had bought for her aunt, to help her forget Marmaduke. Olivia bent down to pick it up and began stroking it. Her daughter, Polly, who was currently staying with a friend, would remain at Truro public school and live with her in St. Ives. Polly loved surfing and horse riding, so she would be fine. Yet, there was one thing that Olivia was dreading telling her daughter, and that was about her grandfather, Jonathan. They had always been so close. Never mind, she would take Polly on a Mediterranean cruise for Christmas, that would cheer her up, as she had always longed to go to Egypt. Piran could see her every other weekend, if he wished.

'Excuse me, Mrs Trelawney, where does the four poster bed go?' a workman asked.

'Oh, sorry, I should have mentioned, my name is no longer Trelawney, it is Trevithick,' Olivia smiled, having removed the 'Bray' from her maiden name. 'Could you put the beds in the house next door. The four poster is for my daughter's room, the double bedroom at the front. My bedroom is the double at the back, so can you put the electric bed in there, please.'

Olivia looked down at the soft bundle of fur in her hands. 'What do you want, little fellow, some milk?' But the kitten had only wanted a cuddle and had seemingly fallen asleep. She placed it down gently on the couch, and then made her way to the house next door.

Using a duster, she began to polish the new brass name plate on the wall. She had changed the name from *Lyonesse Lodge* to *Primrose Manor*, she would have the whole facia decorated with flowers. She had already chosen the colour scheme, yellow primroses and yellow and pink climbing roses.

'Hello, me' 'andsome,' the milkman called out from the milk float.

Olivia smiled and gave a nod.

'Is Mrs Beckerleg coming home, I heard she was taken to hospital?'

'Yes, she'll be back in a few weeks. I'm her niece, I've just bought this house.'

'Oh, that's nice, she'll be having someone to look out for her. She's a lovely lady. And there will be a bit of glamour in the street now you're here,' he flirted.

Olivia blushed; it had been a long time since a man had said something nice to her. She was also feeling more confident due to having lost 6 stone and changing her hairstyle. She had even replaced her spectacles with contacts, revealing large hazel eyes which had been hidden for too many years. Only now she realised why she had let herself go for so long, it was all to do with Piran. He had made her feel worthless. Secretly, she had always had a soft spot for Guthrie, he was a real man, big and muscular.

'Do 'ee be wanting to sign up for a daily pint?' the milkman interrupted her daydream. 'Here's a list of what we supply, although I'll need a day's notice to bring potatoes,' he smiled, handing her the form.

'Thanks, I could do with this.'

'I can deliver bread, milk, butter, potatoes and clotted cream.'

'Okay then. Can I order two pints daily, and a loaf of bread every other day, as my daughter will be living with me,' she explained. 'And a packet of unsalted butter, a tub of clotted cream and a bag of potatoes once every three weeks, please?'

'Certainly. I collect the payment fortnightly on Saturday mornings. If that's not convenient for any reason...'

'No, that will be fine, thank you. You're running a bit late today, aren't you?'

'Ha-ha, no, me 'andsome, I'm just taking the float to the garage for repairs,' he grinned. 'Do 'ee want anything now? I still have some bits and pieces left.'

'Don't suppose you have 3 spare pints and a loaf?' she smiled hopefully.

'Yes, I think I can manage that,' he winked.

Olivia needed the extra milk for the workmen's tea.

Only a few moments after the milkman had gone, her mobile phone rang.

'Hello... Oh, hello, Gemma... Yes, I know... Well. I'm sure you'll manage. Daddy has left a tidy sum for you and the girls... Of course you'll cope... Yes, of course we're still friends. Bring the girls over during the school holidays to see my new home here in St. Ives... No, I'm divorcing Piran.'

CHAPTER TWENTY-NINE

'Moreish,' Brian said, dipping into his creamy dessert, as they sat outside on the terrace. They could view the cool blue Malpas waters from here, and watch the occasional yacht sail by.

'This gateau is also really nice, I love walnuts,' Abigail mumbled, her mouth dribbling cake. Then she turned to face Guthrie. 'Can I ask why Sebastian Dubois chose to involve himself with the Trembaths, I mean, why choose them and not someone else?'

'I think there was a family connection way back due to their bee farming businesses.' Guthrie dipped his spoon into the cherry and cream cake. 'Sebastian Dubois ran a legit bee farm back in Belgium. The product was called King Bee Honey. The problem for him was, how to prolong the shelf life of the sarin, and make the packaging and product unique to the buyer.'

'How would that be possible?' Abigail asked.

'Dubois' contract with Jonathan also included violet and saffron contamination. It's all in my report how it was achieved, and about how the flowers were artificially sweetened.'

'I think I have heard of this sort of thing before,' Gerry frowned. 'Japan I think.'

'Yes, it is known as entomological warfare to be precise,' Brian expounded. 'Lt. General Shiro Ishii used fleas that had been infected with the plague to attack China.'

'I'd always thought it was flies.'

'It may have been both.' Guthrie rubbed his eyes, he was so very tired. Even his throat was sore from talking too much; forced to remember things that he would rather forget.

'Mm sweet violet,' Gerry raised his thick brows. 'Worth a couple of Michelin stars if the Penventon adds that to its menu, ha-ha.'

'By the way, Guthrie, you were recently seen chatting to a chamber maid there, so my spies tell me,' Brian laughed.

'I have several lady friends there, actually.'

'You're not on the game are you?' Gerry quizzed. 'I have heard that black men are twice the size, ha-ha.'

Abigail frowned.

'What's up, honey, don't like my vulgarity?'

'It's not that, Gerry. I was just thinking about what on earth could anyone do with flowers as chemical weapons?'

Brian put down his spoon. 'Well, we know the Trembaths' produced violet and lavender soaps and other toiletries, some had sarin in them.'

'Oh my God!' she cried, her eyes open wide. 'That's why you went mad at me, when someone had sent me the box of toiletries.'

Guthrie gave her a subdued smile.

'I suppose contaminating the flowers would be an easy way of getting the bees to be carriers. Contaminated pollen. What do you think, Guthrie?' Gerry asked.

'Yes, of course. Contaminating the flowers is far easier than injecting every bee,' Guthrie nodded. 'As for the soaps and perfumes, like the flowers, I think the only contaminated ones were the violets. Cornish violets.'

'You mean only the violets had sarin in them?'

'Yes, violets, and maybe honey. I don't think Jonathan had managed to infuse saffron with the sarin yet, he only got as far as contaminating it with cocaine.'

'What does sarin look like?' Abigail asked, as she wiped cream from the edges of her mouth with a serviette.

'It's a liquid that is turned into a gas,' Brian explained. 'It was invented in Germany in 1938 as a pesticide, you know, for killing insects. It's now listed as a chemical weapon of mass destruction.'

'So if it is designed for killing insects then how comes it didn't kill the bees that were carriers?'

'Yeah, good point, Abigail.' Gerry was impressed.

'Jonathan must have produced some antidote in the bee. Very clever I admit,' Guthrie remarked.

'So, perhaps whatever made them immune, caused them to change colour, orange rather than yellow,' Abigail suggested.

'I expect you're right,' Guthrie conceded. 'Maybe Jonathan developed some sort of mixture of Atropine and Pralidoxime chloride – they are antidotes for nerve agent toxicity. Well, that's what my friend Solly thinks.'

'I'm afraid I don't know anything about nerve agents,' Brian admitted. 'What about Jonathan, not so altruistic after all?'

'Well, he was in some ways, oddly enough,' Guthrie sighed. 'Jonathan had initially been dealing with the Emirates to help him with his own research.'

'I know they're over budget at Treliske, but I didn't think they'd resort to killing off the patients,' Gerry jested.

'Scientists in Dubai had claimed that the glue obtained from bees could stop cancer. Jonathan had genuinely wanted to continue this research in Treliske.'

'I suppose it was Dubois' idea to make the bees sarin carriers, so it must have been just pure luck that he met up with Jonathan,' Gerry said.

Abigail considered Gerry's comment. 'Unless of course they already knew each other, Dubois and Jonathan I mean.'

'Why would they have known each other, if Sebastian Dubois was based in Belgium?' Gerry looked bemused. 'And why would a beekeeper have had any prior link to a hospital executive?'

Guthrie decided it was time to speak.

'Because they both, be it sporadically, worked for the MOD.'

*****

They ordered coffees and liqueurs to finish off the meal.

Guthrie handed out cigars for the men and a bottle of Chanel for Abigail as a small treat.

His body still ached from the numerous assaults and bullet wound, his mind fared no better.

Abigail was now sharing a smell of her wrist with her two colleagues, for them to review the perfume. He knew he had got it so badly wrong. He would have to make it up to her big time, some day.

'Brian, why did you tell me over the phone that Guthrie will be charged with murder?' Abigail suddenly digressed. 'You aren't really going to charge him, are you?'

'I'm afraid we have to,' the DI replied. 'Unless he can think of a way to get himself out of it. One corpse was found, and bits of another body, both had Guthrie's DNA.'

'Well, that's not evidence.'

'Guthrie has privately admitted to me that he committed these crimes, in self-defence.'

'Not crimes, Brian, self-defence is not a crime,' Guthrie winked. 'The other guy fell on his own knife, so basically, I had nothing to do with his death.'

'But you got rid of the body.'

'Well, it saved the force a load of work,' he laughed. 'Anyway, please don't worry about me, Abigail, I'm sure things will work out just fine.'

'If only you had been working for the MOD at the time, then you would have been protected from prosecution,' Brian sighed.

Then suddenly, the policewoman asked the one question that Guthrie had been dreading all day.

'You still haven't told me the name of the Godfather behind all this malarkey. Was it Dubois?'

Brian shook his head. 'I'd take a bet it was either Jonathan or Paul Trembath. I'd put my money on Trembath?'

'Jonathan,' Gerry said with certainty.

'Really?' Abigail looked perplexed.

'We know it is a possibility that he murdered the mortician,' Brian reminded her.

'Well, Guthrie, was it Trembath?' Abigail demanded.

Guthrie looked sheepish as he turned to face them; and, in almost a whisper said, 'she's dead.'

'Who is?'

'The Godfather.'

Guthrie kept his head lowered as he said, 'Katie was the boss of the whole shebang.'

'What are you talking about?'

He turned to face Abigail and placed his arm around her shoulders.

'I'm so sorry, I didn't want to tell you, but Katie's dead.'

Abigail just stared back at him.

'Her husband shot her by accident while flying a Sea King helicopter.' He smiled, trying to hide his pain. 'She was married to Wing Commander Paul Trembath.'

'Never!' Abigail turned pale.

'I'm so sorry.'

'Katie's dead? And you let me think you'd had a row and she'd gone back to Ireland.'

'I didn't want to upset you.' But he failed to mention his own part in her death.

'I know that Paul Trembath is being held at Bodmin along with another other suspect,' Brian said.

'The other guy skippered the trawler, Brian, name of Maxime Dubois.' Guthrie put the cigar to his lips and breathed in deeply.

'God, you're so lucky to be alive, Guthrie,' Abigail said tearfully. 'I know this sounds bad, but she seemed such a lovely person... She was so beautiful, and that glorious auburn hair.'

Guthrie gave Abigail another comforting hug. 'I don't know how to tell you this, but that was a wig, her real hair was black.'

'How did you know Katie was wearing a wig, did it come off?'

'When we had sex, Abigail, her pubes were black not ginger.'

'Don't be coy, Guthrie, say it as it is, ha-ha,' Brian teased.

'Yeah, don't beat around the bush – get it, bush?' Gerry laughed.

'I just don't understand how Katie could have got herself mixed up with criminals, it didn't seem to be in her nature.' Abigail squinted, as if her brain was in turmoil.

'But, if I told you that Katie's father was the notorious Sebastian Dubois, then you would understand.' He kept his arm tight around her, but it took all his strength not to break down and weep himself. 'She inherited the business when her father was killed a couple of years ago, in Ostend.' But, he omitted telling her that it had been himself who had killed Dubois.

'I still can't believe it, Katie was so naïve.' Abigail sniffed.

'Her name wasn't Katie,' Guthrie corrected her. 'Her real name was Suzette Dubois. She was from Belgium.' The name was so hard to say, sticking in his dry mouth. 'She wasn't a simple little Irish colleen. At 18 years of age Suzette Dubois studied music and drama at the Sorbonne.'

He swallowed hard. He had made love to Katie, he did not even know the educated, sophisticated woman, Suzette. Then suddenly, he remembered the first time they had met at Tehidy Bee Farm, when she had said: "She's also a classically trained musician. Mrs Trembat' is a very clever woman." How could he have ever guessed that she had been speaking about herself?

'Katie may have been many things, deliciously beautiful, quirky, funny, but the one thing she wasn't was naïve.'

'She was a damn good actress then,' Abigail conceded.

'How did you find out her real name?'

'I received a letter some time back, it contained clues to solving the crime, and it mentioned French Pancake Day. But, it didn't make sense at the time. That was, until I visited the bee farm and saw a painting by the daughter-in-law, Suzette,' he explained. 'And then, as time wore on, I put two and two together.'

'What's that got to do with the price of kippers?' Brian mocked.

'What do they call a thin pancake in France and Belgium?'

'Oh, my God,' Abigail laughed, 'Crepe Suzette.'

'So who was the person who sent you the letter?'

'Have no idea, Brian. It could be someone who works for the MOD or an RAF man, no idea to be honest.'

'I still think Katie cared about you,' Abigail protested. 'I mean; she was always kissing you. It doesn't make sense why she moved in with you, if she had a husband, what was the point?'

'If you remember, she didn't spend that much time with me, she was only in Lobster Rock a couple of weeks,' he reminded her. 'And every other night she claimed to be staying over with a friend in Hayle, when in truth, she was returning to her husband at the bee farm.'

'But what was the point?'

'I would hazard a guess and say she wanted to find out what I knew. From the start her plan was to eliminate me.'

'But she could have done that after the first meeting. I mean, they could have just shot you on the first day you moved down to Cornwall. I think she really did like you.'

'Well, as for the whys and wherefores that she went to all that trouble, I can't answer that.'

'I have to say I agree with Abigail,' Gerry said. 'I mean; why would she have slept with you?'

'Can't answer, don't know. But I should tell you that she was the one who killed Stella Johnson in...' He suddenly stopped speaking, his heart was racing now, unable to breathe. Pouring himself a glass of water he tried hard to hide his emotions. 'She dressed in a gabardine raincoat, black hat, beard and fake side-locks, imitating a Hassidic Jew. Suzette I mean. It was a clever disguise to wear in Antwerp, when there were so many orthodox Jews in the vicinity.'

The others remained silent.

'I know at some point you're going to ask why, if she knew we were in Belgium planning to kill her father, why she didn't kill me.'

Brian and Gerry nodded.

'I'd hazard a guess that she wanted her father dead, so she could take over the firm.'

Abigail, still tearful, asked, 'what firm, the chemical weapons business or the bee farm?'

'Both of course. She had no moral issues about her actions; no doubt due to being raised by her criminal father. Like the night she bumped off the old skipper in St. Ives harbour.'

'Oh, yes, I'd forgotten about him,' Gerry confessed.

'Remember that night we had drinks in that bistro by the harbour, and she was supposedly visiting her friend in Hayle?' Guthrie raised his brows. 'I imagine it was an excuse to get out of the house. I would guess something had gone wrong, otherwise they'd have chosen somewhere far more discreet to kill him.'

'You sound like Hercule Poirot, Guthrie,' Gerry laughed.

'Goodness, don't mention him,' Brian warned.

'Why?'

''Cos he was also from Belgium, ha-ha.'

CHAPTER THIRTY

Cornwall was buzzing. It was all over the headlines:

RAF PORTREATH IN CHEMICAL WEAPONS SCANDAL

VIVIENNE KALEEL ARRESTED

TEHIDY BEE FARM MANAGEMENT UNDER ARREST

TRELISKE HOSPITAL EXECUTIVE HELD IN CUSTODY

Newsagents in every town and village in Cornwall had sold out by lunchtime. Although, it was the height of the season, and some feared that such negative publicity would damage trade long term. But for the present, the hoteliers, publicans and shopkeepers across the county were happy to be inundated with extra customers, including the media, police and inquisitive others. Even Blankenberge and Dubai were feeling the pressure. The story was broadcast on nearly every news bulletin across the world, not least due to the chemical waste dumping old chestnut being brought up again. Even Parliament had been called back from recess, and the Prime Minister had given a press conference.

But not all of Cornwall was buzzing that day. In a small country churchyard near Redruth, a figure dressed in a black suit could be seen handcuffed to a police officer. There were no other mourners, only a police presence and the funeral directors.

The grass was newly mown, the fresh, pungent smell rose up towards the blue sky. The sun blazed down, lighting up the nearby cornfields.

The coffin was wheeled out of the hearse. Silence - not even a twitter of a bird as they wheeled it towards the open grave.

The handcuffed man trembled as he tried to reach out to the coffin, but the shackles prevented him from moving.

The undertakers carefully lowered the coffin down into the earth.

There had been no service or minister. The man had not asked for one, after all, she had been an atheist.

He wondered if his girls had remembered to wear sunscreen today. Now recalling the conversation with his late wife about her desire to move nearer the school, about how they were progressing with their horse riding and music. And now, it was all over for them, they would have to leave their school, their friends. How stupid he had been not to have considered the alternative scenario. Perhaps the girls could live with his parents in Spain, although, in truth, he had no idea where his parents were. It was possible they had also been arrested. After all, his father did own the farm, and he had been the one who had initiated the deal with Sebastian. The alternative option for his daughters was unbearable, he doubted he would ever see them again.

It was as the earth was spaded over the coffin when the tragic figure fell to his knees weeping. The police officer attempted to drag him back up onto his feet, but his legs buckled, causing another officer to rush across the graveyard to assist.

So many memories flooded his mind, as if his brain was a bingo ball dispenser, with all the memory balls bouncing out at him at once. Another memory ball suddenly bounced in - the face of Maxime. Maybe he was still in Belgium safe, if so, he could take the children; and for a brief second the man felt slight relief.

Now, another ball had bounced in – her face, like the 99% of other balls in the dispenser. She always had tight rein of his heart, only her and no other, even though he had been unfaithful with his body. Adultery came second down his long list of shames that he would have to live with. She was his soul mate. After all, they had known each other since childhood.

There were no wreaths or cards, he had not been granted that privilege. One solitary red rose lay on the top of the coffin, the attached card read:

Petals - by Amy Lowell

"Life is a stream
On which we strew

Petal by petal the flower of our heart;
The end lost in dream,
They float past our view,
We only watch their glad, early start.
Freighted with hope,
Crimsoned with joy,
We scatter the leaves of our opening rose;
Their widening scope,
Their distant employ,
We never shall know.
And the stream as it flows
Sweeps them away,
Each one is gone
Ever beyond into infinite ways.
We alone stay
While years hurry on,
The flower fared forth, though its fragrance
still stays."
It was signed – Brian Boru

CHAPTER THIRTY-ONE

Sitting on a bench above the river bank, Guthrie watched the afternoon sun cast a golden glow over the Malpas waters.

It was here where the two rivers of Truro and Tresillian converged. Meandering in twists and turns along its course, bordered by dense woodland. It provided a shelter for the small birds that now swooped down onto the river bed, scavenging among the debris, as the boats sailed away towards the setting sun.

Just along the shoreline curlews were wading in the shallow waters, as if they were secretly planning to cross to the opposite river bank, thick with trees.

Tristan and Iseult were said to have crossed the Truro River here at Malpas, once known as La Mal Pas.

They had been like Tristan and Iseult, acting out their lines in a cursed romance. Or maybe just two spiders ensnared in a self-made web. Yet, he had failed as her knight; never worn her colours, or fought any duals in her honour. Instead, she had shielded him from certain death.

It was her funeral today. Perhaps they had let her husband attend, now that he was in custody. Wing Commander Paul Trembath, living with the knowledge that he had indirectly killed her. Guthrie did not feel guilty for his own part in it, only pity for their children. Yet, morality was such a complex issue. A gallantry medal for the soldier who achieved maximum slaughter of enemy fighters and innocents abroad, or a life tariff prison sentence for a single crime of passion, or accidental road death at home. Was the only difference that the soldier killed the enemy of the state, murder by proxy, commissioned by an unknown other?

'Are you okay?' Gerry asked, making his way to the back of the bench, followed by Abigail and Brian.

'Yes fine, just thinking.'

'It was good of you to pay the bill, but you didn't have to.' Abigail grabbed his hand and nestled it in her own.

'It was just a small thank you from me for your exceptional support in this fiasco.'

'Well, thanks anyway,' Gerry patted him on the shoulder.

'Yes, thank you, Guthrie, very decent of you,' Brian added.

'You're a gem,' Abigail bent forward to kiss his cheek.

'I'd best tell you now, although it's in my report,' Guthrie digressed, as he handed round an open packet of Marlboro. 'There is a hangar full of sarin packed into steel containers up at RAF Portreath, if you could sort that out I'd be grateful.'

'Thanks for that,' Brian nodded, helping himself to a cigarette. 'I'll inform the Chief Constable.'

'Won't the military want to take over the investigation?' Abigail asked curiously.

'They might want to, but they aren't going to get the chance,' Brian laughed.

After taking a few drags from his cigarette, Guthrie added, 'there are also tons of chemical waste up at Portreath. And I found a pile down South Crofty.'

'Probably have to get the army in after all,' Brian groaned.

'Tell them to look for those 5 mounds on the base that I was telling you about, dumping areas for sarin. It could be as much as 40 tons.'

'How did you find out about South Crofty?' Gerry asked.

'Just a tip-off.'

'Wish I got as many tip-offs,' Gerry complained.

'You know they'll send someone to arrest you, Guthrie, probably me. They found your DNA at the Eden Project whilst searching for a missing person.'

Guthrie ignored Brian's warning.

They had all joined him on the seat by now, their eyes fixed steadfastly on the glorious Malpas river.

'By the way, Guthrie, they are exhuming Stella Johnson's body, as you requested, for a second post mortem.'

'Thanks for that, Brian.'

'What about her family, her husband, will they need to be informed?' Abigail turned to face Guthrie.

'No, she wasn't married.'

'I'll read your report and get back to you,' Brian patted him on the back. 'You've lost a heck of a lot of weight.'

'Must be the stress.'

'Think you should join our police force, with you on the team crime would drop at least 80%, ha-ha,' Gerry laughed. 'Don't know how you do it, give us a clue.'

'The philosopher Descartes said: If you would be a real seeker after truth, it is necessary that at least once in your life you doubt, as far as possible, all things. I take it that one step further and doubt all people too, ha-ha.'

As they stood up to go, Guthrie glanced out at the Malpas river for one last time. Then Brian and Gerry both shook his hand and headed off to their car.

'Don't worry about my arrest!' Guthrie called after them. 'It may never come to that!'

'Well, I hope you're right, mate, I really do!' Brian shouted back, and then got into the driver's seat with a heavy heart.

Once they were alone in the car, Abigail asked, 'Did Katie really have to die, was there no other way out?'

'If I'd handed her over to the police, many more lives would have been lost in the future. And, to be honest, what proof did I have that would have stood up in court?'

'What a waste.'

'I must say, Abigail, I should apologise for my behaviour towards you. At one time I was certain you were involved with the Trembaths'.'

Abigail did not answer.

'I searched your bag when you first arrived at Lobster Rock and found an RAF issue pistol.'

'Oh, didn't you know, Guthrie? I'm an RAF reserve.'

'No. I wish you had told me,' he groaned. 'I could have dropped you from my list of suspects at the start. To think how horrid I was to you.'

'My fault, I should have told you. To be honest, I probably should have returned the gun after training. By the way, where do you want dropping off?'

'The Penventon Hotel, Redruth, please.'

Retrieving the letter from his satchel that Abigail had given to him earlier, he tore open the envelope and removed the papers inside.

'Redruth? You know you won't get a train back to St. Ives from there after about quarter to eleven. That's if you're thinking of going to the Twilight Zone.'

'I'm staying there for the night. I've got to deliver a £395 diamond ring set in white gold.'

'Where are you delivering it to, a safety deposit box?'

'No, I'm taking it to a lady.'

'What?'

'Hey, watch the road!'

'A lady. Do you mean your lady, a girlfriend?'

'Well, she's a lady who I've been seeing. We're meeting at the Penventon; I've booked us the honeymoon suite. I didn't want to get too serious while the job was on.'

'But I thought...'

'Sorry, I should have told you.'

'But I don't understand.'

'Watch where you're driving,' he instructed, as the car swerved towards the other lane.

'But you lived with Katie.'

He bit his lip, ashamed of the deception.

'Okay, I'll be honest with you. I did love her in a strange way, the quirky, naïve Katie,' he confessed. 'I never knew Suzette, although I wish I had. Perhaps I had seen beyond her facade, who knows.'

'It was her funeral today.'

'Yes, I know. Were there any mourners do you know?'

'I have no idea, they might have let her parents go, I suppose.'

'I had toyed with the idea of going myself, but thought it too hypercritical when I think about what happened.'

'Yes, what really did happen on Clodgy Point that night, you never did tell me?'

'Top secret,' he laughed, trying to erase the memory.

'So, what would you have done if she had turned out to be innocent, I mean the real Katie, you know, the real Suzette?'

Before he had the chance to reply Abigail threw another question at him. 'So is your new fiancé more beautiful than Katie?'

He was quiet for a moment, as if not certain how to respond. And then his green eyes sparkled, as if he had experienced a sudden revelation.

'Kant, he was a philosopher, and wrote something about the Analytic of the Beautiful.'

'I don't understand philosophy I'm afraid.'

'No wait, let me explain,' he smiled, accentuating the dimples in his cheeks. 'Kant said that beauty isn't a property of a work of art, or natural phenomenon, but is a state of mind. It is experienced by the imagination and the understanding.'

'They're going to arrest you.'

And for a second he seemed melancholy, the smile had vanished, as if it was all too much, even for him. Looking down at the letter he began to read in silence, and then re-read it through again.

'You were like Robin Hood in a funny sort of way. I really wish there was a way out of this for you,' Abigail sighed despondently.

Suddenly, Guthrie burst into a fit of laughter, waving the headed piece of paper in the air.

'Why are you so happy at a time like this?'

'I've just got a £250,000 cheque from Interpol and the offer of a renewed contract with MI6,' he grinned. 'It means, Abigail, that all charges have been dropped. Henry Guthrie OBE, always does find a way out, ha-ha.'

THE END

I would like to thank Nick Catford for his research into underground bunkers and airbases, that partially inspired this book.

THANK YOU FOR READING

"CATCH THE STINGER, BEFORE IT STINGS YOU!"

By

E.R. POMERANSKY

LIKE THIS BOOK?

See more great books at www.creativetexts.com

"RUDY'S PREPAREDNESS SHOP"
"CME: CORONAL MASS EJECTION"
"HOME SWEET BUNKER"
"THE HERMIT"
"SIMPLER TIMES"
"BUGGING HOME"
"THE SLOW ROAD"
"LOW PROFILE"

& MANY MORE GREAT
THRILLER, POST-APOCALYPTIC FICTION
& OTHER TITLES

THANK YOU!

56411750R00251

Made in the USA
Charleston, SC
19 May 2016